BLOOD BINDS

WYRD BLOOD BOOK THREE

DONNA AUGUSTINE

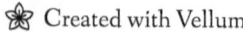

For Camilla, whose brutal honesty is both scary and invaluable. I've lost count of how many books you've helped me with. It's only fitting you should get this last book in the Wyrd Blood series and the happily ever after.

ONE

My ragged breathing muffled the noises around me as I sucked in more air than my lungs could hold. Twigs hung from tangled hair. Rocks dug into my palms and knees. There was a rip in my leather pants, my shirt was torn, and I had scratches everywhere my flesh was exposed.

Burn dropped to the ground beside me and then flipped to his back, his lungs needing more clearance. Sneak was bent over, hands on his knees, the flesh of his neck sucking in with every labored breath.

"Damn, that was close," Burn said in between gasps.

My fingers tightened around the stone, its magic throbbing in my hand. I'd barely lifted it past the ward when a horde of stinging nettle beetles were unleashed. One second there had been nothing, and the next, we'd been running for our lives.

Ryker had yanked me back and then yelled for us to run and get out of range. As soon as we did, wave after wave, the beetles had dropped while we dodged the few that managed to keep pace with us.

It was a good thing my legs hadn't failed me, because within seconds of taking off, I'd been robbed of my magic. This was the second time Ryker had done it. It felt exactly the same as the first time, like a great vacuum had sucked out my insides and then scraped the lining. I knew from past experience that I wouldn't feel human for another few hours.

Ryker stepped into the clearing a few minutes later, looking like a lion after a leisurely stroll. Magic was still pouring off him, his eyes deep and feral. The Cursed King in all his glory.

I wanted to plow into him and knock him on his ass. Anger erupted inside me, ready to explode. We were up to six stones in the last three months, and this was the second time he'd crossed the line and taken my magic, and I no longer cared if it was by accident.

"Let's get going. We don't know what else might be coming," Ryker said.

He was right about moving on. I swallowed the anger, feeling as if I'd choke upon it but holding it down anyway. This wasn't the place or time to have an all-out, throw-down fight.

We weren't sure who the latest stone belonged to, but it hadn't been buried out here in the middle of nowhere by accident. The owner might have felt his ward getting cracked open like a bad egg and come sniffing around for the stench of intruders.

Ryker held out his hand, offering to help me to my feet. I ignored it, standing on my own. We might not be brawling now, but we would be soon. I saw no reason to pretend otherwise.

I threw my discarded bag back over my shoulder and began walking in the direction of the stashed chugger that we'd drive home. Burn and Sneak felt the tension in the air and were staring, mouths hanging open, wondering what they'd missed. I didn't tell them as I walked. If I spoke, I'd be cracking open.

We made it to the chugger in record time, my weakened legs fueled by anger.

I'd almost made it to the door when Ryker walked up behind me.

"Things happen. It was an accident," he said.

His words didn't ring of an apology.

On the trek over here, I'd convinced myself it would be better to not hash this out until we got back to the Valley. But if he was going to rip the subject open, I wouldn't slam it shut. My rage was still boiling over, the emptiness I felt inside giving it that much more room to burn.

I spun. "You *said* it wouldn't happen again."

After the merge, he'd promised me he'd never take my magic without my permission. He'd done it. Twice. The first time I'd accepted it as a slip. I'd buried the hurt and ignored the gnawing ache it had left for hours. I hadn't made a thing over it. After all, I'd made more mistakes in my life than I wanted to recall. Who hadn't?

But how many times was I supposed to look the other way? He couldn't possibly understand what it felt like, to be standing there, stripped of your magic, feeling utterly defenseless in the worst possible moment.

I turned and walked off, putting as much space as I could between us before things took an ugly turn.

He followed behind me, his hand landing on my shoulder and spinning me around. "You're overreacting."

There was nothing he could've said that would've made the fury burn hotter. He'd stepped all over my magic, plowed past my line in the sand, did what he said he'd never do again, and acted like it was a tiny slip-up? As if I was the one out of line?

My fist connected with his gut. I heard a groan. It wasn't from Ryker but Burn, who was cringing as he looked on. Burn and Sneak were off to the side, staying well out of range.

Ryker grabbed my wrist, holding my hand in between us. "You get one shot. That's it."

I narrowed my eyes and jerked my hand from his grip. "I want this connection between us severed. If there's a way to do it, there's a way to undo it."

I tried to walk around him and head back toward the chugger.

Ryker stepped in front of me. "What about the problem that someone might still want you dead? What do you plan on doing about that? Our merge is the only thing keeping you alive."

"We have plenty of stones. We don't need to be joined. We can kill whoever we want now." I moved to the right.

He moved with me. "We don't know *who* to kill." He stared at me as if I were insane.

Maybe I was crazy, but he was the one driving me to it.

I plowed past him and tossed my bag into the chugger. "I'm willing to take my chances," I said, letting my rage answer.

"You're being an idiot."

"It's not only your call," I yelled.

He crossed his arms as he stared at me. "I'm not going to help you get yourself killed. Once you calm down, you'll see it's the right choice."

Those words did the opposite of calming me. They enraged me. "You don't own me. You don't make my decisions. Do we have that clear?"

"Very clear. And you don't make mine. I'm not doing it." He walked around to the driver's side of the chugger, yelling, "Get in or walk. Your choice, but I'm leaving."

I jumped into the back of the chugger, preferring to be bounced around than sit next to Ryker the entire way home.

TWO

One week later...

I glanced up at the clock.

"I have to go." I dumped my bacon, sausage, and half a biscuit into a napkin, shoved my plate toward Ruck, and stood. "Can you get rid of my plate? I don't have time."

Ruck threw his hands up as he leaned back, watching me about to run for the exit. "Why do you have to run out? You just got here. This constant dodging is insane."

"It's three minutes after eight. I don't have time to argue about this right now." I hissed the words through my teeth so the busybodies at the table over, who were leaning as close as they could, wouldn't hear me. It seemed like all people did since I'd merged magic with Ryker was try to stare and listen to every damned thing

I said and did. Once I'd begun avoiding Ryker, they'd quadrupled their efforts.

"You need to sit down and work this out. It's getting crazy. It's been a week already."

"Not now." I needed to be out of here three minutes ago. Ryker had been showing up earlier and earlier, and it was getting harder and harder to dodge him.

I shoved my food in my pocket and ran toward the door, leaving Ruck behind. Another minute and I'd be out of there. Almost gone, almost safe.

And then Ryker walked in.

Our eyes met, and his steps slowed. He wanted to talk to me; I could see it on his face. He wasn't interested in severing the connection. I had no interest in continuing on as is, not when I was getting laid low by my magic being robbed. Things had to change.

There was a large dude in front of me. I darted to the right. I'd duck around him, using the big guy as a human shield, and skirt out.

Then the big doofus noticed Ryker staring. He glanced behind him and must've realized he was in between Ryker, me, and maybe the juiciest encounter he'd seen all week. He stopped short. Instead of plowing into his back, I veered to the right and stepped onto something mushy that was also incredibly slippery. Who the fuck had dropped butter on the ground?

My legs swung up and my back slammed into the ground. The floor stole my breath.

I was sucking wind when Ryker stepped in front of me. I could feel his magic brushing against me, wave after wave. His magic hit like an emotional tsunami, churning up every ounce of mine.

"We need to talk."

The last time I'd been this close to him, he'd offered me a hand up. Not so much this time around. That was fine by me.

I got my air back and my feet underneath me. I wiped my hands on the back of my pants.

"You ready to discuss undoing the merge?" That was all I wanted at this point, a discussion. I might've been hasty in my demands, but I wouldn't live with a dictator. If he couldn't at least discuss it, how was this partnership ever going to work?

"No. I'm not." His arms crossed. Ryker was going to be Ryker. Unmovable to the last.

"Then there's nothing to talk about." Damn him. Didn't he see how he was pinning me into a corner? How he was trampling all over me? Maybe this was why things had never worked out with us. Why it had never moved past a kiss. He wanted a woman I would never be. He wanted one of the girls that would flock to his room and do as told.

I stepped around him with a look that told him we'd be brawling in the middle of the food building if he tried to stop me. He didn't.

I broke out of there and took off, not stopping until my lungs burned and my legs wobbled and there was no one in sight. The only thing I heard were the birds singing, the bees buzzing, and Ruck gasping for air.

The trees rustled as he stepped forward, his chest heaving. "Don't..." He held up a finger and then sank to the ground, his head flopping down in the grass and his knees bent. "Don't run anymore," he huffed out.

I walked over to him, my breathing still labored, but feeling quite good in comparison to how he looked. "You need to get a little more exercise. You're falling apart since we got here, eating biscuits all day. You're losing your sharp edges."

"Hey! You eat your fair share of biscuits." He reached over and gave my leg a halfhearted whack. He might've meant to punch it. Couldn't quite tell.

I sat down next to him. "You're right. I like my biscuits, but I'm not about to blow out a lung after a short run. What if we were getting chased? What if running was our only chance of survival?" If we were back in the Ruins, raiding for a living, we wouldn't stand a chance anymore.

"Trust me, if a monster was chasing us, I'd be able to run. I didn't see a monster. All I saw was Ryker." He leaned up on his elbows, getting his lungs back under control. "You went from watching his every move to running from him like he was going to gut you alive. I know you're pissed off about his slips—"

"Twice. Two times isn't an accident." *Slips.* Everyone liked to make it sound so innocent, like my magic hadn't been violently wrenched from me. If they could feel it, maybe they'd understand.

"Why are you taking this so badly?"

"You don't understand what this magic merge is like or how horrible it feels when that happens." The memory of it still sent a shudder through me.

"Then *explain* it."

I lay down on the grass beside him, wondering how I could put into words everything I'd felt, when I knew even another Wyrd Blood wouldn't understand.

"When the merge first clicked into place, I could feel his magic opening up to me, and it was invigorating to be that close to it. I was scared shitless in one way, because there was so much that it lets off a constant sizzle inside me that is intense. Even now, I can feel it.

"It's like I'm walking around with the blueprint of what makes him *him* inside of me. But he's got the same access. It's like my soul is a book and he can come flip through it anytime he wants. But it's worse, because twice now it's felt like he's yanked it right out of my chest."

Ruck was silent for a few seconds. He reached up and scratched his head before saying, "Damn, that sounds horrible."

"It's worse than horrible." I dropped my head into my hands and then dragged my fingers through my hair. "It's like he steals my soul and then has it to peruse while I'm withering away with nothing for hours. It's intimate in the most unpleasant way. Vulnerable." Even the memory of it made me want to get up and run again. But run where? To what?

I was drowning so deeply in my own misery that it took me a few minutes to realize Ruck had fallen silent. That was never a good sign from him.

The silent judgment was a killer. I let it roll on for another few minutes before I pressed him. "Can you say something?"

"I don't know what to say. That doesn't sound

good." He let the silence drag out for another few painful seconds. "That's why neither of you kissed again, isn't it? It's too much?"

I shrugged, letting his question go unanswered. I didn't know myself. I just knew Ryker hadn't tried to take our relationship to that place again, and neither had I.

"Well, for the record, it sounds wretched." Ruck patted my back.

At least he understood now. In our lives, there were a few things you feared. Torture, starvation, and lagging only slightly behind was intimacy.

Ruck had fucked more men than I could count, and he'd been truly intimate with none. I knew this first-hand, since he'd fucked a lot of them in whatever shack we'd been holed up in, and most didn't have doors. Some didn't have complete walls, either.

Intimacy made you vulnerable. That kind of weakness could land you in a shallow ditch. I could count on one hand the people I trusted enough to be vulnerable with, and that number had diminished significantly.

Ruck grabbed a shedding dandelion, pulling one fuzz out at a time. "Look, you still have to figure this out. You gotta get past this with him. I never thought I'd be the one who'd have to tell you to do the hard work. You've always just done it. You have to make peace somehow. You can't fight with him forever, not if we're going to live here. And what about the stones? Don't you need to get more?"

"We've got enough. When I'm in the same room

with them all, I can nearly feel my skin tingling from all the power they're cranking out."

He plucked up another dandelion and handed it to me. He knew how I liked to watch the fuzzies float away.

"You can't go on like this. Go talk to him and explain it like you did with me. He'll understand. He's not unreasonable. If you can't stand him after that, we can always kill him."

I laughed nervously. "If I'd ever had any delusions of killing Ryker, they're gone now."

"Really?" he asked in the hushed tone of someone greedy for gossip. Ruck ate gossip the way others ate cake. Luckily, he didn't dish it out the same.

"His magic is *vast*."

"What's it feel like?"

I leaned my head back and pointed at the sky above. "Like that. It feels like I'm standing on the threshold of the universe and can't even imagine where it might end. If there's something out there worse than him, might as well pack it up and call it a day."

"Good thing he's on our side. You better go play nice with Mr. Universe, because accidents or not, unless you want to move, it's going to be tough living here and waging war with him."

I let out a long breath with a curse or two floating upon it. He was right, and I knew it. There wasn't even a sliver of doubt. If I stayed here, Ryker and I had to come to terms, and right now, I couldn't see a way to leave.

I stood, wiped some dead grass off my butt, and then slumped.

"Come on there, killer, you can do this."

I nodded and tried to force myself to take a step in the right direction, but my legs wouldn't move. The only thing they wanted to do was crumble.

I fell back down next to Ruck.

His shoulder bumped mine. "Maybe later?"

"Yeah, maybe later."

THREE

Maybe I'd overreacted. I was a big enough person to admit to that. So he'd accidentally pulled on my magic again. It wasn't as if he'd needed it. It hadn't been intentional, right? He'd done it to save us, and I'd blown up at him like a banshee, then punched him in the gut. That might've been a bit severe. Just as him telling me he wouldn't try to sever the merge had been a bit much. He'd reacted to my overreaction. We were both adults. We could talk this out.

I walked up to his place. His window coverings were drawn back, the light glowing inside. I walked past the window, and a flash of movement caught my eye. There, on his couch, was Marly. She was one of the gardeners that I'd caught staring at him over and over again. She was sitting in my corner of the couch, in one of his shirts, her leg bent as she lay there reclined.

I jumped back as if I'd seen a murder.

I turned, keeping my head down as I walked away. I wasn't with him. If I sniffed, it was because the night air was cold. I didn't care what Ryker did. We were nothing to each other. I had no right to be upset. For magic's sake, he hadn't kissed me in months and months. Just because the trail of women in and out of his place had stopped didn't mean he was celibate all of a sudden.

A woman leaned against a building down the way, her smile wide, as if she'd guessed what I'd seen and was happy for it. What seemed like decades ago now, she would've been the first person I sought out when I was upset. Now I kept walking as if I'd never seen Marra standing there.

THERE WAS A TAP AT MY DOOR. I ROLLED OVER onto my stomach, dulling the sound with a pillow over my head. The tapping turned into banging, and it was clear they wouldn't be leaving. Still, I didn't speak, clinging to hope.

It wasn't that I was in the depths of despair. It was more the depths of uncertainty. Was this how I was going to live out the rest of my life? Watching Ryker sleep with every chick that lived here when he was on a break from stealing my magic? Having to make peace with him when he wouldn't even discuss what I wanted? I'd thought this place was the best thing that had ever happened to me, and now I longed for the Ruins.

The door creaked open. I should've locked it. No one respected privacy in this place. If I'd been back at the Ruins, I wouldn't have had a door, but I also wouldn't have had the illusion it provided.

"Bugs? You okay?" Dez walked in, glorious blond hair swinging. It was amazing that someone so beautiful could also be one of the most wonderful people I'd ever met. She'd taken pity on me one day when she'd caught some ugly looks flowing toward me from Marra's table. We'd bonded over biscuits and lost friends. It turned out a lot of women struggled with being friends with a goddess.

"Hey. I'm fine. Just tired." If she was a good friend, she'd ignore the crack in my voice.

"What happened?" She walked over and sat on the bed beside me. So much for that.

"It's nothing. An off day." I sat up a bit straighter and smiled. *See? I'm fine.*

"It's Ryker, isn't it? I've seen his casualties before." She toyed with a blond lock. "Plus, I saw you heading from that direction."

I was shaking my head before she finished, leaning an elbow on the windowsill by my bed and looking out at the stars. "It's complicated. This whole magic merge thing..." I waved a hand in the air and shook my head again.

She flopped back on the bed, bumping me a few inches off to the side as she did, and stared at the ceiling. She took a deep breath then shredded on her exhale. "I get it. I was in love once. He didn't want me."

She bit her lip, but I'd seen the tremble in it. I wasn't sure if she'd been in love once or still was to a certain degree.

"Are you sure? I've seen the way men look at you." Dez was perfect. When she walked into a room, every other person in there looked like they had troll blood. And on top of it, she was a Wyrd Blood. Although no one actually knew what she could do. She didn't like to talk about it for some reason, and I'd never pressed the issue.

"Yeah, well, not this one." She sat up and turned her head away from me, and there was a suspicious swipe of her arm before she turned back. We now had matching fake smiles. The day was not ending well.

"Look, I think you've got to get out of here for a while," she said. "Take a break and regroup. Knife and I are going back to Dorley for a little while. Why don't you come with us?"

"Not an option. I'm linked to Ryker in more than one way. I lost a challenge to him, and now my magic is merged with him. I'm stuck here." I got out of the bed and paced in front of it. How many times had I thought about doing that in the last couple of weeks? If it were only that simple.

She sat up, her brow crinkling. "I think you're wrong. If I know magical theory as well as I think, the merge would cancel out the forfeit of the challenge. In essence, because you're merged, you're never that far from him, even if you physically are."

I stopped pacing. "You think I could just get up and leave here? No problem?"

"Yes. And I bet Ryker realizes it. Plus, it's not like the King of Bedlam is a problem anymore. After they lost the dragons, Harvo got pushed out."

"He did?" What the fuck? Why hadn't Ryker told me? Was this where we'd gotten to? Withholding and dictating?

"Let's face it: whatever his reasons, Ryker wants to keep you here, but it's not fair to you." She took in a deep breath and then relaxed back on the bed. "Look, he's not a bad guy, but I think you need some space. Maybe it'll help him see the situation a little clearer. Sometimes the hardest thing to do is walk away."

I wrapped my arms around myself. I could actually leave. I could get some space to clear my head and figure things out, maybe stomp some feelings away while I was at it. The idea made me feel split in two. Every part of me should want to go, right? But it didn't. Still, could I keep going on like this?

"It's not like you can't come back," Dez said.

"When does Knife want to leave?"

"Two days."

Two mornings, two nights. Not a lot of time. But she was right. I needed to go, get out of here so I could think straight.

"What about Ruck? He'd have to be welcome."

She threw back her head and laughed. "Are you kidding? Knife would roll out the red carpet for Ruck if it meant you'd come."

I didn't doubt it. Ryker and Knife had an odd relationship. I didn't doubt their loyalty or competitiveness. In another life, they might've been brothers.

"Maybe I will," I said.

"Good."

FOUR

I CLIMBED UP TO THE TOP OF THE TOWER platform. Ruck had another five hours left on his shift and I wouldn't make it another twenty minutes. If I was going to leave, and I wanted to, I needed to know if Ruck was going to come. It would be hard enough to make the break with Ryker as it was. There was no way I was leaving Ruck at the same time.

I hit the top of the tower landing. Ruck's back was to me as he watched the horizon. He waved for me to come sit by him. "Just tell me. I already know that whatever you're here to say is bad by how slow you climbed up the rungs and how you stopped halfway up."

Only Ruck would notice the difference in my climb. Why couldn't he be into girls? Life would be so much easier.

I walked the few paces to where he was sitting, his legs hanging over the edge. He moved his canteen and half-eaten biscuit so I could sit down beside him.

A few minutes later, I still hadn't spoken, and the ripped hem of my shirt was a lot worse off than it had been.

"Whatever it is, it can't be *that* bad." He held out his half-eaten biscuit, as if that could cure all the woes in the world.

I waved it off and took a deep breath. "Before I tell you, you need to know there's no pressure. You make your own choice, and I won't fault you for your decision no matter what." *But please say you'll come with me. Please. I can't lose you both.*

"You're scaring me." He turned toward me, taking his eyes off the horizon.

I *really* must've been alarming. Ruck had told me countless times how the watch was serious business. If you didn't keep a good lookout, you lost tower duty. That didn't sound like a big deal until you were digging ditches or chopping up onions for weeks. Or even worse, cleaning the bathrooms. There were stories of one tower watch person who'd fallen asleep on the job. Word was they were still on bathroom duty a year later.

"I want to go to Dorley for a while. It would be nice to have a change of pace."

Ruck's mouth parted slightly as he stared back off into the night horizon. His confused wrinkles finally smoothed into something a little sadder. It didn't take him long to fit all the pieces together.

"Ryker? I guess the talk didn't go so well."

I leaned back so he'd have a hard time seeing my face unless he turned away from his watch again. "I need some space from here. Between the magical slips and the..." It wasn't the girls. It wasn't. It was the magic only.

"The what?"

Fuck it. If I couldn't tell Ruck what was eating at me, who could I tell. "I feel like I'm stuck in this holding pattern where I can't move on and he's banging everything that walks." I pulled a heel up so I had a place to bang my forehead.

"If it helps, I haven't seen anybody coming and going since—"

"I just saw one splayed out on his couch."

"Oh." The seconds ticked by as Ruck rubbed his palm over the top of his pants leg. "I mean, you guys weren't really a thing."

"I know, and I can't seem to accept that. I think space would do me good. It's not like we set out to make this place home. Why stay if things are taking a bad turn?" Before he spent another hour rubbing through his pants leg, I said, "I get it if you don't want to leave here. I don't expect you to drop everything and run away with me because I can't be near someone. If you don't want to leave, I'll make it work, and it's not like I won't come back." But it was going to be hard. Ruck had been my rock, my family, the one constant in my life.

"No. If you want to go to Dorley, we go to Dorley. That's it. Done." He made a fist and held it out to me, like we used to do before raids, way back when.

"Ruck, are you sure? I don't want to take the best place you've ever had away from you. This has become your home too."

"Bugs, we've been together since we were kids. This place isn't home. You're home." His forearm bumped me as he lifted that still-clenched fist toward me. "You going to leave me hanging here?"

I made a fist and brought it down atop his, trying not to sniffle as I did. It didn't work.

His head tilted slightly toward me.

"It's getting cold." I gave him a face that said he was crazy if he thought I was getting choked up that easy.

He rolled his eyes. "You know, there's a big upside to this for me."

"What's that?"

"I'm running out of worthy indulgences."

I hadn't heard him say that since we'd lived in the Ruins. "Here? But this place has so many more guys. You couldn't have gone through all of them." Although he might've. I'd seen Ruck in action. His name should've been Rut.

"You like to live like a prude. I like to be generous with my love."

"Nobody you want to maybe wash and repeat with?"

"No. *He's* not here. Maybe we're supposed to go to Dorley. Maybe *he's* there. This was probably meant to be." He was nodding, a smile budding on his lips. *He* was how Ruck had always referred to the one. Ruck had a romantic streak that was wide and never-ending.

"Going to Dorley might be a great idea." He patted my leg. "I'm glad we made this decision."

I wished I had the same optimism he did.

FIVE

Ryker was standing in my door. No need to hide the bag I was packing. He knew. His riled magic filled the space. The confrontation I'd wanted to avoid had come and found me, and I had no idea how bad this would go. There was no good ending here, not the way I was feeling inside. Too painful to stay, too miserable to leave. My only hope was that getting away would soothe the ache.

I'd been so close to getting out of here without this conversation. There were so many things I wanted to say but could never voice to him directly. The note I'd written him was still on the table beside me.

It was all in that letter that I'd probably never have given. I would've chickened out and jotted down something fast and inadequate a few minutes before we left. I would've snuck out like a thief in the night.

I heard him stirring behind me.

"I told them that Bugs wouldn't sneak out of here

without saying a word to me. She'd never do that. I didn't believe it, but I guess I should've."

I glanced over as he stared at my full bag sitting on the bed.

"I was going to let you know." I paused only a second before I threw a few more items into it.

"When? After you left?" He leaned against the wall, watching me.

I couldn't answer without being a liar, so I bit my tongue instead. The vision of the girl on his couch hammered in my head. I forced myself to think of how awful it felt when he'd taken my magic. Worse, he'd refused to try and undo the merge. Truth was, now that I'd had some space, I didn't know if that was smart. But to be unwilling to discuss it with me? Those were his choices. Leaving was mine.

I threw the last of my things in my bag and then refolded the already folded items, looking for any distraction I could find.

"What about the fact that someone out there still might want to kill you?" His voice was calm, as if he already knew whatever he said wouldn't make a difference.

He was right.

"Nothing's happened for months. The merge fixed that problem. There are enough stones that there is no threat anymore."

"What about the Debt Collector? You know I'm still trying to pin down his location for you. Doesn't that matter anymore?"

"Of course it does, but that could take years. I know

how slippery he is. With Switch, I could be back here within minutes. There's no reason I have to stay here and wait."

"And years are too long to get stuck here, is that what you're saying?"

I didn't answer, waiting for where he'd go next. I'd dreaded this conversation enough to have rehearsed it for days. There wasn't a question I wasn't ready for.

"What about the challenge you lost? The one that indebted you to me?" he asked.

"Dez thinks that once we merged, it neutralized it and made it null, since our magic is always linked at this point. But you knew that, didn't you?" I looked at him, daring him to deny it.

"It's possible, but we don't know anything for sure," he replied, as if that made it okay to have not told me.

"Then I won't get too far." I went back to my bag, struggling to find new items to fix but not having the strength to walk away from him either.

"Is that for me?" He stepped forward.

There was only one thing he could be talking about, and it was the folded note on my table. The one I'd dreamed of slipping under his door, which in all truth, would never be read by him.

"No." I grabbed the folded piece of paper and shoved it in my bag, and then my hands finally stilled. I took a shaky breath.

He was so close now, just a couple of feet away. Our magic was doing that same dance it always did, pulling me toward him, as if I were meant to be by his side. It was another reason to leave. I didn't know where my feelings ended and the magic took over.

Still, leaving was like tearing myself in two.

"Are you going to try and stop me?" I asked, almost hoping he'd say yes.

"No. You want to go? Then go. I won't beg you to stay."

He might as well have shoved his hand in my chest and squeezed as he spoke those last words. I wanted to crumble, fall onto the bed, and cry. I stood still, not even a muscle twitching.

He walked out, his magic leaving and creating a vacuum until the void was overwhelming. I leaned forward over the bed to look out the window, trying to catch a last glimpse of him as he left. At least leaving had been easy for one of us.

I tied my bag closed, breathing past the pain. In a couple of days, this would fade. Maybe a couple of weeks. Maybe a month, but I'd get past it. The pain would dull, and then maybe I could come back a stronger person.

Dez popped in a few minutes later. She leaned against the doorjamb. "How'd that go?"

I dropped onto my bed, feeling like the energy I needed to remain standing had been sucked from my veins. "Well enough, I suppose. No teary farewells. That was probably a given for him." I laughed at my own joke and gave her a half-smile.

She smiled back, sans the laughter and with a sadness about the eyes. "Knife is ready. Let's get going. Better to do it quick, then."

"Yeah. You're right," I said. Still, it took me a few more moments to get up. I slung my bag on my shoulder and walked from the room. I tried to keep my breathing even instead of the jagged mess that my heart wanted to shred it into.

I walked through the Valley, smiling and nodding to the people I'd become so familiar with, while I pretended everything was fine. That I wasn't leaving here, maybe for good.

I wished Ruck was beside me, but he hadn't been able to get his tower shifts covered. He didn't want to leave Ryker high and dry, so he was going to follow a week later.

We made our way to Knife's place, having to pass right by Ryker's. His door was closed. Just as I'd been able to take a breath, it opened. He stepped into the doorway and watched as I walked past. Dez gave a wave, which he returned with a nod. Ryker and I didn't do anything but stare.

He watched me with something akin to anger, as if I were a defector. My stare might've had regret. That was how I felt, deep down. Regret for all of the moments that hadn't worked out, all of the hurt. Everything.

I broke the contact first, not caring about winning anymore. I was already defeated; he just didn't know it. He'd won. He'd stolen my heart, taken it all and left nothing behind. He was the victor of the spoils and me the empty shell.

"It's for the best," Dez said. "Get a little distance, regroup. You can always come back."

"Yeah, maybe." If Ryker would take me back. I wasn't sure he would, not after that last look he'd given me. My steps felt heavier the farther I walked.

"Wait up!"

I spun around at the sound of Ruck's voice to see him running toward us, a bag slung over his shoulder.

"I'm coming now," he said as he stopped beside us.

Dez pointed toward Knife's place up ahead. I nodded, indicating we'd be there soon, and then turned my attention back to Ruck.

"I thought you couldn't get coverage?" I wrapped a hand around his wrist, and there wasn't anything that was going to make me let go of him.

"Ryker told me to go."

Holy magic, the man hated me so much he was purging the place of my people. Marra had lucked out. She probably got to stay because she'd cut me off.

I wrapped Ruck in a bear hug and could feel myself smile.

We turned to catch up with Dez and Knife, my grip still firm on Ruck.

Knife gave me a nod as our party got ready to depart. He didn't say anything else, but I could tell from that single look that he thought I was doing the right thing.

We all made our way to the chugger we were taking together. A lot of Knife's people were staying behind at the Valley, but we had quite a few looking to go back to Dorley. Knife and Dez climbed into the front cab, and I waved them on, hopping in the back with Ruck.

The back of the chugger was wide open, and a few

benches had been nailed to the sides, where we settled in together.

Ruck leaned forward, resting his arms on his legs, looking at the scenery as the engine roared to life. "Nice to be starting a new adventure, right? The Valley was a good time, but I'm interested in what Dorley has to offer."

I rested my back on the side. I nodded and watched as we began moving away. At that moment, not one part of me wanted to leave this place. I put my hands on my knees to help keep my feet glued to the floor.

For Ruck, it was different. He thought maybe the love of his life would be around the next corner. I'd already found the man I wanted, and I was driving away from him as we spoke. Not that it mattered—he'd already been a million miles away where it counted.

"You look off. You nervous about the distance because of the merge thing? Dez thinks it'll be okay, right?"

"Yeah, she thinks it'll all be good."

As we got farther away and the towers of the valley were the last landmarks I could make out, my heart sank a little more. Physically, I felt fine. Dez had been right. The merge wouldn't force me to stay close to Ryker, nor the lost challenge. My last secret hope of an out was dying with every new mile.

I'd never have to see Ryker again if I didn't want to, and it felt like a knife was repeatedly stabbing me in the heart.

SIX

Six months later...

SHE WAS SIXTEEN, TOPS, SITTING CROSS-LEGGED IN front of me on the ground. The knees of her pants were paper thin, and the color of her flesh tinted the area. The hems were so frayed that they had a coating of mud on the dangling threads.

A year ago, I wouldn't have thought she was that bad off. Her clothes were better than what people in the Ruins wore. If that was the bar to judge by, she was in good shape, as long as you didn't hear her stomach growling. Showed how quickly your standards changed.

For some reason, I'd assumed the people of Dorley would be better off, closer to how the people of the Valley fared. I'd learned only some were. Most weren't.

I was working on that. Knife wasn't an inherently bad guy, after all. Just a tad on the selfish side. There were worse crimes, and I was certain I could get him to loosen the coin purse if I harassed him long enough.

"Will I get the raise I was promised?" the girl asked, her fingernails dirty, hinting at a job in construction. Made sense that Knife wouldn't allocate a lot of money her way. He paid a premium to Wyrd Blood, but it was a steep slide after that.

I didn't need a worm for this answer. Knife didn't give anyone raises. Still, I went through the motions, because that was my job here, and I'd rather have the worm be the bearer of bad news.

I reached into the bucket by my side, filled with a smattering of dirt and one of the last pre-dug worms of the day, all happy to return to the ground. I cupped my hands, whispered the question, and placed it into the circle that had already been used forty-nine times today. The worm went to "no" as soon as it hit the ground.

Her face fell and the crease between her brows deepened. I leaned back, waiting to see if she'd put up a fight. She didn't. She stood, gave me a quick thanks, and walked out of the tent. I liked pragmatists best. They accepted the truth faster. I was tired of explaining that I couldn't ask the same question repeatedly.

The bell chimed in the tower, marking quitting time. I tipped over the bucket, and the last of the worms wriggled their way to freedom.

Ruck cast a shadow over where I knelt. "You done?"

He had that tone again. It was going to be another talk. More and more, I was hating the talks.

"Yeah, that was my last client of the day."

He looked over his shoulder as the girl walked slowly across the field, probably heading to one of the shacks in the southern corner. She might as well have had weights tied to her ankles with the way her feet dragged.

His head bobbed as he exhaled. "Yeah, saw her dejected form leaving."

Yep, definitely going to have the talk again.

"Oh, great." His voice had the enthusiasm of a slug crawling in hot sand.

I raised my head and saw Knife heading over. "Looks like he spotted another unhappy customer. Probably looking to give me another pep talk." That talk didn't bother me. I considered it part of the cause. The worms helped the people here realize how lousy they were treated. Hopefully, one day they'd demand more.

Knife made his way over and glanced at Ruck, giving him a brief nod, as he often did. Knife tended to treat Ruck as my accessory, like he was a scarf or something. It didn't help relations much.

Knife focused on me. "Bugs."

"Knife, what's going on?" I asked.

He scratched his jaw, stalling for a few seconds before he launched into his tirade. "Bugs, do you remember the talk we had a week ago, and the one the week before, and all those others before that, about what we'd do differently?"

We. I wasn't sure why he thought pretending he was part of this worming business would make a difference. The only part he'd done was ordering this ridiculous tent erected. Why he thought that was a good idea was beyond me. Maybe it was because it broadcast to all that came here he had a "psychic" on duty full-time. My guess was that word was spreading on how well it was working out—and laughter was following close behind.

"Do you remember the part where I told you I had no control over what the worm did?" Even in the tent, it wasn't a *we*. The worm wasn't even on my team. When it came right to it, the worm did what the worm wanted and didn't care what I said. I'd wanted to squish more than one myself.

He walked over to my dirt circle and pointed. "What about doing something a little differently here? Maybe not marking the circle so clearly? Do you have to use a 'yes' and 'no' with it? What about a couple of Xs?"

Ruck was shaking his head, slapping his palm to his forehead behind Knife.

There had been a time that I'd marked my circles with Xs before I knew how to write. I'd never mark anything with an X again, unless it was a treasure map or a target.

I stared down at the circle as if I were giving it some serious thought and squinted for a few seconds. "Nope. That would break the integrity of the worming process. Can't do it."

Knife took in a breath that made his chest nearly

explode. He grinned like it was his job and then nodded rapidly. "We're going to have to work a little harder on this after I think it over a while."

"Sure." I didn't bother saying it like I meant it.

He closed his eyes and took in a few more deep breaths. "Okay. We'll work on it. We'll work it out." He walked away looking about as convinced as he should be.

I *almost* felt bad for him. Yes, Knife was greedy, and he skirted the line between decent and dingy a lot. But for all his faults, I liked him. Deep down, he had some good in there. That didn't mean I'd lie to his people.

Worms gone, Knife handled, I grabbed my canteen and bag. Ruck was at my side like we were stuck together by a bad batch of hollyhoney.

He angled his head toward me. "Has he said anything about wanting you in his bed recently?"

"No. I think he's given up on that for now."

The first couple of weeks here, Knife had put out feelers on a regular basis. I'd shied away from all advances. Then he'd stopped. Dez had a hand in it. I couldn't prove it, and she was all about the denial, but it had to have been her. Every time I'd gotten annoyed by Knife, you would've thought he'd insulted her as well.

"Trust me, he hasn't given up, or you wouldn't get away with all the shit you do. He's biding his time. The guy is a lot more patient than I'd imagined. Although that's the least of his sins. Having you set up like this, it's a mockery of your gifts. He's turned you into a sideshow." Ruck pointed a thumb over his shoulder.

"The red and white striped tent certainly doesn't help it any."

I tried to keep my mouth in a flat line. It lasted two seconds before the corners shot up and I laughed. "Yes, I'm a spectacle. It's not his fault. My particular skill set lends itself to that, no help needed. It's not all his fault. I agreed to this."

"I don't care what you agreed to. Stop doing it anyway."

"No. I said I'd do it. What else can I do here?"

"Leave. We don't have to go to the Valley, but that doesn't mean we need to stay. We can find somewhere else. Seriously, look at these people."

As we weaved in and out of the crowd, all you saw were long faces, ripped clothing, and dark circles. The only people who had it really good here were Wyrd Blood and Ruck, not that it made him happy. Still, it was probably our safest bet at the moment.

"You know there aren't that many places to go. Do you want to end up back at the Ruins?" I asked, weaving around a particularly cranky woman lugging a bucket of water that splashed anyone who dared come close.

"There might be other options we don't know about."

"It's not safe." The idea of leaving here felt like taking the first step into the abyss. I'd be ready for that at some point, but not quite yet. Maybe in another week or two. Maybe another month.

When I first got here, I'd daydreamed that Ryker would come after me. I'd been gone for a few days, and his heart would start to ache the way mine had, a deep, throbbing pain that felt like it invaded every part of my life. It had sucked all the flavor out of food, robbed jokes of their laughter, and the only things I noticed about sunny days were the deep shadows they cast. He hadn't shown.

Then I'd told myself he'd come because he needed me—if not emotionally, but for what I could do for him. The scene would be simple. He'd stride into the great hall of Dorley and demand I come back because of some other urgent issue. I'd put up a fight for a little bit, but then I'd relent, all the while knowing what I was doing—condemning myself to a lifetime of purgatory in order to escape the immediate hell of pain that I was struggling to make it through.

But Ryker hadn't shown. He hadn't messaged. He'd left me alone. The one thing that had kept me here was my pride. The same pride that would sit under a striped tent every day.

"You're killing me slowly. You know this, right?" Ruck asked, as if he were the sideshow attraction.

"What are you complaining about? You've never had it so good." Ruck's sole job was spot-checking the guards whenever he felt inclined, and reporting any problems he noticed. In reality, Ruck's job was to visit and chitchat with his buddies. Sometimes he'd bring them coffee or a mug of ale. He'd yet to find a problem, and no one seemed to notice or care.

"We aren't people who sit in striped tents. Dogs who perform tricks belong in tents. It's too much." The anger had seeped out by the time he'd finished. His attention had shifted toward the short wall that ran along the castle walkway.

"I'll catch up with you back at the room. I've got to go do something," he said.

I tried to stand on my tiptoes to get a look at what he'd seen.

"Who's over there?" I asked, taking a couple of steps back to get a better view. Being short really sucked sometimes. "Is your new boyfriend over there?" I knew there was one. Ruck had been sneaking off a lot, and at hours that could only mean one thing. "Why won't you tell me who he is?"

I looked for a place to scale the wall. There had to be a foothold somewhere.

"He wants to keep it a secret for now, and I can't betray his trust. I gotta go." He waved and started back the way we'd been walking.

"This isn't fair. You blab on me all the time," I yelled after him.

His only response was another wave.

"When are you going to tell me who it is?" I yelled.

I didn't even get a wave this time.

"Bugs, I've been looking for you," Dez said as she headed toward me from the opposite direction Ruck had taken off in.

I spun, meeting her halfway.

"You coming next week?" Dez asked as we started toward the castle together.

This was definitely the day for having unwanted conversations.

"I don't know. I've got some things I wanted to do."

I kept my gaze forward, not wanting to see her suspicious eyes. I could still see her hands fluttering and her head shaking, blond hair whipping all about her.

"There's only one party like this every five years. There isn't a Wyrd Blood this side of the Great Ocean that doesn't go, as long as you don't count the people afraid of Ryker, or Knife, or... Whatever, there's a lot. No way am I missing it, and neither should you."

"It wouldn't be a big miss for me. I'm not a party person." I walked into the side entrance of the castle and headed to the meal window. There wasn't a large line yet, and I needed to get dinner before the crowd came.

Big Beth looked down at me and placed the two available options on the counter. One was covered in red sauce and the other in brown. When you couldn't figure out what was being served, there was a reason.

I let out a soft whistle.

"Which one should I go with?" I asked.

"It's not going to make a difference," Big Beth said in her signature flat tone.

Dez was on the side, looking down at the plates and sniffing, then pointed. She wouldn't be eating this. She'd only eat in the Wyrd Blood food hall.

I went with Dez's instinct and grabbed the red sauce plate, since it smelled slightly savorier. "Thanks."

"See yah tomorrow," Big Beth said, stepping back from the window to ready more mystery plates.

"I know how you feel about Wyrd Bloods getting better food, but I don't know how you can eat that,"

Dez whispered as we weaved our way through a crowd of dulls, all heading toward the food window.

I hit the stairs that wound up toward the upper suites, taking a quick bite as I did. It wasn't like the food at the Valley, but it wasn't hollyhoney either.

"If you'd lived in the Ruins as long as I did, you wouldn't mind it."

I opened my door to the sitting area. It was connected to the two bedrooms of the suite I shared with Ruck. It was called the Sweetheart suite and was one of the nicest suites in the castle. When I'd first gotten here, it had stirred up a lot of rumors about what was going on between Knife and me. When it came down to it, Knife would do whatever it took to make me happy enough that I didn't go back to the Valley.

The suite was nice, the bed was comfy, but deep down, it meant nothing. I'd rather be sleeping in a tent back at the Valley.

Dez fell onto the couch in the sitting room. "You have to come. If you don't, then Switch is going to transport Knife, and I'll have to take a chugger over. Switch can't transport more than one of us without you.

"And I don't care what you say about not liking parties. When it was mentioned at breakfast a week ago, you were all big eyes and ears." She crossed her arms and legs before raising an eyebrow at me.

I settled into the chair opposite her. "I didn't know where it was then. I thought it was here. I didn't know it was *his* party. I'm not going to *his* party." That done and out of the way, I could get back to choking down dinner while trying to not look too closely at what I was eating. The sauce had slid off the main course, revealing something grey and slimy lurking beneath.

"It's not his party. It's only held there."

I swallowed down a bad chunk. "Don't you need to go get dinner?"

She looked down at the couch fabric, moving her fingers over it to make the velvet go in different directions. "Are you *scared* to see him?"

Holy magic, she wasn't going to quit. What was it with everyone today?

"I'm not scared." I'd said that way too forcefully and much too quick. I'd shot it out at her like a cannonball.

Her head was bobbing "yes" as her forehead was scrunched up in a much more convincing "no."

"Really, I'm not worried about seeing him." I added a shrug to bolster the redo.

"I get not wanting to see him, but—"

"I'm not scared."

She threw her hands up. "Okay. I'll believe you."

I hated when people said they believed you when their tone called you a liar. They might as well continue on and say the entire thought. *I'll believe you, but only because I think you're too fragile to call a liar at the moment.* That was where Ruck really shone. He never thought I was too fragile to hear the truth. If I was, he would tell me to toughen up.

Worse part of it all was that she was right. She shouldn't believe me. I *was* full of it. The idea of seeing Ryker again made me want to shiver inside until my entire body broke into hairline cracks.

Ruck walked through the door, a becoming flush on his cheeks that hinted he'd seen his boyfriend for more than a minute or two.

He held up the piece of paper in his hands. "I have to go back to the Valley tomorrow and stay for a couple of weeks."

My fork bounced off my plate and dropped to the floor, taking some of the red sauce with it. "Why?"

"Ryker sent me a message. He said he was short on people to work the tower and asked if I'd come and fill in for a little while."

"Short on people?" There was no way he was "short" on people. He still had half of Dorley there. My gaze shot to Dez, who was rolling her eyes. She was big on the eye roll, but this one was warranted. "And you believed that?"

He shrugged. "The guy gave us a place to live when we had nothing. If he needs a favor, I have to do it."

"When are you going?" I put my mystery meat on the table, the news ruining my appetite worse than the bad taste.

"Tomorrow night. Switch said he'd bring me over." He stretched, letting out a long yawn. "I'll see you later. I'm beat and I've got to pack."

I was nodding as he walked into his room and shut the door.

Dez barely waited for the knob to click before she snorted. "He's trying to steal Ruck. Now you've got to go, if only to tell him hands off the Ruck Man."

I dropped down beside her. "You're right. I'm going. I have to."

"Good. What are you going to wear? You're not going the way you usually dress, right?" She used her fingers to wave at my stained shirt.

I didn't bother to respond. I had bigger issues. Ryker was not stealing Ruck. I'd go to war before I let that happen.

SEVEN

ONE CORNER OF THE CASTLE COURTYARD DIDN'T have a bunch of busybodies hanging around. It was still too early for people to be in bed as I made my way to the forgotten spot along the back wall, where a line of shrubs fenced it in. It was the only place I could get some privacy when I had my own worming to do.

I knelt, missing the feel of dirt in my hand instead of scraping a bucket. I plucked up a worm and cupped my hands around it, getting ready to whisper my question. The thing wouldn't settle down, as if I were infusing it with my tension.

"Will you relax and listen?"

It didn't. I'd have to deal with an agitated worm.

"Is Ryker trying to steal Ruck?" I put down the wriggler and waited. Instead of moving toward an answer, it went straight down into the ground.

Hmmm. I'd never plucked a bad one before, but there was always a first. I dug into the ground for another. He was a wiggler too, but not as bad as the last.

"Should I go to the party?" I placed him in the circle, and he went straight down, as the other had. I started to sweat.

I was digging up another worm when the bushes beside me rustled.

"I knew you'd be here," Ruck said, coming to squat beside me.

I nodded to him as I whispered to the worm, "Party. Yes or no?" There. No room for miscommunication. I placed it in the circle, and it dug straight down. The sweating spread to my palms.

"Hmmm. Never saw that happen," Ruck said.

"Neither have I. It didn't want to answer."

"Do another."

"Yeah." I dug in a different spot for a worm, my hands shaking a hair as I plucked it out. Hopefully this one would be more cooperative. As soon as its little body wouldn't settle down in my palm, I knew it was going to go the same as the last three times.

Still had to try. "Is Ruck going to eat tomorrow?"

"That's a dumb question," he said.

"I know. That was the point." I placed the worm in the circle. It crawled directly into the ground again. What the hell was wrong with me?

Ruck pointed at where the worm disappeared. "Why aren't they answering?"

"I don't know."

"Your hands are shaking."

"It's chilly out here." I leaned forward and dug both hands into the dirt.

"Are you going to try and go all out?"

"Yes." I'd give it everything I had and see if I could jump-start the answers. I asked the dumbest question I could think of and gave it as much juice as I had.

"Am I alive?"

By the time I stopped, I had to fall back and sit on my heels, completely drained.

Nothing happened. There was no line in the ground. No worms wiggling around. No answers.

"The worms looked normal." Ruck reached down and grabbed a chunk of dirt before letting it drop. His forehead wrinkled as he shifted focus back to me, where I sat depleted on the dirt. "Holy magic. Are you broken?"

I held my arm out. "Grab me."

"Really?"

"It's important."

He did and immediately yanked it back, waving his hand in the air. "Fucker."

"Sorry, but I had to check." I held a hand up, trying to construct a ward and feeling the magic flowing to my fingers. "Only partially broken. I think I can still do wards, too."

He sat down next to me, his shoulder brushing mine. "Doesn't magic mature as you age? Maybe it changes, too? You might not be broken. What if you're evolving?"

"Maybe." I didn't feel different. I felt exactly the same. I lifted a hand to my forehead. Was I sick? I wasn't cold and felt good.

"If you're worried, I could say something to Ryker

tomorrow. Or if you go to the party, you could tell him yourself."

We'd left months ago and yet he still wanted me to go running back to Ryker for everything. "No. I don't need him."

"Sending a—"

"I'm not sending a message. I'm not telling him anything." I narrowed my eyes. "And you don't say a word when you get there. I can't worm for one day. That isn't a problem. It's a fluke."

"But—"

I was shaking my head before he could continue. "No. Last problem he fixed for me led to more problems."

"Look, I didn't come find you to fight. I'm leaving early tomorrow and wanted to make sure you knew that I'm definitely coming back."

I looked down, trying to hide my smile. "I know you will." Because I was also going to that party and telling Ryker in clear terms he couldn't keep Ruck.

I got to my feet, feeling like I was ten hours past due for sleep. A warm breeze blew over me, bringing with it the smell of something rotten, as if to accent what else was wrong with this place.

"What is that? What are they burning now?" I lifted my arm to my nose to block the odor.

Ruck lifted his head. "I don't smell it."

"I don't know how that's possible. I have to get out of here. Unlike you, my sniffer isn't broken."

Ruck had gone upstairs to finish packing while I made my way to the dungeon level and walked down the long hall. The light was still shining underneath the big wooden door.

I laid knuckles to wood. "Alba?"

"Come in."

I opened the heavy door to the dank, dark place. I used to think she was being punished for something to get stuck down here. Turned out she was a Wyrd Blood with a very strange magic. She absorbed moisture. When she'd been in the other rooms, they had to mortar the walls every week because of crumbling cement. According to Dez, this room used to have puddles before Alba moved in. Now it was the perfect climate, unless she got upset.

"Can you rearrange the schedule tomorrow?" I asked, trying to stay by the door and not get too close. She hated rescheduling anything, and I didn't have any moisturizer handy.

"What's wrong? Are you ill? Do you need the healer?"

I scratched some dry skin on my arm and edged back another step, hoping she wouldn't notice my retreat and become more agitated.

"Nothing major. Magic seems off a little. Not a big deal." I scratched at my scalp.

Bushy brows rose. "'Off' how?"

"Just glitchy or something." I leaned in slightly, wondering if she had a water pitcher around. My tongue felt like sandpaper.

"Okay. I'll post a sign on your tent tomorrow that

the day's appointments will need to see me for rescheduling." She grabbed a large book from her shelf, flipped it open, and tapped the pencil to page. "I'll have to push everything until after the party. This glitch of yours, do you think it'll be a short-term glitch? Or is this a longer-term thing?"

I could see the paper of the book start flaking, and my leg was itching like crazy. I took a few more steps back. "To be safe, let's keep the schedule clear until after I get back from the Valley."

"That long?"

"Yes. Thanks." I turned to get out of there before she sucked all the moisture out of my body.

EIGHT

Ruck was long gone by the time I was eating my morning slop, something like oatmeal but with none of the taste and flavor. The book on my lap was my only company.

I'd just gotten to the first kiss between Eric and Iselda when the door creaked open. I wanted to slam it shut. Obviously, whoever was popping in had no idea how many pages I'd had to wait for this moment.

"Hey," Knife said, forcing me to acknowledge him.

I shut the cover on Eric, swearing I'd come back to him soon.

"Hi." I took another bite of oatmeal while I waited to hear what was wrong. Knife didn't make morning visits.

He dropped onto the opposite side of the couch. I ate another spoonful of oat-something-or-other while he grinned, as if that would disarm me.

His smiled seemed fixed upon his face, and I was getting whiffs of stress from his magic.

"I heard you're 'glitching'?" he asked.

Another one with raised brows and curious eyes, as if I were the only one that had off days. "I'm fine. The worms weren't cooperating, is all. Not a big deal. I'm sure it was a fluke."

He placed a hand on the back of the couch as he leaned forward. "So it's true, then?"

"The worm wouldn't answer. That's all."

Maybe it wasn't even me? Maybe the worms were on strike because they didn't like working in this place either? If I didn't want to get back to Eric and Iselda so badly, I would've told him this. But I did, so I wouldn't. He really needed to go. I had places to be that weren't of this world.

He rubbed the back of his neck, working out a kink. "This only happened once, then?"

I hated how hopeful he sounded. I was going to have to pop that hope like a needle to a bubble. Had to, even if that delayed my reunion. What if the issue persisted for a while? I wasn't going to have these morning talks on a daily basis. "Maybe more than once. I'm off, but I'll get back to normal."

I will. One night doesn't mean anything. I wasn't sure who needed to hear that more, him or me.

"How many times did you have the problem?"

"I don't know, maybe three." Or four. The fifth hadn't involved the worms, so no need to include that time for sure.

He leaned back, as if an invisible pair of hands had shoved him and sucked all the energy from him, so the only thing holding him up was the back of the couch.

Did he not hear me? It wasn't a big deal. Why was everyone acting as if it were the worst thing ever?

I got to my feet, abandoning my half-eaten oat thing to the side. The stuff was curdling in my stomach anyway, and the smell didn't help matters. "What? You've never lost some of your magic for a little while? You've never had a bad day?"

"No." His answer was immediate, leaving no doubt. It was as strong as if I'd suggested he pay all the dulls the same wages as Wyrd Blood.

I tilted my head and leveled my best *don't give me that line of crap* stare. "Never? Not once have you lost some of your magic?"

"Ne-ver." He punched each syllable, making it sound like two words. "No Wyrd Blood I know has."

I crossed my arms and continued to stare. If he thought he was going to shame me into being nervous, he was wrong. While I'd lain in bed last night, I'd decided that I wasn't going to freak out.

"Fine. But my magic glitches. I'll let you know when I'm back up and running again, whenever that happens." Maybe Ruck was right and this was the perfect time to ditch this sideshow.

I walked to the corner of the room. There was a stack of books I needed to return to the swap room. I was going to do it later this afternoon, but right now seemed like a perfect time. Except maybe the book with Robert. He'd been yummy. He might need another go. I pulled that one out and grabbed up the rest of them.

Knife beat me to the door, holding it open. He

should've made a right turn. He made a left. Great. He was going to follow me.

"Dez said you're going to Ryker's party. You seem cranky. Is that why?" he asked.

"Dez also said it *wasn't* Ryker's party, and can you keep your voice down? These halls echo." I made it to the stairs. I should've said I was going to the bath hall or the knitting room. That would've lost him for sure.

Knife huffed. "It's at the Valley. It's his party. He's going to be there."

It didn't matter if Ryker and Knife didn't want me to go to the party, or that I didn't want to go myself. Even if the worm had answered and told me not to go, I'd still be going. If I didn't, Ryker would think I didn't have the balls to show up and then think he could steal Ruck. I wasn't taking that lying down. A play for Ruck meant war. All-out, no-holds-barred, bloody war.

Ruck might've said he was definitely going to be back, but I couldn't have Ryker think he had a shot. If that was a stupid reason to go, it didn't matter, since nobody but Dez knew.

"I know you and Dez think he's making a play for Ruck."

The blood exploded in my head so suddenly it was hard to hear what else he said over the ringing noise. Why did my two closest friends have the biggest mouths?

I stopped walking halfway down the stairs. "I'm going. It doesn't matter what else you say. I have to go, but you can relax. I'm not going to fall into his arms the second I see him. I'm way past that."

Knife stopped on the stairs right below me. "I'm glad, because even if you're the right woman, he'll always be the wrong man. I'm saying that as a friend."

I wasn't sure there was a right anyone in my future, but I didn't bother arguing with him.

"You, me and Dez can catch a lift from Switch. We'll walk in together. It'll be easier this way." Knife turned and descended the stairs at a faster clip.

He always took off after he did something nice, like he couldn't face himself. That, right there, was why I didn't leave the sideshow. He'd taken me in when I wanted to leave the Valley. Other than a few raised eyebrows, he didn't give me grief when I did everything he didn't want me to. Now, when he knew I was tense about the party, he was going to be a buffer, whether I said I needed one or not. It wasn't all a long game about sex for him. Knife liked to hide it, but deep down, there was a decent guy in there.

"Thank you," I called after him.

He didn't respond, but I was sure he heard.

NINE

It would've taken days to walk, or hours to take a chugger. I juiced up Switch and we were at the Valley in seconds. As soon as my feet hit the ground, I realized the ride would've been preferable. A chugger would've been a slow reentry in stages instead of being slammed into the heart of the Valley. It was as if I'd jumped into icy water and couldn't catch my breath. Before I could ask for a redo, Switch was gone and I was surrounded by memories.

I hadn't had much of a dating life, but I could only imagine this was like seeing an old boyfriend again. One who had brought you flowers and candies, treated you like a princess, but you had dumped because you didn't like his father.

My body reacted as if it had been slammed as well, spinning this way and that, searching for a sign of Ryker. The place was empty. From what I'd heard, all the Wyrd Blood would be at the party, which was held in the grove. Everyone was invited, but the dulls would be hanging close to home with all the strange magic about.

There wasn't a Wyrd Blood alive who knew dulls as well as I did. I'd lived like one of them for years. Most were in awe of magic, secretly hoped to have Wyrd Blood offspring. They liked the safety magic could provide them. But having too many Wyrd Blood descend upon their home all at once would send any dull scurrying. Maybe they thought if too many got together, strange things would befall them. It was probably true. If I were a dull, I'd be hiding tonight.

"Come on. Why are you dragging your feet?" Dez asked from a few steps ahead of me, where she was waiting with Knife.

She dashed back and grabbed my hand, her face lit up like she had an inner fire burning brightly. Knife watched as we caught up, his eyes running over the outfit Dez had lent me. His gaze then shifted toward the direction we were heading, as if that same fire lighting up Dez was going to be used to roast him alive. That made two of us who were about to be cooked on the well-done side.

"Hey, I forgot to ask, did you try again this morning?" she whispered.

That was Dez's nice way of asking if my worming was still on the fritz. She'd caught me trying to worm earlier in the day. She'd *accidentally* stumbled into my favorite corner.

"Still not working."

"It'll be okay." She squeezed my hand and didn't let go as we made our way through the familiar streets.

All those nights I'd lain in bed and thought about this place, and here I was again, knowing I couldn't stay. It was almost worse to come back and see everything I'd missed. The houses weren't too big and they weren't too small. The roads were the perfect width, with just the right amount of trees lining them.

"Hey!" Ruck yelled down from the tower.

"Ryker's making you work?" I yelled up. That bastard. He'd do anything to screw with me. I'd assumed Ruck would be at the party.

He waved his hand, telling me to calm down. "No. I'm covering a shift tonight for Tommy, who wanted to go check out the party. Don't leave without saying bye and bringing me some food, okay?"

"I'll be there." Probably sooner than he'd expect.

He disappeared to the other side of the tower, and it might've crossed my mind to ditch the party altogether and go hang out there. Except that bastard wanted my Ruck, and I'd be making things very clear to him tonight.

Laughter rang out in the distance, mixed with the sound of music. The smell of a roast made my mouth water. Nothing prepared me for when we saw the gathering.

The grove looked like something out of the fairytales I'd read. Fires burned and fairies flew overhead, leaving sparkling trails in their wake. The light bounced off dancing bodies. Bottles were passed around as hundreds of Wyrd Blood mingled and weaved, danced and laughed.

There were familiar faces everywhere. Burn and

Sneak stood across the distance mingling. I gave a nod in their direction and received a wave and a smile in return.

I'd make my way over there eventually and give them a formal hello, but not until there was more booze than blood fueling my body. Burn and Sneak were from a lifetime ago, and attached to someone I wasn't sure I was ready to see. As to *him*, he wasn't here. I would've felt him already, even mingled with the heady sizzle of magic filling the area.

Dez grabbed my arm, her fingers digging in. "Oh my magic. I haven't seen him in a decade."

Him who? I followed her gaze until I landed on a hulking piece of man that Ruck would've given his stamp of approval. He'd noticed her as well, and gravity was about to take over.

"Come on, I'll introduce you," she said, tugging on me as she let the blond god's gravity suck her to him.

I wriggled my arm loose. "That's quite all right. I think this is a meeting meant for two. I'm good here."

"You sure?" she asked, even as she struggled with the gravitational pull from across the grove.

"Positive. If things get ugly and I need you, you'll know. We rarely keep our fights quiet."

She bit her lower lip. She was half turned away from me but not moving.

"Trust me, I'll be loud enough that you'll hear me." I gave her a small shove.

She smiled, and then her feet moved. Knife had already fallen into a small group, mingling.

I circled the place, waving at a few people here and

there. Stopping and making small talk with others. Jeanette was on her fifth child, and none of them showing any signs of magic yet. Zane was chasing after a dull who had no interest in him or his ability to see through walls. Moto was forcing himself to eat a spoonful of hollyhoney every day because he swore it was increasing his magic.

By the time I'd made my way back around, an hour or so had passed.

Knife stepped closer.

"You see Ryker yet?" He tilted a bottle he was holding to his lips and then held it out to me.

"Nope. He'll show eventually. That'll be soon enough." I took his offer, letting the liquid burn my throat before handing the bottle back.

"Come on." He took a few steps toward the mass of dancing bodies, and then turned back, his hand extended.

I held up a hand. "I'm good."

"No, you're not. You're strung worse than a coiled snake about to strike." He inched forward, wrapping his hand around mine. "Come on. He's going to show eventually, and you don't want to be standing here looking like you're counting down the seconds"—he leaned in with a knowing smile—"even if you are."

I opened my mouth to deny it. He raised his eyebrows and cleared his throat.

"Fine. We'll dance." I let him tug me closer. He had a point. Did I really want to be happened upon standing by myself while I watched everyone else dancing and laughing? No. I wanted to be one of the happy people. I wanted to have fun, and drink and cavort because I didn't care if this was Ryker's party or not.

Knife pulled me forward, an arm wrapped around my waist, and spun me into the crowd to the beat of the band.

People passed bottles around while others smoked. Some did nothing, simply enjoying the music and zoning out.

For the first time in my life, I was surrounded by nothing but Wyrd Blood. These were my people. They understood the persecution, the hiding, the fear. They also knew the thrill of magic pouring through you.

Dez sidled up to me, dancing to my right, her blond god beside her. The musicians launched into a new song with a slower rhythm and a bass that reverberated through you. The magic was flowing, commingling in a way that tingled on my flesh. At some point, I stopped becoming a spectator and was pulled into the larger blend of power exuding and mixing all around. If I were a coiled snake, the magic was the charmer, luring me into the moment, the music, the dance. It was headier than the alcohol flowing.

A half-hour—and half a bottle of booze—later, I'd almost forgotten about Ryker. Until I felt him approaching, his magic a magnet for mine. He was much stronger than the rest of the people here combined, except for me and maybe Knife. When he entered the area, he packed a heady punch.

I wasn't the only one who'd noticed as soon as he'd stepped into the clearing. I caught sight of him as he made his way through the crowd, people parting as he walked. A woman I only knew by face made her way to him, trying to lure him into a dance, her hips signaling an invitation to much more. My blood instantly spiked. This was why I'd left. My feelings had continued to grow into something unhealthy, while his hadn't grown at all.

He walked past her, shrugging off a hand on his arm as if it had been a gnat. His stare was on me and he was heading our way.

He stopped, watching me. I pulled my gaze away from him. I'd talk to him, but when I decided, not him. I took another swig of liquor and then moved closer to Knife, resting my forearm on his shoulder, moving my hips in time to his. I didn't look at Ryker again.

I'd known I'd see him here. Had planned to. But I hadn't been prepared for the pain. The gaping hole in my chest, which had barely scabbed over, was torn again. Months away and it changed nothing. It might as well have been hours.

Knife said something, and from the smile on his face, it might've been a joke. I forced out a laugh that was hollow, which echoed in my ears and rattled my hollowed heart. It was for the best this way. Full hearts only led to pain.

I forced my eyes to look anywhere but the spot I'd seen Ryker last, as his magic burned my senses and called to me in a way nothing else in the universe ever had.

Ryker's presence grew stronger, and I fisted my hand on Knife's collar. Knife's gaze was guarded and fixed over my right shoulder. If that wasn't enough, all the eyes around us were fixed on the same spot.

I stopped pretending Ryker wasn't right behind me, dropped my grasp on Knife, and turned around to face Ryker.

He was standing there, barely a foot away.

"Do you have a minute? We need to talk." The hard look of Ryker's eyes wiped away the softness of the words.

How many times had I dreamed of him saying we needed to talk? Except in those dreams, he'd shown up at Dorley and begged me to come back. The reality was dismal in comparison.

Not even a single note in six months. Ruck he'd messaged. Not me. If I hadn't come here tonight, I might never have seen him again.

I could've refused. He wouldn't force me. I knew Ryker enough to know when he'd make an issue and when he'd walk away. Our eyes locked for a few seconds and then he turned and left, giving me the option to follow or not.

I stood still as my heart pounded in my chest, as if it were trying to leave me behind and follow its rightful owner.

I glanced at Knife. "I'll be back in a little bit."

He nodded, looking as happy as I was.

I made my way toward where Ryker had disappeared down a trail that would lead back to his place. He was still near. I could feel him. A little farther and I could see his form up ahead as he waited for me in the dark.

I didn't stop until we stood almost toe to toe. His smell, the feel of his magic, all so familiar, called to me like I'd been a long time from home. Why was it that the Cursed King, maybe the most dangerous man to have walked this world, made me want to curl into him? Wrap myself around him?

Why hadn't all these months away dimmed the need I felt when I was around him? Was I equally cursed? Would I always feel this emptiness gnawing at me, which only he could fill? I'd barely seen him and yet I dreaded leaving. I never should've come back here.

He turned on his heel and began walking again.

"I see you've settled over at Dorley quite well. Heard you're in the sweetheart suite." He punctuated the sentence with a short scoff, in case the sarcasm of his words hadn't been blunt enough to bludgeon me to death.

"Dorley is an easy place to settle into. I can't complain about the accommodations, either." So I wasn't the only one who'd heard my rooms were typically given to Knife's current flings. If I *had* fucked Knife, it was none of Ryker's business. Just as it was none of mine when *he* fucked every woman in this place and probably the five countries around it. I'd never say a word to him, even as it shredded me on every level and made me wonder what was wrong with me as I lay in bed at night.

I walked behind him as if every minute with him wasn't my own personal purgatory of want. My head told me to run from here and never come back. My heart told me to leap into his arms and beg him to want me. Convince him I could be whoever he wanted. Unfortunately, I wasn't drunk enough to give in to either notion.

We walked the rest of the way in silence. I wondered a few times if I should find some excuse to scurry on back to the party. He'd stop and turn, as if sensing my need to escape. I'd continue to walk forward as if I'd never had the thought.

He opened his door, a dim light burning in the corner of the room. He crossed the distance to it, making it burn slightly brighter, but still dark enough for the shadows to blur together.

I watched his every move, soaking it in. He turned back toward me, his eyes meeting mine as he walked back over, stopping a few feet away.

Ryker's gaze landed on my face and then my lips. They followed the line of my waist and the curve of my hip before meeting my eyes. He was doing it again, making it seem like he wanted me when he didn't. Toying with me, making me want something more from him.

We'd had a few moments before we'd merged magic, and then it changed. I didn't know why, but I was tired of the chase. I was ready to do the running.

As much as I'd wanted to see him, had thought of this grand plan of confronting him about Ruck, if Ryker hadn't sought me out, I wouldn't be standing here right now. Pride had driven me to the Valley, but fear had me wanting to leave as soon as I'd arrived.

We stood in his living room, not too far apart but

not close enough either. Like always, our relationship was in some sort of murky middle ground that neither of us could quantify, and I didn't want to be in this place anymore. For the millionth time in minutes, I wished I'd never come. I felt as if my wounds were lying open, my blood gushing out as I wanted to beg this man for mercy when he didn't know the word.

There was only one thing he knew—war and battle. If I wanted to survive, I needed to fight my way out of here and never come back.

"Why did you ask Ruck to come here? I hope you're not thinking of trying to get him to stay. He won't. He's mine." Unlike Ryker, Ruck *was* mine. He was my family, my rock, the one person I could count on, and no one was taking him from me.

"I needed him, but I won't make him stay."

He needed Ruck. Not me. Not now that he had his stones. There'd never been anything else between us, and yet I couldn't turn and walk away.

Deep down inside, hidden in a place I didn't share with anyone, I'd hoped that maybe when Ryker saw me, he'd finally realize how much he wanted me. It was sad and pathetic and hard to admit. But I stood there, letting him take his sweet time with whatever it was he wanted. That was what kept my feet in one spot. The hope that maybe seeing me would change something for him. It would hit him like a lightning bolt that he wanted me as much as I wanted him.

Odds were that wasn't going to happen, but my feet didn't budge. I needed to get out of here before more damage was done. "What did you want?"

His eyes narrowed, as if he'd not understood the sudden impatience. "How long do you plan on staying at Dorley? I've got leads on other stones."

Oh yeah, he wanted something. It was a good thing I'd stayed away. Better yet that I was going back. Being here, seeing him—none of this had been a good idea. I'd walked into this place, girding myself to be like those stone statues I'd seen in the ancient temples. If I could be hard as stone, then I'd be okay. But even stone crumbled.

I crossed my arms, turning slightly away from him and looking at the door. After tonight, I wouldn't come back here, no matter what. "Send me a message when you know where they are. I'll go get them. I'll keep every other one I get. That's the deal."

I was done with this inequitable distribution. This was business. I didn't need him anymore. No reason he should get them all.

"You can't go alone."

"I won't. Knife will back me up." He'd be happy to if he got a stake in my share of the stones.

After tonight, it was clear what this was. This would be the last time I had any stupid delusions of something happening between us, any romantic notions that Ryker really did want me. That he could ever fall in love with me.

"Was that it? I want to get back to the party." I wanted to get back to Dorley, away from this man that crushed me. When he didn't say anything, I walked to the door, slower than I should've. If I had any common sense, I would run from there, but my heart was still reaching back to him, arms outstretched, begging me to stay. Pleading with him to want me.

I was nearly to the door when he said, "Bugs...hold up."

I turned. *Give me something.* Anything I could cling to. It would be so easy to stay. I *wanted* to stay. I'd never wanted anything more. He walked out of the room, and I waited.

He walked back in and tossed something at me. I caught it before I saw what it was. The second my fingers closed around it, I felt the hum of its magic.

"That's the largest. Its mass roughly equals the same amount I have. That should settle us up."

My chin dropped. My eyes watered. My heart sputtered.

I looked at him, forcing everything warm and soft in me to ice over and freeze. I gripped the stone in my hands and nodded.

Then I did the only thing left to do: I walked out of his place, away from him with a confidence that was all show. I kept my back straight and leashed my emotions until I got well away from him.

TEN

I STEPPED OUTSIDE AND WALKED TO THE RIGHT. Left would've brought me back to drunken revelry, and there was no part of me that would be able to blend in with that crowd at the moment. I could go see Ruck, but he'd take one look at me and immediately question what was wrong. I'd rather have my tongue cut out than talk.

Instead, I walked the streets of the Valley alone, saying goodbye to this place like I hadn't done when I'd left for Dorley. When I left six months ago, part of me had at least suspected I'd be back, or hoped. This time was much different. I'd never set foot here again if I could help it. I never should've returned in the first place. It was idiotic to think it would be a good idea, or even a mediocre one.

At least I could say goodbye in peace, since the streets were empty. Any Wyrd Blood would still be at the grove. Any dull would be asleep, and I had no delusions of Ryker chasing after me this time.

There were memories everywhere. The shower building, where they wouldn't give you a bar of soap if you were even a day early for your ration. No one cared if your buddy Ruck had lost his and you'd been sharing for a week. Somehow, that made me smile now.

The food building appeared around the bend, and I could almost smell flaky biscuits covered in butter. The first time I'd walked in the place, I was shocked at all the heaping piles of food laid out for anyone to take. I'd had to fight the urge to pocket more than my stomach could hold, and usually lost. I ran a hand over the closed door, knowing I'd never eat there again.

An autumn breeze blew through the brilliant purple leaves of the Harlow trees with their strong floral scent. That smell alone made my stomach grumble, as if it signaled the feast to come.

It was followed by another smell that brought my arm to my nose. It was like I'd been walking through a clean, crisp forest and then been plunged into a smelly bog.

I recognized its greasy foulness as it settled over me. It was the same smell I'd noticed at Dorley, but stronger. This time, I knew it wasn't just a scent on the air, but the smell of something wrong nearby. I could feel it with my magic.

This was something dark. Something magic. Something that my most basic instincts rebelled against, urging me to run.

I glanced around, searching through the night shadows and crevices, trying to find what I sensed to be there. I reached out with my magic, trying to identify what it was.

I couldn't see anything but couldn't shake the feeling that I wasn't alone, or lose the clinging sense of dirty magic. I turned around and began strolling back the way I came, toward the grove and the partygoers. Hopefully, it wouldn't know I sensed it. If there was something here, if I ran, it would chase. That was what monsters did after all, right? If they didn't, they wouldn't be very good monsters.

Had this thing followed me from Dorley, or was this a coincidence? I wished I still believed in those, but I didn't. I was being stalked.

I had to get to the grove, where there would be backup. Not even a monster would want to mess with the amount of magic that was concentrated there right now, even if it were mostly drunken. If the grove was too far, I'd have to settle for Ryker's place.

Just a few minutes ago I'd told myself I'd never go back there willingly. Now look at me. I was one smelly monster away from banging down his door.

If things went bad before I made it to either of those places, fighting was a tough option when I couldn't see my opponent. Even if I could see it, I wasn't optimistic. I could hold my own with someone my size, but who knew what would appear? Better off erecting a ward thicker and stronger than anything I'd ever made before. Something not even a monster could get through.

"Chiara." The voice was a blend of squeal and rattle, coated in sugar, that couldn't have come from a human. The name carried on the air, seeming to come from everywhere.

I should've run. Instead, I froze, feeling as unmoving as the ice filling my veins. I hadn't heard that name in a decade. Whatever was here, it knew my given name. Whatever is was, it was here for me. It hadn't happened upon me again by chance. Sometimes it sucked to be right.

"Show yourself." I turned in a circle, trying to find the thing that had called me.

Nothing appeared, but the feeling of dirty magic was brushing up against me. A tickle over my skin.

"Who are you?" It didn't answer, and the feeling of a feather brushing my skin turned to metal teeth grazing it. A pressure pushed on me from every direction.

I turned, belatedly deciding to run for it, and found my legs had gone weak. They collapsed underneath me, and I crashed to the ground.

I opened my mouth to scream but couldn't hear my voice leave my body. I didn't know if this thing was muting the sound or if I'd lost the ability to speak.

I tried to think past the pain, to build a ward. There was nothing left to do but build a ward around me and hope it held. Except I couldn't seem to build anything.

Pressure built around me, churning and chafing everywhere it touched. Pushing and prodding. I locked everything I had inside, barricading my mind and body as best I could as it felt for a way in, a soft spot it could exploit. It wanted in, and I didn't know why.

The force around me grew until it was pressing at

me from every angle. I curled in a ball, trying to find some relief.

I'd been up against some bad things in my life, but this was the worst I'd ever felt. It wasn't just the pressure and the chafing, as if I were being rubbed raw. I felt as if it were violating me everywhere it touched.

The stone. I wrapped my arms around my middle and felt for its outline in my pocket. I gripped it though the fabric, and a surge of magic shot from me, thrusting the foul thing away. The pressure broke, and I gasped, breathing in fresh air once again.

I got to my feet and ran. The closest thing to me was the tower, and I scrambled up the ladder as quick as my feet could move.

When I got to the top, I nearly plowed into Ruck. I turned and scanned the area to see if I could find what had attacked me and put a name to this new enemy.

"What's wrong?" he asked from behind me.

I kept looking, searching for any kind of anomaly, a stray wind through the trees, a shadow in the field, a gust of foul air. Some sign that this thing hadn't just appeared and disappeared with no trace.

Something grabbed my shoulder, and I whipped around to a stunned Ruck, who quickly jumped back.

"Why are you so freaked out? What happened?"

I turned back to scan the horizon. "Did you see anything weird?"

"Like what?"

I turned back to him, grabbing his arm. "I don't know. Anything that isn't normal?"

He braced a hand on one of the posts as he looked

at my white-knuckled fingers digging into his arm. "No. Other than the partygoers, it's been quiet."

I lifted my head, sampling the air in every direction. Was it really gone or was it cloaking its smell somehow? I shoved my hand in my pocket, wrapping it around the stone, just in case.

Ruck stepped closer. "Bugs, what's wrong with you?"

"You know that smell I told you about the night before you left Dorley? That smell belonged to something magical." I stepped closer to him, the crushing feeling, the greasy magic, still so fresh in my mind. I wasn't sure if I'd ever be able to scrub it out of my senses.

"What was it?" he asked, his shoulder bumping mine.

I breathed deeply of the scent of his freshly laundered clothes and shampooed hair.

"I don't know. I couldn't see it. I only felt it. It was like something trying to swallow me whole. This time, it spoke."

"What did it say?" he asked, his gaze back to the horizon, searching for the threat.

"My name."

He continued to scan the area with me for another few minutes. "Are you sure something was really there? Nothing can get in here without Ryker knowing it crossed his wards, not to mention I've been on my post all night, and so have the other guards. Your magic *has* been acting up lately."

"I'm not crazy. There was something. I *felt* it." I

took my hands out of my pockets, keeping the stone gripped in my hand as I crossed my arms. "There's a monster out there that is trying to get me."

"Okay, I believe you," he said. His eyes narrowed, dropping and then freezing on my arms, where I'd shoved the jacket sleeves up. "What's wrong with your skin?"

"Nothing." I looked down at the strip of visible flesh. It looked like I'd been scrubbed with tree bark for a good hour. It looked exactly like how it had felt when I'd been attacked.

Ruck grabbed my sleeve, yanking it further up my arm to reveal more bright red flesh. His eyes slammed back to my face. "If you were attacked, you gotta tell Ryker."

This was the last thing I wanted to deal with right now. The run-to-Ryker speech. "No, I don't. Why would I? I'm barely speaking to him. If I tell anyone, it'll be Knife."

"What if this has something to do with the people who died?"

"Six months ago? Not likely." Ruck's man crush was showing again. I was starting to think he'd do anything to get us out of Dorley and back here.

"Fine, maybe it doesn't have anything to do with that, but what if he could help? What if this monster is dangerous? He knows more about magic than anyone I know."

"You better take a sledgehammer to that pedestal you've got him on. He doesn't deserve it. You want me to run to him for help, but I'm not doing it." I stabbed my finger at him.

His hands went to his hips as his chin lowered until all I saw were eyes poking out from underneath bushy brows. "Bugs, you're not running to him. You're asking someone who cares about you if they know anything that would help, like you would do with me."

"Cares about me? Are you kidding? The man basically gave me a going-away present tonight. Only thing missing was him telling me not to let the door hit me in the ass on the way out. I go to him now asking for help and that is the definition of running to him. You want to run to Ryker so bad, you do it, but not until I leave." My close call of having to beg Ryker for help had been averted. I wasn't speaking to Ryker again, not tonight, not ever. My night had gone as badly as I could possibly handle. I was barely escaping with my sanity.

The second Ruck's eyes switched from scanning the perimeter to the ground in the wrong direction, I knew what he was up to.

"Ruck? Don't you do it."

Ruck leaned over the platform. "Hey, Tommy, I got a problem," Ruck yelled down.

I loved Ruck dearly, but if I could've tackled him to the ground right then, I would've.

I leaned over and spotted Tommy, walking over with a furrowed brow. His bag was slung over his shoulder, and he looked like he'd recently gotten off a shift at one of the northern towers.

"No, Ruck doesn't need you. I'm sure you're tired

and want to get home." I waved a hand, gesturing for him to head the other way.

Tommy stopped, looking back and forth between us. He scratched his head, looking from the ladder to the way he'd been headed.

"Tommy, get up here," Ruck barked.

That got Tommy's feet moving again with an urgency that looked like I'd have a hard time stopping.

I turned toward Ruck and stared. If I could zap him with my eyes, I would've. "When did you get like this? What happened to you? Did I steal too many of your biscuits? Not bring you enough snacks on the tower? Tell me, where did I go wrong that you prefer Ryker?"

Ruck gave me his full attention. "I know you're mad at him for myriad reasons, but he knows more about this stuff than we do. If there's something magical coming after you, he's the man we need to talk to."

"I can talk to Knife or Dez. He's not the only option." I wanted to shake Ruck until his teeth rattled.

"They're not Ryker, and you know it."

Tommy had barely hit the landing when Ruck's head was disappearing downward. "Ruck, I swear to magic, you better not say a word."

There wasn't a peep in response. That bastard.

I hung over the edge of the platform. "If you're my friend, you'll keep your mouth shut."

"A friend would get you help whether you wanted it or not," he yelled up, not even pausing in his descent.

"That's bullshit. A friend keeps secrets," I screamed down, still on the platform like a big old chicken.

"Not with this," he said, leaping off the last few rungs and heading toward Ryker's place.

If he got Ryker, which he was on his way to do, staying on this platform wasn't going to save me. It wasn't like Ryker had a weird fear of heights or something.

I glanced at Tommy, who'd already made himself comfortable and was acting as if he'd been deaf to Ruck's and my discussion. He certainly wouldn't be any help against Ryker, and I didn't want to get stuck up here with an audience.

I was doomed if I waited here. Trapped like a cat in a tree. I never should've told Ruck about the invisible monster. Only thing to do was get down as fast as I could and find Switch. I'd get out of here fast. I'd worry about the monster later. I had a Cursed King about to press down on me.

I scrambled down the ladder, slipping on a few rungs in my haste. Switch was probably going to be poking around the grove soon. Or I could hope, anyway. Otherwise, I wasn't above hiding.

An arm wrapped around my waist before I hit the ground, but it wasn't Ruck's. It was Ryker's.

"What the fuck? Get off me," I said, trying to squirm out of his grasp, digging my fingers into his forearm.

"Hold on to her. She'll take off, and this is something you need to hear." I heard Ruck's voice before I was swung around and saw him.

"I think I can manage," Ryker replied.

I lifted one hand from where I'd been trying to pry

Ryker's fingers off to point at Ruck. "You're in deep shit."

"Had to do it," he said, lifting his head proudly before walking ahead.

I refused to scream, because that might draw eyes. The houses all looked dark, but I knew this place. I'd lived here. They'd all scramble from their beds to peek through the curtains for a worthy show. It was bad enough I was being towed along. I wasn't above scratching, though. One arm quickly relocated over my two, pinning them to my body.

Fine. I had other limbs. My heels connected with his shins. He wasn't lugging me around like this and not paying a price.

ELEVEN

MY FEET DIDN'T HIT THE GROUND UNTIL I WAS standing in Ryker's living room. Ruck was already inside as Ryker deposited me by my old spot in the corner of the couch, from back when I'd lived here and I'd considered him a quasi-friend, ally—some kind of check in the positive column.

Ryker stood in between me and the door.

"If I want to leave, you're not stopping me." I crossed my arms, not making a move to prove it. I wasn't a total idiot. I knew how that scene would go down, and it wasn't very flattering for me. Not like I could count on Ruck backing me up. He'd made this mess.

Ryker glanced down at the nail marks on his arms and then back to me with a raised eyebrow.

Dick. No matter what he thought, I could've done worse. I'd been trying to act with decorum. He'd know nothing about that.

"Can we argue later? We've got bigger problems,"

Ruck said, stepping in between us.

Ryker glanced at him and then shifted his entire attention back to me, leveling a stare my way that could've given me frostbite. "Where are my stones?"

"Huh?" Ruck's head jerked to Ryker.

"You mean the one you gave me? Here, take it back. I didn't ask for it anyway." I lobbed it at his head. I didn't *really* want to give it back. It was the only thing that had saved me a little while ago, but there was no price too steep to get away from him.

He caught the stone and held it up. "This is the one I gave you. Now you can tell me what you did with the ones you *took*."

"I didn't *take* anything. If I wanted the stones, I would've taken them, but I didn't. If you lost them, that's on you, you..." *Dick? Asshole? Dick* wasn't vile enough for him. Both were so overused. I needed something horrible. *Fucking dick?* That was almost as lame. Why was my brain short-circuiting on me when I needed it most? It was taking me so long to come up with a fitting insult that I was losing the moment.

"They disappear on the night you get back. As soon as I gave you one, it weakened the ward around them, and before I have a chance to redo it, they're gone. I'm supposed to believe it's a coincidence?" He stepped closer. "Where did you put them?"

I moved forward as well, shoving Ruck out of the way. Ryker's magic was churning. I could feel it in the room and inside me where we had that strange connection. I didn't want Ruck anywhere near it.

"I told you. I. Didn't. Take. Them. If I wanted

them, I wouldn't need a weakened ward, and you know it. I risked my life to get them. I trusted you to keep them safe. It's not my fault if you lost them."

"You're saying that you, the only person who could've gotten to them, didn't?"

"Yes. That's exactly what I'm saying. I didn't steal what was already half mine."

"But they disappear the night you get here?" He edged forward, crowding me back a step.

Did he really think he could scare me? I shoved at his chest with both hands. I dropped them fast as I felt the sizzle of our magic connecting. "Yes. You are. Because I didn't take them. If I wanted them, I would've demanded them. You said that stone was equal to half of them. We're even."

I stepped around him, walking to the door. He beat me there. I would've shoved him out of the way, but then I'd have to touch him again. That sizzle between us had been more than enough for the night.

"You think you can steal from me and walk away?" His palm was flat on the door.

"You're going to have to get out of my way or kill me, because we're done here."

It was a bluff. I didn't think he'd kill me, not if he wanted more stones in the future. Me killing him was still on the table if he didn't get his hand off that door.

"This isn't finished," he said, but then finally moved away from the door.

I was swinging it open when Ryker's attention shifted to Ruck. "What were you calling me for? What was the problem you had?"

Shit. I turned, staring at Ruck. *Now do you get it? He can't be trusted.* I gripped the door handle, my knuckles white and my palm sweating. One more straw on this camel's back and I'd never get out of here tonight.

Ruck's eyes met mine and then dropped for a second, before he looked at Ryker with a confidence he wasn't feeling. "Nothing. I wanted to give you a heads-up that I was cutting out early. Tommy is on the tower now. You need to find someone to relieve him, because I'm going back to Dorley tonight with Bugs."

Ruck's voice dropped a little at the end. Dammit. Now Ryker was making my boy feel bad? It was horrible enough when he'd crushed me. Now he was breaking Ruck's man crush too, stepping on it and squashing it like a bug. We never should've come back here. Ryker was toxic. This whole place was wrong. I couldn't believe I'd gotten all sappy about leaving again.

I stepped back into the room and grabbed Ruck's hand. We'd walk out of this place together. I turned to leave as Knife was walking in the door.

"What happened? Tommy said something was wrong?"

His eyes darted about the room, taking in the tension radiating off each of us. Then he stood right beside me, making his alliance as clear as day, even though he didn't know what was wrong yet.

I had to bite the insides of my cheeks to keep from smiling.

When we got back to Dorley, I was going to cut Knife a little more slack. I was way too hard on the guy.

"My stones are missing," Ryker said.

"So?"

"It's a little coincidental that the only person who could break through my ward happens to be here the night they disappear."

"Did she say she took them?"

"Obviously not."

"Bugs isn't a liar. If she said she didn't take them, she didn't." Knife wrapped an arm around my shoulders.

Ryker finally dragged his gaze from mine to where Knife's hand rested on my shoulder. By the time he looked back at Knife's face, his stare had gone from icicle cold to glacier frost. It was a steep contrast to the magic filling the room with sweltering heat.

Knife was trying to help, but I'd been so close to getting out of here before he got involved. The last thing I needed was for the two of them to go at it. The night had already tanked. All I wanted was to get the hell out of here and call the whole visit a mistake.

"Then where are they?" Ryker asked.

Knife stepping inside had reignited the whole matter, and I was going to crack if I didn't get out of here.

I lifted my arms. "Search me if you want, for magic's sake, if that'll finish this up."

Ruck was shaking his head. "I don't know if that's..."

I ignored him. He'd already done enough damage

tonight. I'd forgiven him, but I wasn't listening to him now and getting stuck here for another hour.

I yanked off my jacket and flung it to the floor. I would've stripped out of my shirt and pants next, except I heard Ruck groan. I suddenly realized what I'd forgotten in my desperate urge to escape. My arms were a mess. Now there'd be more questions.

Knife froze.

Ryker's eyes narrowed. "What happened to your skin?"

The three of them were staring at me. I glanced down, realizing the damage was worse than it had initially looked. Bruises were forming up and down my arms, and the sleeveless shirt was displaying them all.

"I fell." Technically, the monster had shoved me down.

Ryker reached forward, grabbing my wrist and pulling me closer. "Did he do this to you?"

I could feel the room about to explode.

Knife stepped forward. "Me? You're the one who just manhandled her."

Ryker pulled on my arm until he was standing between Knife and me. What was wrong with him? Knife had a very good point. Ryker *had* dragged me in here.

Ruck was staring, shaking his head, eyes as big as I'd ever seen them. He turned to me. "Do something!"

I barely heard him over the buzzing of magic that I thought even Ruck felt.

If it didn't calm down in the next few minutes, Knife was going to be dead. Even with sweat breaking out all over his body, Knife was all in. He wasn't going to back down.

Ryker let go of my wrist, and I tried to dodge back around to step in between him and Knife but was blocked by two forearms. Well, at least they agreed on something.

"I told you what would happen," Ryker said, nearly nose to nose with Knife.

"Do something," Ruck said.

Someone was going to be dead if I didn't come clean. Dammit. Did I really have to?

"Don't act like you're the one trying to protect her when all you've ever done is use her." Knife's chest puffed out as a bead of sweat dripped from his cheek to his shirt, and his face had gone red.

"And you haven't? Everyone knows about the fucking tent."

Really? Everyone? Tents were nothing to be embarrassed of. It was a job.

Damn, it was getting uncomfortable in here.

I had minutes, maybe seconds, before Knife dropped. Fuck. I pushed forward again, ramming into Ryker's arm, the one that sprang up as soon as I moved. "It wasn't either of you two. I was attacked by something else."

Both heads swung to me.

"What?" they asked in unison.

TWELVE

I was curled up in the corner of Ryker's couch, wondering how this night had gotten worse as the chatter in the room buzzed in my ears. I'd thought I'd bottomed out when I was curled in a ball in the center of the street. Somehow, curled in the corner of Ryker's couch was worse.

"Bugs," Ryker said, jerking my attention back to him. He stood in front of me, not looking fatigued despite the fact that we'd been at this for hours. "You're sure there isn't anything you left out?"

Ryker had been leading the interrogation. Knife had tried several takeovers, but they'd been unsuccessful. Dez, Burn, and Sneak were hanging back, listening like it was the first time they'd heard speech before.

Ruck was on the other side of the couch, an elbow on the armrest and his palm holding up his chin. I tried not to make any fast movements, because a firm rattle of the couch and he was going down. At least one of us could catch a nap.

I shrugged. I'd lost the urge to argue an hour ago. I was on to the part where I was blindly repeating everything in hopes this would end soon. It was torture by repetition. "There was the time at Dorley I smelled it, and then here." This was the fifth time I'd answered this question, and I didn't think it would be the last.

Ruck squinted, as if he were in physical pain. He leaned back and said, "Wait, didn't you tell me you noticed something after Knife's birthday dinner?"

"No. I don't remember anything being off."

Ruck rubbed his eyes and then yawned. "After he blew out the candles? You were complaining they smelled weird."

I sucked in a breath. I'd thought it was a funny-smelling smoke. "Yeah, he's right. I did."

It had been so subtle I'd completely forgotten it.

Ryker took a few steps away, shaking his head. He'd finally gotten additional information and now he was more annoyed?

His silence didn't last long. "Why wasn't I told about this?"

"That I smelled something funny?" He'd lost his mind. Completely and utterly lost it.

Knife edged forward, crowding Ryker. "Or me? You live with me. I should've been the first to know."

The only reprieve I got from Ryker's death eye was when he switched it to Knife. "You can't handle this situation. I should've been informed, though."

If there weren't several layers of people in between me and the door, and my wingman Ruck looked as energetic as a plucked turkey, I would've made a run for it.

"There wasn't anything to tell. It was a smell." I pulled a knee up to give my arm a resting place. If my skin wasn't raw, no one would've believed I'd been attacked. Now we were debating the threat level of a smell.

I looked at Burn and made a gesture like I was tilting something to my lips. He broke away from next to Sneak to come to my side. He tugged a flask out of his pocket and handed it over.

I knew he'd have something on him. I took a swig and then another until I finished it.

"You okay?" he asked, pointing to my skin, while Ryker and Knife argued about who should've been informed.

"Yeah, I'm good. Looks worse and all that."

He nodded, rolling his lips in as he continued to watch me.

"I'm fine, really. It was just—weird." And slightly terrifying, like a living nightmare, but I didn't have the energy or inclination to whine at the moment.

He smiled a little and then looked at his feet, like if he looked at me for another minute he'd call me on my bullshit.

"So it said Bugs, that's it? Nothing else?" Burn asked.

Ah shit. "Well, no. Not that name."

"What did it say?" Dez asked, moving forward, taking the seat in between Ruck and me.

Ryker and Knife had stopped speaking and were back to interrogation mode.

"It called me by the name my mother gave me," I said.

Ruck's mouth went so wide I could see his tonsils. "Seriously? The monster knows your real name before *me*? I didn't even think *you* remembered it. That's fucking bullshit."

"To clarify, it called you Chiara?" Ryker asked.

My head snapped to him. "How do you know my name?"

"He knew it too?" Ruck threw his hands up. "What the fuck? You think you know someone and they're hiding all sorts of shit."

"I didn't tell him," I yelled at Ruck, as he got to his feet and waved a hand at me.

"Then how'd he know?" Ruck pointed at Ryker.

"How did you know my name?" I asked Ryker.

"It was on the contract your parents signed that the Debt Collector showed us."

Showed? That was a stretch. The show he was referring to was more like a fluttering piece of paper in the air. We'd barely seen anything, or I hadn't.

"Anybody have a guess on what this thing is?" Burn asked.

The room fell quiet for the first time since they'd all come shuffling in here. Leave it to Burn to cut to the heart of the problem.

Ryker was running a hand through his hair like he was sorting through ideas in his mind. Knife was scratching his jaw. Dez was leaning forward, her hands steepled on her legs.

"Maybe it's a Gorgol?" Dez mumbled through her fingers.

Ruck's forehead grew about ten new wrinkles as he looked at me and mouthed, *What's a Gorgol?*

I shrugged. I know but didn't like the sound of it.

"No, I'd sense one of those a mile away, and they aren't strong enough to break an outer ward." Ryker said.

"What about Snarg?" Sneak asked.

Ruck kept flashing his gaze to me, checking in. If he thought I had a clue, he was wrong. I might be a Wyrd Blood by birth, but I'd lived the life of a dull, not run in magical circles where this sort of thing was discussed.

Ryker was shaking his head again. "They can't disappear like that. Their mass is too heavy, and wrong type of magic anyway. I've never encountered something that could be invisible and not trip off one of my wards."

Wasn't I special? I had a brand-new monster all to myself, never seen before.

Sneak cleared his throat from the other side of the room. "Maybe you should worm it? See if we can narrow it down?"

I hadn't thought up a reply to shut this down when Knife said, "She can't worm. She's been on the fritz for a few days now."

"He said it. Not me," Ruck whispered in my direction.

"You can't worm?" Ryker was tilting his head

down, crossing his arms. "No one thought this should be mentioned earlier? That it might be important?"

Did he think he was in charge of running my life? Thank magic I'd left when I had. One night back and he was trying to take complete control again.

"No. I didn't. And I didn't sign over my life and everything I am when we merged magic. Now I've had enough. I'm going home. Where's Switch?"

Ryker stepped forward. "Now you're going to be stupid and think you can handle it alone?"

I stood. "Stupid was when I trusted you wouldn't take my magic."

This was getting too intimate. It was feeling like old times. Even the bickering. The anger toward him. It was as if all the feelings were getting dredged up from the abyss and set loose, running wild. Feelings I wanted to freeze up, dry out, and bury six feet under.

The longer I let this conversation go on, the worse it would get. He was already trying to take the reins. Next he'd be telling me what I was supposed to do and with whom while I watched him do everyone else with everybody.

"This isn't your problem. It's mine, and I'm ready to go." I looked to Knife. "Where's Switch?" I asked again.

Ryker stepped closer. "You're not going anywhere. There's a creature in my territory and my stones are missing. You might prefer to fuck him, but he can't protect you."

"You don't have a right to talk to me about who I want to fuck or where I'm going." We were standing toe to toe, his magic crashing against mine and becoming something else altogether. And I knew I had to get out of there.

I stepped away from Ryker, and he didn't try to stop me.

"Who was the last person to see Switch? I'm leaving." I'd walk if I needed to. I turned around the room, looking from one person to the next. They were all staring at Ryker and me, as if we'd been groping and kissing in the middle of the room.

Knife was staring the hardest, squinting as if he were trying to read tiny lettering.

I moved closer until I was right in front of Knife. "I *need* to go. Where is Switch?"

He finally broke his concentration from Ryker and focused on me. Before he spoke, I knew something was off. "You know, maybe it would be best for you to stay here for a little while, just until this is resolved."

"Wh-what?" There was no way Knife had suggested I stay here.

"I'll stay too, but I think it's better. Just for a little while, at least..."

He kept talking, repeating his argument for me staying.

His words faded into the buzz that was ringing in my ears. It was on the tip of my tongue to refuse. I could see in Knife's eyes as he continued to repeat the same thing in different ways, that he'd deny me my home in Dorley.

What was going on here? Was he afraid that Ryker would kill him? Was there something else afoot? Did he not trust Ryker? Did he think Ryker was behind the attack and wanted to remain close in order to catch him?

Either way, if I walked out of here with nowhere to go, Ruck would follow me. I might be dooming us both to death without the protection of a city and fellow Wyrd Blood. There was a monster stalking me. What if I died out there and left him stranded alone?

"You want me to stay? That's what you're saying?" I asked, even though he'd said it in every way imaginable over the course of five minutes.

"Only for a little while," Knife said, his eyes already pleading for forgiveness.

He must have a plan of some sort. It was the only thing that made any sense. Okay. I'd play along, but he better supply some answers as soon as we were alone.

I threw up my hands and turned around. "Fine. You all want me to stay? I will, and I'll get you your damn stones back." I didn't know how I was going to do it, and from the looks around the room, they were all stumped on that matter too. Well, fuck them all. Except Ruck. I was going to need some help, after all. Everyone needed a little backup. And Dez too. She didn't have any guilt here. Actually, just fuck Ryker.

I marched toward the door and then stopped. "I still have a room, right?"

Ryker nodded, and I swore he wanted to smile. He didn't, but I could feel the happiness on him. I could smell it. Gloater. He thought he'd won, but I wasn't going to be here long.

"Hey," he said, right before I walked out. The stone came flying toward me.

I caught it and then pocketed it. He was wrong about one thing: I might be stubborn, but I wasn't stupid.

THIRTEEN

I JERKED AWAKE TO THE SOUNDS OF PEOPLE starting their day. It took a minute to remember that life had gotten upended last night. If the sounds hadn't done it, the stone jabbing through my pocket and into my ribs would've. I'd slept with my jacket on in order to have a close place to keep it.

Back in my room. Back at the Valley. Back to seeing Ryker at every turn. There was one other thing back in my life that I could be happy about, though. Biscuits! Piles of fresh eggs and sausage. I might've eaten the dull fare at Dorley, but I hadn't liked it.

The food would have to wait for a few, though. I needed to find Knife and find out his plan. Whatever he was thinking, it would surely need some fine tuning if history was any indication. Plus, I had my own plans to lay out. I'd been winging it for months, and where had that gotten me? Back here.

I was out my door five minutes later and kneeling in a fresh batch of dirt a minute after that. This had been one of my favorite spots to worm when I'd lived here. Plenty of cover, with bushes facing the busy part of the Valley, but plenty of sun, too. Maybe my worming issue wasn't me. It could've been Dorley soil and unhappy worms.

The minute the worm landed in my palm, its wiggling made it clear that there'd be no answers today. Guess it wasn't Dorley. I dropped it without asking anything and headed off to where Knife's room had been last time he'd stayed here. Odds were, we'd all be back in the same places.

I banged on his door several times to no answer, so I opened it. It wasn't locked, and his ward was pathetic. Other than a nosey dull, I doubted it would keep even the lowest-level Wyrd Blood at bay. After last night, I wouldn't put it past him to try and dodge me.

No Knife. I stepped out of his room and headed toward Ryker's place. It was on the way to breakfast, and I might as well get my business settled now so I didn't have to back track later. I had some things I needed to handle with him, too.

Ryker was standing in the living room drinking coffee and talking to Burn when I barged in without knocking. No Knife, though.

They stopped speaking as soon as I walked in, making me suspect I'd been the topic of conversation.

The aroma of black brew drew me over to the side table, and I made myself a cup as they watched, as if they knew I had a bomb to drop. There was also a plate of biscuits by it. No wonder Ryker was always the last to show for breakfast. It was surprising he showed at all. He was getting in-house catering.

Biscuit and coffee in hand, I took a seat on the couch. I'd been sorting through this fiasco since last night, and I saw only one way that I'd be safe here for the time. I choked down a couple of bites before I laid out my demands. "I need more stones. I need enough to be able to ward off a nice chunk of real estate around where I'm staying while we figure things out. I'm thinking six should do it."

Ryker leaned a shoulder against the wall. "You were going to retrieve my stones. Now I have to help you get more?"

I took a sip of coffee, and then another bite of biscuit. I'd seen this question coming the second I decided what needed to be done. "Yes. If you want your original stones back, that's part of the deal. When I leave, I give you three back and keep the rest."

And then if I still had a monster issue, I'd be better protected.

I angled away from him, looking across the room. There was a tan bag sitting in the corner that would have a stain on the other side. A sleeve with a ragged cuff was hanging out. Knife hated that shirt. How many times had he threatened to throw it out, saying it made it look like he didn't pay me enough? Technically, he didn't, but I hadn't stayed at Dorley for the money. I'd stayed there to avoid the man now standing in front of me.

I'd worn that shirt at least once a week when I lived at the Valley. If Ryker had noticed, he'd never mentioned it. It was the one I was wearing the day I'd gotten caught. It was a shirt I'd never throw out because it would always remind me of my life in the Ruins, the days of hunger and the years of looking over my shoulder for threats.

Whoever had packed my stuff up hadn't taken much care. Had they gone through all my things? Everything? I abandoned my coffee and walked to where it sat, my face lit up like the Eternal Volcano, exploding for all to see.

I dug a hand through it searching. *It* wasn't there. Unfortunately, that might not be a good thing. Why I'd hung on to it for so long was stupid. Should've burned it, but I hadn't.

"Why's your face red?" Ryker asked.

If he had to ask, then he didn't know. If he did know, he definitely wouldn't have brought it up.

"It's hot. How did my bag get here? Who packed my things?" I patted it, just because someone going through my stuff deserved a firm hand movement.

"Knife sent Switch over to do it last night. What's in there that you were searching for?" He walked closer, staring at it as if he could see through cloth.

"Your stones. Would you like to search it?" I raised an eyebrow, in case the sarcasm that dripped from my tongue hadn't made it to his ears.

I grabbed my bag and turned, calm as a sunny day. I was done letting this man rattle me. I'd do what I had to and get out.

I walked to his table, took the last three biscuits on

the plate, and headed for the door. "Let me know when you get a lead on more stones."

"Stop calling Dorley your home. It's Knife's place, and you're stupid to think of it as anything different," he said before I'd made it out the door.

"Why? It is. Would you rather I say I was home-less? Does that work for you?" What was wrong with him? He might as well have waved chocolate in front of a sweet tooth. Now I was going to call Dorley home over and over and over again.

His eyes told me he wasn't happy with that solution either.

"No? I guess it's back to Dorley, then."

My hands were already shaking. If I stayed another second, I was going to get violent. My threshold was lower than it used to be, at least with him. I walked out.

Ruck nearly ran me over the second I turned the corner out of sight of Ryker's. He must've been lurking in the shadows.

"We need to strategize," he said.

"Agreed." That was as far as I got. My facts were too few and my mind too overwhelmed by the ones I had to think further at the moment. "Well? What do you have?"

He squinted. Clearly he hadn't expected to have to lead this strategy session. "Well, there's two things we know. One, there's an invisible monster that talks to you. Two, Ryker's stones were stolen."

"If we could refer to them as *the* stones, I'd prefer it. I did help steal them. They aren't exactly *his*."

"I called them the stones."

"No. You called them Ryker's stones."

He stopped walking. "There's an invisible monster talking to you and this is what we need to clarify?"

I stopped as well. "If we don't start with clear facts, how are we going to move forward upon a false foundation?"

"Fine. From this point forward, they will be referred to as *the* stones." He began walking again. "You might be Wyrd Blood, but you don't know that much about magic. We need more resources."

"Agree again." As much as I should've been thinking about the invisible monster, I had other worries I couldn't shake loose. "Have you seen Switch?"

"Switch? Why? I don't know. What do you need him for?" He was scratching his head and not looking at me. And walking fast, which he did when he got a case of the nerves. You would've thought he was the one who was on the verge of a massive humiliation.

That was when it hit me like a stone to the skull. "When you left Dorley to come back here, why weren't you upset about not seeing your new boyfriend for a while?"

"It wasn't going to be that long," he said, keeping one step ahead of me.

I grabbed his arm, dragging him back. "It wasn't because your new boyfriend could travel easily, was it? It's Switch, isn't it?"

"Maybe. Kind of." He side-eyed me, not holding my gaze.

It had been me and Ruck for a long time. Even

when we had a crew, it had still been the two of us at its core. From the way he was acting, we might be expanding to three after a very long time.

I gave him a pat on the shoulder. "I like him."

His eyes snapped to mine. "You do?"

"Yeah. I do. Now, enough with the mushy shit. Where is he? I need him. They sent him back to pack up for me, but there was something in my room that I don't want to be found." I scanned the area, knowing Switch wouldn't be in the food building. He didn't like people enough to be surrounded by them. The only chance I'd see him over there was when he was flashing past on his way in or out.

"What? The note?"

"How do you know about the note?"

"I borrow your shit all the time. How would I not know about it? It was in your drawer."

"Folded in my drawer. Why would you read it?"

"It was *right* there." He waved his hand down, as if an imaginary drawer was in front of him.

"Fine. Just help me find him. I've got to go tackle another issue." I tilted my head in the direction of the food building, watching the people come and go. If Knife wasn't at his place or Ryker's, he'd be in there. He didn't like to go without his breakfast. How many times had I heard him saying he thought his blood sugar was getting low?

"Knife?" Ruck asked.

"Keeping us all here better be a scheme, or he's in deep trouble. I'll see you soon." I turned and headed into the food building.

Last night I'd laid my hand on the door of this place, saying goodbye to my memories. I'd been brimming with emotion and drama. What a waste. Who knew I'd be back less than a day later?

I swung open the door, and heads turned. I ignored them as they got their fill. *Yes, ladies and gentlemen, I'm back.*

Soon enough, my steps were slowing. I paused a couple of feet in, old habits dying hard.

Don't do it. Don't.

I did it. I looked. Marra was sitting at the same table as the last time I'd eaten breakfast here. Looked like she still had the same replacements sitting next to her. I guessed her new Ruck and Bugs were working out better than the originals. Only thing that had changed was shock had her looking straight at me with an expression that said I didn't belong here. She better not push it. Made me want to move back in for good.

I kicked back into gear and scoured the building. I found Knife quickly. He was sitting at a table with Dez, their heads bent down, glancing around the crowd periodically.

He caught sight of me as I approached, and leaned back. I took the seat beside Dez, but my eyes nailed Knife to the seat.

"What was that bullshit? First I get the spiel about how I shouldn't roll over and welcome Ryker with open arms. Then you help tighten the chains to keep me here?" I leaned forward, and he was lucky I didn't leap over the table. "What game are you playing?"

He didn't answer immediately and looked across

the room to dead space. I waited. I wasn't leaving here without an answer.

His eyes dipped down before he finally turned to look at me. "It's not a game. It was the right thing."

"Right thing? How so? What are you getting out of this?" I leaned back with a huff. The only "right thing" in Knife's life was one that benefitted him.

"Nothing." His tone was flat.

"He's not," Dez said softly. "We were just talking about it. He thinks it's better for you to stay here."

"You're telling me you don't have a scheme or payoff?" I asked. "You threw me under the chugger and you aren't even getting anything out of this? You aren't trying to spy or trick Ryker somehow? You just kicked me out?"

"I didn't kick you out," Knife said. "I'm staying here with you, and so is Dez. We'll all be in one place in case this turns ugly."

"Is that what this is? Strategy? You're afraid I'll lure the monster back to Dorley with me and staying here lets Ryker deal with the brunt of it?"

Knife opened his mouth, but Dez cut him off. "Yes. That's exactly what he's thinking."

Knife looked at Dez. He didn't say anything for a second but then nodded slightly.

I leaned back and crossed my arms. I didn't like the plan. I liked not being consulted even less, but at least this made some sense. If anyone was good at killing, it was Ryker.

"We hang back, figure out what's going on, get him

his stones back, and then we all go back to Dorley?" I asked.

Dez smiled. "Yes."

Knife nodded but was looking across the room again.

FOURTEEN

SWITCH WAS WAITING FOR ME OUTSIDE THE FOOD building when I walked out, skulking in the shadows across the way as if he were guilty of something. I made my way over and didn't bother telling him he could've come inside and gotten me. He knew that.

"Ruck said you were looking for me?" he asked, his gaze constantly shifting, as if he were about to get jumped.

"Yeah, you packed up my room, right?" I settled into the shadows with him, hoping it would take the edge off his jitters.

"I only did what I was told." He instantly switched from guarded to a fear you could smell. He sidled a couple inches away.

"I'm not mad. I appreciate your help." I said it so fast it nearly sprained my tongue to get out. I couldn't risk him disappearing.

He scanned my face for a lie before his shoulders

slumped an inch. "Sure. I wanted to help, and Knife said you really needed me to do this."

Now to the hard part. "When you emptied my drawers, did you notice a folded piece of paper?"

"The letter to Ryker?"

I breathed in through my nose, taking a long, calming breath. It didn't matter if Switch read it. He didn't speak to anyone.

I couldn't get mad, either. He was too socially awkward to know he shouldn't have read it, and worse, told me. If I'd been in his shoes, I probably wouldn't have read the whole thing, but I might've given it an accidental couple seconds of perusal. The only difference between us was I wouldn't have told anyone.

"Do you have it? It wasn't in my bag."

"I left it behind, you know, just in case someone went through your stuff."

"You have to take me back to my room. I need to get that letter." Who knew how long I'd be here? I had prime real estate in the castle. No way would my room sit empty. They'd be like vultures on a carcass within days.

He inched back. "I was told by Ryker, and then Knife, that I can't take you anywhere."

Those interfering fuckers. They shouldn't be allowed to speak. They were too alike. I wondered who started this new rule. I'd have a talk with both of them, right after I got back from doing exactly what they thought I shouldn't.

I grabbed Switch's arm in a death grip. He wasn't getting away from me until he took me back there.

"We're going to be two minutes. In and out. No one will know."

He was shaking his head rapidly as he stared down at my fingers. "I don't—"

I changed my grip to his shoulders as I pressed his back against the building. "Switch, do you want to spend the rest of your life only doing what you're told? Being controlled? Fettered? Chained? You've got magic that's invaluable." I paused for a couple of seconds as I stared at him, really trying to nail the dramatic impact of my next words. "You could be a *god*."

He shook his head violently. "Oh no! I don't want to be a god."

Uh oh. Misstep. I should've read that one better. I didn't want to be a god either. *Back up. Different approach.*

"And you don't have to be—you're better than a god. You should be free to do whatever you want..." Like what? I needed a close. "Like a *bird*."

His eyes lit up. That one hit the bullseye. I should've guessed. The guy slept in the middle of bushes.

I lifted a hand, waving my fingers as I raised it. "Soaring free, weightless. Above all the petty disputes and bickering and power grabs. Just you, soaring through the air. That's how you should live. Like a great, free bird."

"Yeah." His voice was a whisper as he looked at the clouds above.

Time to strike. "So you'll fly free and take me? And we'll both be free birds?"

"I'll take you."

I smiled and grabbed his hands before he could change his mind and fly off without me.

"You said only a couple minutes, right?" He cracked his neck.

"Swear. Now let's go, and quick." If he started to remember he didn't fly so well in reality, things would go south quick.

———

THE SITTING ROOM WAS EMPTY WHEN WE POPPED into it. I dashed into my bedroom, not wasting any time. Twitchy was going to be counting down the seconds, and he'd drag me out as soon as we hit two minutes. This bird wasn't used to flying yet.

I pulled open the drawer I'd kept the letter, cursing myself for not throwing it out. It had made no sense to keep it. Or read it over and over again. Or pretend he was hearing it and saying all sorts of words back.

The drawer fell forward with a clunk. It wasn't there. I pulled the drawer out all the way and shoved my hand behind it. Nothing. I dropped to my knees, looking underneath the dresser and then behind it, while Switch watched from the doorway. Where could it have gone?

"Are you sure you didn't take it?"

He walked over and looked in the empty drawer. "I'm positive. It was there," he said, tapping the inside.

Had someone come and cleaned out the room that fast? Maybe it got stuck to some of my clothing and

Switch accidentally shoved it into my bag without knowing. I looked under the dresser again and then around the back, just for the sake of it.

I dragged both hands through my hair. "It's gone."

He shrugged. "Things happen."

Twitchy Switch was going to lecture me on letting things go? "You read it. You know what I wrote."

"Only briefly." He tilted his head, all of a sudden afraid to commit to any particular knowledge.

"If that was your letter, would you want it circulated?"

He sucked in a breath between his teeth.

"Exactly. Thank you."

"Either way, it's been two minutes. Can we go?" He held out the watch Ryker had given him when we'd gone to Cacoy ages ago. It was as if everything Ryker did was somehow planned out to make my life harder.

I looked back at the dresser.

"Please," he said.

I grabbed his hands. No reason we should both be tortured. It wasn't here.

We didn't have the easy landing I'd expected. Normally when Switch brought you somewhere, you were standing in one place and then you were standing in another. That was it. The only thing startling about it was the seamless transition. Better than walking, better than a chugger. He was my preferred mode of transportation, until now.

Lying on my back in the middle of a forest, I felt like I'd been flung against the side of a mountain. I reached to my pocket. The stone was still there. I rolled to my side to find my transporter next, but he wasn't there.

"Switch?" I called out, getting to my feet.

No one answered.

"Switch?" I called a little louder, spinning in a circle. "Switch, you better not be messing around with me."

That wasn't Switch's personality. He wouldn't mess with anyone on purpose. Maybe he'd crashed harder than I had? I ducked behind bushes and searched the immediate area, afraid I'd find a bloodied body.

I looked everywhere in a fifty-foot radius but found nothing, not even a drop of blood. Did he make it back without me? And where exactly was I?

The only landmark was a mountainside. I'd never realized how similar they all looked until right now. Where had he dropped me off? Logic said it had to be somewhere between the Valley and Dorley. Did magic travel work in a linear fashion? Maybe I was on the other side of the world. At least it wasn't too cold yet. Judging by the temperature now, it probably wouldn't drop below freezing, another sign I wasn't too far away.

I could hear water flowing in the distance. If I *was* in between Dorley and the Valley, that would be the Chichi River that ran in between the two countries. Or I wasn't and I didn't know what river it was.

Waiting wasn't a good option, not when I knew the

kinds of creatures that roamed regular forests. For all I knew, I was in the Ruined Forest. Standing still and waiting would be the worst thing possible when Switch might not know where he lost me. Nothing else to do but walk out of here, and the sooner the better.

I'd only made a few feet when I felt the magic. There was a stone nearby. I could feel the ward protecting it. They had a distinctiveness to them I could nearly taste at this point.

Did I try and get it? There were some serious reasons to leave it. I was alone, with no backup, and no idea where I was.

The same reasons I had to leave it were the ones that made me think I should get it. I wouldn't be as vulnerable with another stone on hand. I knew the kind of ward I'd be able to create with two stones. If I was stuck out here for a while, at some point I'd have to sleep.

Go for it or not? I'd managed to get them out before, and about half of those times, I might've made it out alive. Barely, but that was better than falling asleep and dying in the woods.

No, leave it. One stone was probably enough.

But, if the ward around that thing was any indication, it was a large stone. Larger meant stronger. Maybe the strongest I'd seen. If someone else passed by this way, they might feel it. What if they got it before I could get back here with help? Was there any real harm in checking it out a little more before leaving?

Now I had to zero in. I walked in a small circle

until I narrowed down its location. Then I looked up. Figured. It was halfway up the mountainside.

"What the fuck? Why'd you let go?"

I jumped at the sound of Switch's voice behind me. I swung around, glad he was alone.

"I didn't let go." I wagged a finger. "You dropped me—not that I'm holding any grudges."

"I don't drop people. Or I haven't in a decade. Either way, I was gripping your hand when you yanked away."

"There's a stone close. Maybe it called to me or tripped me somehow." I walked closer to the pull of the magic, looking at a shadow halfway up. Was there a ledge?

Switch followed me, reaching for my hand. "We've got to go."

I pulled away and crossed my arms so he couldn't catch me unaware. "Did you not hear me say there's a stone?"

"We have to get back. He's waiting for us, and he'll kill me if I don't hurry. He said so."

I didn't even need to ask who he'd told. Ryker. I let out a groan that a grizzly would've been proud of.

"I had to. I thought I lost you." He took a step back, and this time, I didn't care if he ran away. I wasn't eager to get back anyway.

"I've been gone for five minutes, tops."

"I panicked." There was a tiny shift of his shoulders.

"Did you tell him where?"

"No. I said I lost you trying to bring you to the

grove. Then I got scared and disappeared when he started threatening me with death."

Hmmm. Could be worse. He thought I was still in the Valley.

Switch reached for my hands, but couldn't seem to get past the fact that they were pressed against my breasts. I was a literal boobie trap.

I walked over to the side of the mountain and pointed up. "You want me to leave, I need to get up there. There's a stone, and I'm not leaving without it. I'm going to get it, and then you get us out of here as quick as you can."

"I don't think that's a good idea."

"Switch, you can do this. You can help me get this stone because you're stronger than you ever imagined and you're as free as a bird. Now it's time to learn to fly. You with me?" I held out my hand, hoping he wouldn't grab it under false pretenses.

"Okay, I guess if we're quick." He didn't look so sure, but he was saying the right words.

"You can." I took his hand. "You get us up on that ledge, I get the stone, and then you get us out quick."

He nodded, and then we were teetering on a two-foot ledge. I grabbed on to a ridge as we both shuffled, trying to find our footing.

There was some wobbling as we shifted around, bumping into each other here and there.

"Do you have a solid hold?" I asked Switch.

He nodded.

"Good. Give me your hand." I wrapped a hand

around his and let go of the mountain. "I'm going to kneel down. It's in the crevice by our feet."

Switch looked down but didn't see it. Neither did I, but I still knew it was there. I felt its power pulsing.

I knelt and ran my free hand over the area, feeling for a weak spot. They all had one.

"When do I move us?" Switch asked, his twitchiness showing.

"Not until I tell you." I pushed forward, pausing my fingers over a weak spot. "I think this is going to be easy, but be ready, just in case."

"Ready for what?"

I gave the weak spot a push and my hand crashed through. My fingers grazed the stone at the same time as heat swallowed me.

Before I could scream for Switch to get us out of there, we were standing in the middle of Ryker's living room and multiple pairs of hands were patting burning embers from my shirt.

Then Ryker's hand wrapped around my wrist, holding up the stone in between us. "If Switch was bringing you to the grove, how did you end up with a stone?"

I yanked on my arm, and he let go of my wrist. "We stumbled across it."

"Where? It wasn't in the Valley, I know that."

I tossed him the stone. It wasn't quite as big as I'd hoped, but it was close. "Here. You can keep it. And if you lose them again, it's not on me. I'll replace them once, and once only."

Ryker held it up. "This doesn't end with me getting

replacement stones."

I looked like I'd been drop-kicked here and still had gotten a stone. Now he was going to harangue me? I gave up sitting and flopped down on the couch.

Switch looked like he was about to take off. Ryker pointed at him while he continued to stare at me. "Don't move. Where did you go?"

I yawned, as if he weren't infuriating. "You know where you're going wrong? You keep thinking you can dictate to me, and you can't. I don't have to listen to you, and I don't have to answer to you." I sure as hell wasn't telling him why I'd gone back to Dorley.

"Switch, where did you go?" Ryker asked.

That got my eyes open as my head jerked toward Switch so fast it was in danger of coming off my shoulders.

He looked over at me and then back at Ryker. His pulse fluttered in his neck as he wrung his hands in front of him. "A bird flies free," he said with a tremor.

"What bird?" Ryker asked.

I bit my lip as I watched. Would Switch hold up? I wasn't sure he had it in him.

Switch's eyes met mine and his chin tilted upward. His shoulders went back and his spine went straighter than I thought possible, since I'd only seen him hunched over.

After a deep breath, he stated, "Me. I'm a bird. I soar high and free."

His arms rose, as if he were envisioning himself flying.

"You go, birdie!" Even if he hadn't saved my ass and

wasn't Ruck's new man, I would've cheered him on.

He smiled, his eyes gleaming. Then he was gone.

Nope. I was wrong. I could be prouder. He hadn't even stuck around to let Ryker harass him for answers. He'd given him a big Switch "fuck off."

Ryker focused all his attention back on me. "What is this bird thing about? Why is he saying he's a bird, and why do I think you've got something to do with it?" He didn't wait for me to answer. "Do you realize how stupid it was to go off without telling anyone and without backup? With everything going on, you pull this now?"

I stood, having had enough. "Really? You wouldn't have done the same if you'd had a chance at a stone? You would've hunted me down for permission? That's the song and dance you're trying to sell?"

Ryker remained quiet, and I leveled my stare on him.

For the first time since I'd known him, he broke the stare first. He angled his head to the side, giving me a clear view of the tightly strung tendons in his neck. "It's different. I can kill anything that gets close to me. We merged magic. That doesn't make you invincible. You can still be killed."

I huffed. "Everyone can be killed. Even you."

I walked past him, and he grabbed my wrist. The stone landed in my palm.

"You can't be replaced." He let go of me and then beat me out of his place, leaving the door wide open.

As he walked off, I could feel the frown lines on my head wrinkling. Well, that had been almost—nice.

FIFTEEN

Two stones. I might not be able to ward this whole place, but I could still protect myself with two.

But how to do it best? That was the problem with magic that I hadn't understood when I'd started. Yes, there might be certain spells you could find, but the best stuff was unique to the user. There wasn't anyone who could break or make a ward as well as I could, so how could they tell me how to make the best one I'd ever made? And that was what I was about to do.

I stepped inside my place and pulled out both of the stones, one in each palm, magic sizzling and arcing through me. I moved to the center of my room and closed my eyes.

I stirred up the magic within and let it rise until I could feel it warming me. It grew hotter and larger, and I pushed it outward a foot or two. Then I started to build again, until the heat was nearly burning me. I pushed outward again.

Over and over, I built it up and then pushed it

farther until my entire place was protected. Then I collapsed into a puddle on the ground, feeling drained of everything. It was worth it. Whatever had attacked me wasn't going to touch me again, not in here.

"Bugs!" My door burst open and Ruck rushed in.

"What's wrong?" I asked, leaning up on an arm.

"What's wrong? Your place lit up like the damn sun and you looked like you were dead."

"Sorry. I was warding the place. I'd closed my eyes. Hadn't realized everyone would see that light." I walked to the door he'd left open and saw the crowd of people hanging around, watching. I gave them a wave. "All's good! Just a magic surge. Nothing to be alarmed over."

I could feel another set of eyes on me, could see a shadow off in the corner. It was Marra. I stared back, waiting to see if she'd come forward or turn away.

She held my gaze for a moment before leaving, and I shut the door. I walked to the bed and flopped down on it.

"If it's warded, how'd I get in?" he asked.

"I focused on blocking only those who would harm me. The more precise the threat to me, the stronger the ward works." I waved a hand toward the table near my bed that had a basket of biscuits. "Can you get those? I need sustenance, and I don't want to move again."

He grabbed the basket, and my canteen from near it, before dropping down beside me.

"Where's your boy Switch?" I grabbed a slightly chilled biscuit. I'd buttered them all in preparation for this a couple of hours prior.

"He's lying low, trying to avoid Ryker—said he might ask him more questions." He ate half a biscuit in one bite, barely chewed it before he swallowed, and then continued. "He told me what happened earlier. Then he kept talking about being a bird or something. They better not have broken my boyfriend."

My eyelid twitched. I rubbed it, hoping it would stop before he noticed.

Ruck wasn't looking at me, and yet somehow he'd caught it. "Why does your eye have a tic? Did you break my boyfriend? You only do that when you feel guilty."

"I can't break another person unless I kill them. If anything, I tried to give Switch an uplifting pep talk."

"Uplifting? Like maybe a bird? Is that how you got him to take you to Dorley?" He leaned over, his face inches from mine.

"Maybe." I threw an arm over my eyes, trying to hide the evidence. "I didn't mean to mess him up. To be honest, he needed it."

"I know. That's one of the reasons I came here. We have to talk. I don't want to go back to Dorley, and neither does Switch. Don't tell me you want to be there either. That sideshow scene was a joke."

My lower lip tasted really good all of a sudden as I tried to think of a reason Dorley still might be better than staying here. There was only one, and its name was Ryker.

"Are you really going to lie there and say you want to go back?"

When I didn't answer, he lifted my arm up.

"I don't know." I rolled over onto my stomach to avoid the all-knowing gaze.

"Because you still want to get in the big man's pants and have him tell you you're the one and only?"

"Yes, if we must spell it out. I don't know why I can't seem to get past it. I don't even like him most of the time." And yet I had to give myself a pep talk to keep my shit together whenever I was around him, and it wasn't just the way our magic reacted.

Ruck flopped onto his stomach next to me. "You know what my suggestion is. Climb on a different dick." His voice was very sincere considering his words.

"I don't want another dick. I haven't had a first dick to compare."

"It still might help. Hair of the dog that bit you."

"But I didn't get bitten, and that refers to drinking."

"It's just as relevant. I have more experience. You need to trust me on this." He gave my hand a pat. "Look, wherever we end up, Switch wants to come with us. He doesn't want to go back to Dorley and he's afraid to tell Knife. He says he needs to be free like a bird."

Switch had really grabbed on to this bird thing. I'd needed a lift to Dorley, which had taken him all of ten minutes. Now I was going to have to negotiate his release. Somehow that didn't seem like a fair swap.

I lifted to my elbows so Ruck could see how serious I was. "Knife isn't going to let him go easily. Do you realize how special Switch is?"

"That's why I need your help. I know how special he is too, and not just for his magic."

I was glad I was lying down, or I would've fallen. There wasn't a hint of humor or a smirk. He was serious.

I leaned a little closer, watching every nuance of his expression as I asked, "Is he the one?"

He nodded, smiling shyly at first. The smile morphed into a giggle. I didn't know Ruck even knew how to giggle.

Wow. Switch was the *one*. I groaned and dropped my face onto the bed. "You had to fall for Knife's most valuable Wyrd Blood? Seriously?"

He sat up, taking another biscuit. "He's still got plenty of other Wyrd Blood, like Dez, even if no one knows what the hell she can do."

"How am I supposed to get Knife to let him go?" I asked.

"I don't know, but Knife doesn't even talk to me. Hard to negotiate with someone who doesn't acknowledge your existence." He took another bite of biscuit, as if all his worries had been handled now. "These could've used a little more butter, by the way."

It didn't stop him from grabbing two more before he left.

I shoved the stones under my bed, just in case someone not meaning harm stumbled in here and moved them. The thought of not having them on me all the time was nearly painful. The idea of being attacked in my sleep was even worse, and I couldn't ward this place every night.

SIXTEEN

I'D BEEN AT DORLEY FOR SIX MONTHS, AND WITHIN a couple of days back in the Valley, I was already looking over my shoulder for Ryker and trying to do the dodge. I'd scrambled in and out of breakfast before most people were wiping the crust from their eyes. I'd done a lap of the area where the monster had made its presence known before most others had reported to work. I wasn't ready for another talk about where I'd gone with Switch and how I'd found another stone. Silence and distance was my foreseeable plan of action.

A moving target was harder to hit, so I'd scoured every inch of the Valley perimeter that was close to where the monster had attacked me. If it had come in, and it was no longer here, it must've left. I'd spent hours upon hours trying to find a trail. By the end of the day, I snuck into my room like a thief in the night, my feet throbbing and my legs shaky.

I stripped out of my clothes in the dark and shrugged on my sleep shirt before crawling into bed.

My head hit the pillow and exhaustion made my limbs feel like they were a thousand pounds each. There was no bed that existed in the universe that felt better than this one in this moment.

Ryker's voice broke the silence and ripped my peace to shreds. "You ready to talk yet? I didn't want to wait until you did five more laps around the place tomorrow."

Fuck. How had I not felt him in here? I'd just...

"Did you watch me change?"

"You've stripped in front of me before. Didn't realize you'd become bashful in the last few months." A match was struck and the lantern by my bed flared, casting Ryker in harsh shadows.

"How come I didn't sense you in here?" Before the merge, his presence was unmistakable. After the merge, it was a punch to the gut. But not right now.

"While you've been hiding at Dorley, I've been working on subduing it." He walked to the corner and dragged the chair to the side of the bed, its back facing me. He sat down, his arms resting on it. I knew then that my night was going to be ruined, because he was too big to physically drag out of my room, no matter how that appealed.

Had I gone to the bathroom before I went to sleep? Yes, but maybe I needed to go again. I sat up. He was shaking his head before my feet hit the ground.

"I need to—"

"No. We're talking and you're not running away. Drink if you have to, but you aren't leaving." He reached into a back pocket, and a flash of silver glinted. I caught the flask before it hit my lap.

Being told what to do had always chafed, like nails dragging over raw skin. I leaned my back against the wall, stretched out my legs, and crossed my arms.

"I need answers, and I'm getting them tonight. Whatever is going on with the missing stones, the creature attacking you, the attempts to kill you, it's no coincidence."

I didn't open the flask, but I didn't give it back to him either. I set it on the table next to me, just in case.

"I need to know what you remember from your past, your parents, where you grew up. Any detail you can give me." His stare said he'd sit there all night until he got them. His eyes never lied.

I picked the flask back up and took a swallow.

"Why?" Talking to him was always a bad idea. I should've made a run for the door and then fought until I lost consciousness.

"The Debt Collector sold you to somebody. The Queen of Cacoy made an attempt on your life. There's more here than you're saying. You can't tell me that it's not all connected somehow."

"This has nothing to do with where I came from. I was born to dulls."

My attention shot to the door. Could I make it past him?

"Neither of us are leaving this room until you come clean. We can't afford the secrets anymore. I'm trying to keep you alive. You might want to help."

"You have no idea if that thing came for me or was here for someone else and stumbled upon me."

He let out a half laugh. "It didn't come for anyone else."

"How do you know? You can't be sure."

"I know the history and three generations back of every person here but you. I should've pressed you on this before you left and I let it go. Not anymore."

Was he joking? Surely he was exaggerating at least. There were too many people here to know everyone's history. If he wanted to press me, it was one thing. I could understand why he thought digging into my history might lead to something, but I disliked being bullshitted.

"Kenny the tailor," I said, daring him to supply the evidence.

"I'll play your game, but then we're playing mine." He watched me, waiting for an agreement.

"Fine," I said with a shrug.

"Kenny was born in Barkle. Came over with his parents, who were also born there, as well as his grandparents." There was a gleam in his eye.

Cocky bastard. One person didn't mean anything. "Sylvia, the cook who makes the good biscuits?"

He leaned back, stretching his neck. "Born here. Her father and mother came together after one of the wars broke out with Bedlam and Dorley. Her grandparents were born in both of those countries and died in that war. By the way, her biscuit recipe was handed down from her grandmother on her mother's side, in case you were wondering."

"Burtie the burier." The little fucker wasn't even human. Good luck with that one.

"Burtie was a mountain gnome, from a long line of gnomes before him. I can't tell you where they originally hail from because if I say the name, you'll die instantly. It's a spell that was cast by his ancestors to guard their home. Are you happy with that, or would you like to continue? I can do this all night if you'd like. Feel free to ask for a substitution, but I don't feel right about you dying over a name."

I grabbed the flask and downed half the contents.

"Good thing I didn't bring you the bottle," he said.

"My full name is Chiara Rokke. I was born in a place called Crisp." I watched for recognition. Even as a child, I knew the place I'd come from was small, even by this world's standards.

He nodded. "I know of it. Keep going."

"My mother was a lower servant to the ruling family. My father was a farmer. There was nothing out of the ordinary about either of them." There, all my secrets were on the table. As I'd told him, there was nothing special.

His expression was intent as ever. "How did you end up with the slavers?"

I downed the rest of the flask. This was where things went bad, at least memory-wise. I'd had a warm and loving family one night and then been in a living hell the next. I had no desire to relive it. "I went to bed on a day like any other. I woke up in the dead pile the next morning. Before I knew what was happening, slavers grabbed me. That's my long and illustrious tale of woe, and all I know."

"I'm going to go there tomorrow. You don't need to come with me." He stood, grabbing the chair and swinging it back into the corner.

"You really think I'm going to let you dig around in my past and not be there?" He was begging to get tackled if he thought he'd do this alone.

He let out a short laugh, this one warm and genuine. "Of course I didn't."

"If we're going, and you want to actually find something, we need to bring Sneak."

"Why?"

"Because everything you might want to know about my family history will be in one place, and it'll be easier with him there. They keep records of all the family trees of everyone born in Crisp."

"Do you remember where it is?"

"Won't know until we get there."

Ryker nodded and then left, taking any chance of sleep with him.

SEVENTEEN

THE SUN WAS STILL SLEEPING, BUT I WAS UP AND digging around in the dirt. The fourth worm of the morning was wiggling like it had been zapped with a hit of adrenaline. Before I could even ask it a question, it leapt out of my hand like it was on fire and hit the dirt.

Shit. I shoved my hands in the dirt, giving another push of magic until I wavered a little to the right.

Nothing.

I caught sight of grey dreadlocks swing in the breeze as the healer made her way over to me.

"Ah, my best client. Having some issues?"

"Nope. Not at all." I stood up, transferring the dirt on my hands to my legs. The last thing I needed was her trying to con me out of a few years for payment. I'd just gotten my life back and was planning on being very stingy with it.

She was looking at the unused circle I'd drawn. "Looks like you can't worm anymore."

"I can't, but it's not a problem." I dragged a boot over the dirt, smearing the circle. I turned toward Ryker's as the sun began to rise. No way I'd let him leave here without me and some flimsy excuse that I'd been two minutes late.

"I know what the problem is, but you're not going to like it," she said.

I stopped like I'd hit a brick wall and looked back at her.

She smiled like she'd just caught a big, fat fish.

I crossed my arms, pretending that my insides weren't wiggling like I'd gotten dragged out of a pond. "How many years is this going to cost?"

"For my best customer? Free." She walked toward me.

"Am I sick again?" My hand went to my chest. I didn't feel sick, but there was something wrong. I didn't glitch for this long and think everything was great.

She tapped a finger on my chest. "No. Not sick. You're too conflicted, and it's screwing with the worm. It's all over you. You're a walking mess."

"I'm not a mess, and I'm hardly conflicted." I smoothed back some strands sticking up. The woman was a con artist if I'd ever met one. Her next words were probably going to pitch a cure that would cost me a decade.

"If you say so." She tipped her head in my direction and sashayed away.

"I do," I said, hoping she heard me.

RYKER WAS STANDING OUTSIDE HIS PLACE WITH Sneak and Burn beside him when I walked up. Switch was standing several feet away.

"Where's Knife? Is he coming?" I glanced around, expecting him to walk up at any second. "Didn't you tell him we were going?" I asked, looking at Ryker.

"No," Ryker said. "We need to get in and out light. You ready?" Before I had a chance to answer, he was waving Switch over. "Come on."

"Who's going? You two?" Switch inched away like we were a pack of rabid dogs.

"The four of us," Ryker answered, waving again, as if that would quicken Switch's pace.

Switch stopped moving. "Four? I can't do four. I've done three tops for short hops. That's it."

Ryker took a step toward him. "She'll juice you. It'll be fine."

Switch was beginning to twitch again. "I'm going to need one hell of a lot of juice to pull that off."

"How much more?" I crossed my arms, edging closer to him. Every part of me felt sucked dry since the ward, like I'd spent the night with a pack of leeches and now someone asked me to open a vein.

"Like twice what you gave me when we went to Cacoy to see the Mushroom Man?" Switch nibbled on his cuticle like it was a link of sausage.

Twice? I shook my head. "I don't think I have it. I was warding my place all yesterday, and then..." They didn't need to know about the failed worm attempts and the lack of sleep. "It was a lot. I don't know what I have left." If I were to use my magic alone, I definitely couldn't do it. But there was a way.

I knew how horrible it felt to have my magic taken. Hopefully it wouldn't be so bad on the other end, being a taker. Ryker had tapped into my magic enough. It wouldn't be so bad for him to see what it felt like. At least he'd know it was coming, which was more than I'd gotten.

"Give us a minute," I said, and broke from the group, knowing Ryker was going to follow me. His steps were right behind as I walked far enough that the perked ears wouldn't hear. That didn't mean they wouldn't lean forward to listen.

His tense jaw told me he already knew what I was going to suggest. He was a smart man. It wasn't a surprise he'd known this was coming.

I breathed until I couldn't get one more ounce of air in and then held it. As soon as I exhaled, I let the words fly out. "I think I've got to tap into your magic and take a little taste."

I cleared my throat and gave him my best smile. I'd been working on it. It wasn't horribly awkward anymore. Dez had said it was only mildly so now. And the truth was that I wanted to do this. I'd dreamed of having a reason to do this.

He didn't speak right away, but at least he nodded. "Fine."

"Good." Why'd he agree so easily? Did he know something I didn't? Was there a bad part to taking too?

"You don't think it's going to get..." I rubbed a palm on my hip and shifted my weight from foot to foot.

Freaky? It was already that. Freakier? How much worse could it get when you already felt like you were peeking into the abyss every time you felt it? "...weird?"

"I don't know. I guess we'll see." His words were clipped with a razor's edge, and the set of his shoulders did nothing to soften them.

I fisted my hands at my hips and jutted a foot out. It was fine to take my magic at a whim, but magic forbid I had to take his. "We don't have to do this. This isn't *my* choice. I'm trying to get us there in one piece."

"I know, and I didn't say it was." His words were right, but he looked at me like I was about to slaughter everyone at the Valley. What the hell? I nearly wanted to shove him in the chest. "If you could juice Switch, I'd gladly let you do it with mine if you *asked*." He'd never done that, though.

"I said it was fine." His words came through a clenched jaw.

Clearly it wasn't, but he'd deal with it as I had. Maybe it was better he hated it. He'd think twice before doing it to me again.

We stood, saying nothing for a few seconds. I could see the guys staring our way. They were probably wondering why we weren't talking or moving.

"Do you know what you're doing?" he asked.

"As far as taking some of your magic? No. But I'll figure it out." After all, he had, several times.

His chin dropped an inch and his eyes narrowed. "Don't pull too much."

"Seriously? I'm not looking to use your magic any more than I need to." He was so lucky we had an audience or I'd try to kick his ass right now. He was even luckier that I knew I'd lose, or I might do it with the audience.

"That's not the problem." The way he stepped closer made me think he might've wanted to kick my ass just as badly.

"Then what? There definitely is a problem."

He turned, creating a wall between me and the guys. "I don't know what will happen if you pull too much. I'm not sure what you can handle. I don't know if it'll hurt you. Your magic is younger."

"Oh." The fists at my hips fell limp to my sides. I shuffled my feet, and the stone wall of the building beside us was suddenly fascinating. He was worried I'd get hurt? That was why he was mad? This nice stuff he kept pulling lately was a real head trip.

"What did you think?" he asked, not sounding so nice anymore.

I shrugged and waved a hand in the air. "I had no idea."

Definitely not that he'd been nervous about me stealing his magic. I'd take that to my grave.

"I'll push my magic toward you, but be conservative." He turned toward the group and then waited for me to precede him.

I stopped beside Switch and gripped his hand tightly, and then did the same to Ryker's. Burn and Sneak completed the loop. I looked around the circle, making sure everyone had a firm grip on the person next to them. "We ready?" I asked.

I heard a chorus of yeses and deafening silence from my right.

Switch was staring at me, his palm was sweaty, and his nose was twitching.

"Is there something wrong?" I asked.

I dipped my chin to rub it on my shoulder, scratching an itch as I waited for him to reply.

"Nah, no. Nah." His eyes shot to the guys before coming back to me. "No. Nothing is wrong."

I let go of Ryker's hand. "We need a minute. We'll be right back."

I pulled at Switch, and he didn't hesitate. I waited until we were ten feet away. "What is it?"

"Did you talk to Ruck?"

"Yes. Congratulations. Now what's wrong?"

"Knife has been looking for me. I know he wants me to go back to Dorley." He had the look of a cornered cat in his eyes.

"I'll figure something out. Dodge him until I do."

"You promise?" he asked.

"I promise to try. It's the best I can do, but I mean it. I'm not going to leave my best friend's man behind if I can help it."

Switch wrapped his arms around me, and I felt the tingle of his magic brushing up against mine. It was all warm and fuzzy, like a puppy's kisses. Did Ruck feel this when they were together? Dulls didn't usually feel magic, but I hoped some of this made it through. I pulled away before Switch turned me into a bigger mush ball than him.

"Come on. Let's get going."

We rejoined the group and Ryker asked, "What's wrong?"

"Nothing. He needed reassurance."

He gave me a nod, as if he accepted the answer. I knew him well enough to know he didn't.

"Juice me up as soon as you're ready," Switch said as we re-formed the circle.

"Okay."

I held his hand while I mentally tiptoed next to the abyss that was Ryker's magic. He was right. I was going to need to be careful. The closer I got, the more I could feel the waves of it crashing against me. It was nothing like mine. It was aggressive, like it wanted to come out and play. Wanted to be used.

"You almost ready?" Switch asked.

It had only been a few seconds, but I could already feel the eyes on me, as if they were sensing something wrong. I nodded vigorously. "Yeah, I'm ready."

Do it. Just do it and get it over with. How bad could it be?

I stuck a figurative toe into the abyss, trying to tap into a small ripple of magic. What I got was a tidal wave.

EIGHTEEN

"Bugs, come on, wake up."

Strong arms were around my waist, my head lolling on my shoulders as the haze cleared. I felt like I'd been swept up in a blast that had ricocheted me to the other side of the world. From the chill in the air, it had. I'd forgotten how cold it was in Crisp.

"I'm good. I'm here." It took me a second to find my feet underneath me. I pulled out of Ryker's embrace before the sizzle of our magic took care of the chill.

I shook my head, trying to clear the rest of the haze.

"Did you not hear me tell you to take only a little?" Ryker asked.

"I only dipped in. Maybe you pushed too hard?" I crossed my arms, trying to keep my body heat from escaping quicker than I could generate it.

"You dipped in too far," he barked as he pulled off a woolen sweater. I was freezing, and he was stripping. That just proved he belonged in the underworld.

I was counting heads, making sure we didn't lose anyone, when I was temporarily blinded by wool over my eyes.

"What are you doing..." I stopped yelling as I found the armholes and my head broke through the top. Damn this man and his nice gestures. He needed to cut that out. He was making it impossible to keep my needed quota of anger toward him.

I was about to give Ryker an evil glare to get him back in line when I saw Switch sitting on the ground. His legs were sprawled out in the snow and he was shaking his head. I must have channeled too much of the blast through me and into him. "You okay?"

Please be okay. It was bad enough he was calling himself a bird these days. If I did any more damage to Switch, Ruck was never going to shut up about it.

He looked up, his head tilted at a funny angle. "Yeah, a little stunned, is all."

Sneak held his hand out, and Switch took the help, standing.

"If it's okay, I'm going to get going." Switch was rubbing his arms and took a step sideways that didn't look intentional.

"Be back at dawn," Ryker said. "Dawn here, not dawn back at the Valley."

Switch nodded. He gave me a last glance, a hint of the promise he was going to hold me to in his eyes. Then he was gone.

Sneak took off to go check the perimeter, and things were feeling oddly familiar. I knew the drill. It was like when we'd gone hunting stones. Sneak was clearing the area. Then Ryker and Sneak would go up ahead, scouting, flushing out any possible threats. Burn and I would follow after. We'd follow the same plan as always, except Ryker hadn't been depleted all those other times. This time he was.

Why was I getting a knot in my stomach over it? He was a grown man. He'd lived a lot longer than me. He knew his vulnerabilities. He didn't need me to list them.

"The border to Crisp is an hour from here. I'll go up ahead with Sneak." Ryker grabbed a stick, drew a rough shape in the dirt, and pointed to a spot. "You'll meet us at the forest's edge near the northern corner. There's an entrance there not many know about. We'll be waiting."

Did he not know he was weakened? No. He had to feel it.

Sneak came back. Ryker tossed down the branch he'd been using, acting like things were normal. It wasn't normal at all. Maybe he did need me to spell it out for him? Dumb man. He was going to get himself killed.

"What happens if you run into trouble when you're drained?" I asked, shifting my hands to my waist.

"You didn't take all my magic."

Wait a second. This was so wrong. The wrongest thing ever to exist. "You don't feel that gaping hole, the soul-sucking feeling? Is that what you're saying?"

"No." Ryker shrugged. "It didn't feel like much of anything."

My face scrunched, and I wanted to lob every curse

I had at him. How was this possible? Of all the unfair, rotten things. He was supposed to be miserable right now. Like I'd been. This was supposed to give him a taste of what he'd done to me. I wanted to scream, but the injustice of it all turned me mute.

Burn wrapped an arm around my shoulder as he told Ryker and Sneak, "We've got this. We'll be there."

Ryker jerked his head to the trees before turning to Sneak. "You're sure we're clear?"

"Positive. Snow was fresh. No hint of magic," Sneak said.

Ryker kept his attention keen on the distance for another minute. If there was magic nearby, I wasn't feeling it, and Sneak would've seen a dull a mile away.

Ryker turned and took a step toward me. He paused, his eyes narrowing as he stared at my midsection.

"You didn't bring the stones?" he asked, as if he couldn't quite believe it.

"I couldn't. I didn't want to break the ward I set up at my place. That took a lot of work." He had no idea how many times I'd thought about running back and grabbing them. Only with every step I'd taken. I'd forced myself out of my room by sheer will.

He cursed under his breath and stared off at the trees as the rest of us watched on. It did nothing to cool him down, because his eyes were still burning up, along with his magic when he turned back around. "I didn't give them to you to leave behind."

At least the air was warming up. That was something.

"Actually, I gave them to you first so you were only giving them back." The swell of magic told me that probably hadn't been the reply he was looking for.

The line of his shoulders told me he was still annoyed, but he turned to leave with Sneak.

"Don't be late," Ryker said as he was walking off.

As he left, a great swell of cold filled in behind him.

I LEANED CLOSER TO THE FIRE, POKING AT IT WITH a branch to adjust the logs.

Burn dug into his bag, pulling out something covered in cloth. "When you can't have comfort booze, there's only one alternative left." He unfolded it and held out some biscuits. "It's a poor runner-up but they're already buttered, and Ryker won't kill us if our stomachs are full of these."

I plucked one from his hands. "Thanks."

"What's going on with you and Ryker?"

We had at least an hour before the second moon rose. An hour was going to feel like a month if this was the topic of conversation. "Absolutely nothing is going on between us other than some missing stones."

"You know I have eyes in my head, right?" He took a big bite of his biscuit.

"I'm not sure who you're looking at with them. Maybe the other women coming and going out of his place?" I edged closer to the fire, but that wasn't what caused the burn inside. Every vision of Ryker with someone else lit its own little torch inside me. If it hadn't stopped bothering me by now, it probably never would, which was why I had to get away from him. I could live my life or I could continue to watch him live his.

"But not the *right* kind of woman." Burn stared into the fire. Clearly he'd been giving this a lot of thought and was thinking it over again as we sat there.

"I don't know. There were a lot of coming and going. I find it hard to believe they were all wrong for some crazy reason." Not to mention Ryker didn't want my company, not like that. There'd been a blip, but it had disappeared after the merge and never come back.

Burn shrugged and then swatted an ember away. "Not wrong, per se, but not right for him."

"And what's right for him? Is this a Wyrd Blood thing? You're not some sort of secret purist, right?" I'd heard about people like that back in the ruins. Wyrd Blood who would only sleep with other Wyrd Blood and thought others should do the same. Burn had plenty of dulls he'd been interested in, but maybe he held Ryker to a higher standard?

It wasn't only a Wyrd Blood thing, either. There were dulls that said they'd only sleep with other dulls. That was a lot easier to accomplish, since there were many more of them. Of course, there were also dulls that said they were holding out for a Wyrd Blood, and Wyrd Blood who hated having magic so would only be with dulls. People got really weird when it came to sex.

"He needs someone who's more..." Burn took a deep breath, trying to find the word, but only exhaled air as he rolled his hand.

"More what?" Couldn't wait until he figured this one out. What was I more of? Crazy? Desperate? Destitute? The options could roll on and on if I wanted to dig myself right into a depression.

"Just *more*. Like you. Like how when you walk into a room, you're instantly the center of it."

"That's hard to believe, since I don't talk half the time and I prefer the wall space."

"It just happens. Everyone is always checking on you because there's this thing you do that is hard not to notice."

"But I'm not doing anything." All I'd ever wanted was too lie low and not be noticed. Hanging toward the back, not speaking a lot, and definitely not saying anything too provocative unless I got pissed off. I'd perfected not doing anything for years. The only glitch in my game lately was that Ryker pissed me off an awful lot.

"You don't have to. It's there in the way you talk, or don't talk. The way you move. It's like the magic in you is bubbling up and spills out, and waves its hands at people and says, *Hey, something interesting is going on over here.* Maybe you'd be like this without the magic too. I don't know. But you're more, and Ryker was never going to fall for someone normal. He needs you."

Oh, damn it all. He thought I was going to save his friend's soul or heart or some goofy shit. This was what happened when you hung around mushes. They contaminated you with their softness and tried to make you think a lion was a pussycat.

"I hate to break this to you, but Ryker isn't falling for me, and I'm not sure he needs anyone's help."

"He's hardened, but he needs this. When he commits, it'll be different. You'll see," Burn said, as if we lived in a world filled with doves and rainbows.

The last rainbow I'd seen had been after a week of horrendous storms. Hadn't seemed worth it.

"Maybe he's better off being hardened. Love, marriage, family—that's not who I am, and it's not who Ryker is either. We're not meant for that kind of life. Live lean, that's who we are. Who we have to be." My life couldn't take any more complications. My head count couldn't increase any more either. I'd lost too many people too quickly. Best way to stop the loss was to limit the lineup of possible casualties. I needed to become harder, not softer.

Burn didn't say anything else, letting me have the last word. I didn't care if he was tired of arguing or agreed. I'd take the silence.

We passed the rest of the time with idle chitchat about who was on latrine duty, who was moving out, and who was looking to move in.

By the time the second moon began to rise, I was antsy to leave. I hadn't walked in the place of my birth for many years, and I wasn't sure how I felt about doing it again. Better to be done with the mess.

Burn pointed to the second crescent. "You ready for this?"

"Yep. Time to go to work." I got to my feet and kicked out the fire. I slung my bag over my shoulder but couldn't kick Burn's words out of my head. He acted like I was this great catch, and yet other than Knife and Ryker, no one was pounding down my door.

"If I'm so special, why isn't every man in the Valley falling all over themselves to get me?" I asked him about fifteen minutes into our trek as we entered a field.

"I didn't say special, I said *more*. First off, even if they were interested, you're too connected to Ryker. No one is touching you when they aren't sure what's going on there.

"The other issue is not every man is going to want more. You're a lot. You're always on the verge of dying. That's a real buzzkill." He softened it with his signature Burn smile.

I couldn't help but laugh. It was surprising I heard the twig snap at all. I paused but managed to catch myself before I swung toward the noise. If we were being followed, better if they didn't realize we knew.

Burn continued walking beside me, but I saw the look he threw out of the corner of his eye.

"See that silhouette of a building up ahead?" Burn asked.

It was a partial remains a couple of hundred yards ahead. In the center was a room that looked somewhat intact, roof and all. It might be a trap or it might be our salvation. It was also our only shot. We'd never make it back to the tree line.

"We get into that thing and we blowtorch whatever comes close," Burn whispered.

"Is it smart to back ourselves into a corner like that?"

"You have any other ideas?"

I looked around. "Nope."

"Then it's barbecue time." The words were followed by the sound of a stampede. There had to be at least thirty men, all running toward us.

Burn grabbed my hand, forcing me to keep up with his longer stride. We didn't slow down until we were slamming into the wall of the building.

In a split-second move, we switched grips. I had his arm in my hand, and he lit up like a dragon breathing fire. Thankfully, my magic had replenished while we'd been waiting, but I still wasn't operating at a hundred percent.

The fire kept them at bay as it arced around us. I heard footsteps above our heads as they climbed onto the partial roof.

"Who are you? What do you want?" I yelled.

No one answered. Another two edged closer, and it was hard to tell who was in charge. Their clothes were nondescript, but that didn't mean anything.

"I don't think they're local," I said to Burn. I remembered the army at Crisp enough to know they'd be wearing a grey and gold uniform. This group looked like hired mercenaries. Or an army disguised.

"No, I don't think so either."

One by one, they'd come at us and then backed away as we shot flames at them. We waited until they were closer this time before we blasted fire in their direction. We caught an arm here or there, but no serious damage.

They'd fall back and then come again, like a scripted dance. Over and over again, coming just close enough that we'd have to use our magic. This was planned. They were draining us intentionally, and there was nothing we could do about it. If we left our protected spot, they'd swarm us. I didn't have enough magic left in me to make it worth the try. I'd been running low before we started. I wasn't sure how I'd managed this much.

Another one came close, and there was only a whimper of a flame this time. I'd barely juiced Burn at all.

Burn glanced at me, and I launched into action before his shock blew our cover.

"We know you're trying to drain us, assholes. It's not going to work. We're not that stupid." Couldn't believe we'd been that stupid. I'd let them drain us. To Burn, I whispered, "Don't light your flame at all, and get that nervous look off your face before you broadcast it."

They were watching, edging closer. Waiting. They hadn't bought my story.

"Come on, take a few more steps, asshole," I yelled, taking a step toward them and dragging Burn with me.

The attacker paused, but I didn't know how much time I'd bought us. At least Burn wasn't broadcasting the *oh fuck* look anymore.

One of the men was making hand signals, and then they all edged in together. They weren't as stupid as I'd hoped.

"When they rush us, which will be any minute now, you need to run," I said to Burn.

"What the fuck you talking about, Bugs? I don't run from a fight."

"They're here for me. They don't care about you. You need to run. It's our only shot. You break free, get help, and come back for me."

From the second they cornered us, it had been clear they were hunting me. Their eyes never left me. If they glanced at Burn, it was only for a few seconds, as if he were a nuisance to get around, not the target.

I didn't think I'd be alive when he returned if the past attempts on my life meant anything. It didn't matter. At least one of us would live, and I didn't want Burn to die for me.

They edged in closer. Minutes were dwindling to seconds. It was nearly over. "Promise you'll run."

They charged. Time was up. They were almost on us, and then all I could see was a black cloud around us, whipping as if we were in the eye of a tornado.

The familiar feeling of greasy, oily magic was everywhere. There was nowhere to run. Every direction led into the greasy magic. We'd gone from a bad situation to worse.

Burn was spinning beside me. "What the fuck is this?"

He didn't know, but I did. My monster had decided to make an appearance.

I grabbed his arm, dragging him back to the center of our eight-foot circle. "Don't touch it."

I could hear screaming beyond us but couldn't see what was going on. All we could see was the dark cloud surrounding us.

"Bugs, I've seen a lot of shit, but this is creeping me out."

"It's okay. It'll be okay." No. Nothing would be okay. Not if this thing was after me. My fingers were dug into Burn's arm—for his sake, of course. I didn't want him to do anything foolish and touch my monster's inner bowel somehow. Couldn't believe I had nothing left. Nothing in the well.

"We've got to get out of here. This doesn't feel right." Burn wouldn't stop circling, forcing me to turn with him. "Bugs, we have to get out of here."

"I know." There was Ryker's magic. I could feel it churning beside my empty well of nothing. Would he want me to use it to save Burn? Probably. But what if he was in the weeds right now and I took it? I could cost him his life.

There were screams rising on the other side of the dark magic. Burn stepped closer, nailing one of my toes. I didn't care.

"Bugs?"

Burn was about to lose his shit, and I had to get us out of there now. Ryker said I hadn't drained him before. What if I took just a little? That might be all I needed. I braced myself and gripped Burn's arm, ready to blast us out of there. I hadn't been ready last time. I could do this.

"I'm going to try and pull from Ryker," I said, hoping he'd be good with it too.

"Do it!" he screamed.

A whoosh of power surged into me, and my magic went from depleted to overflowing. I was ready for it this time. I channeled it all into Burn's arm, yelling, "Make a flame."

I couldn't hold on to it. I had to let it out. Ryker's magic was just like the man, aggressive and impossible to subdue.

Burn's eyes lit up a second before his hand.

The burst of flame that shot out nearly knocked me backward. Burn managed to keep to his feet, and I didn't let go of his arm.

White-hot flames pierced the wall of my monster. A howl, so loud it was nearly deafening, filled the air. I didn't need to tell Burn to keep it up. I didn't think he'd stop until we were back in the Valley. It was a good thing, because I didn't think he'd hear me over the roar of agony that was all around us.

A hole appeared in the black cloud of magic. Beyond it were dead bodies that looked like they'd been thrown around like rag dolls, misshapen and broken, limbs askew. The only ones still alive had their backs to us as they fled the scene.

We burst through the hole we made as the thing continued to roar in pain. We circled together as a team to see what had surrounded us.

It was immense, its form shifting and flickering in the moonlight, as if it were struggling to hold its shape. What a shape it was. It stood on two legs with leathered grey skin that looked like arrows would bounce off it. Horns twisted out of its head, eyes glowing white and red. It opened its mouth, and the howl of pain was ear-piercing.

Burn and I took a step backward at the same time.

Its gaze focused on me for just a second before the creature was gone.

"Holy fucking magic. What was that? I've never seen anything like it," Burn whispered, as if the creature would hear him and come back.

"*That* was my monster."

NINETEEN

"This is a mess. What are we going to do with all these bodies?" Burn sounded like a novice to killing, like he hadn't been hanging with the Cursed King for probably a solid decade and had at least a bucket of blood on his hands.

"Can you manage to get past your shock and awe and help me search them? Let's see if we can find something that tells us who they are." I was already on my third corpse, checking pockets and avoiding fleshy bits, while Burn tiptoed around the place like he was afraid to stain his boots.

"Burn." I called his name as a teacher would to an errant student. And people said spying was bad? If I hadn't spent all those hours peeking through the school room window in the Valley, I never would've mastered the tone that got Burn moving.

He bent down by the nearest body, using two fingers to lift a jacket away from a shirt. "Then what? Do we leave them out here?"

"I don't know. I haven't thought that far." I glanced over from my fourth body while he worked on his first and looked like he'd be there a while.

A small smile lit his face. "Maybe we should torch them?"

I ignored the part of that suggestion that made my stomach flip-flop and focused on the man who'd turned into a large kid acting as if he'd discovered a new toy.

"The torch was very cool, but I'm not sure a bonfire of bodies would be better than leaving them as is. Their friends who got away will be back. We're already late, and I don't want to draw more attention to us than the big demon in the field might've."

I was on my sixth body and still hadn't found anything. It wasn't like people usually walked around with identifying objects, but there wasn't even a coin to hint at an origin. It was as if they were told to empty their pockets before they attacked. How had they planned this when we'd only decided to come last night? Had they been lying in wait for days hoping? Figuring we'd eventually come this way in search of clues? My gut had screamed that this was a bad idea from the start, and now it was chanting, *I told you so.*

"You're worried about being late?" Burn asked, still by the same body.

"Yes, I am. They'll never get to the right place without me."

I stood, trying to figure out which bodies I hadn't checked yet, when I felt Ryker nearing. He broke through the line of trees looking ready for war and scouring the area for an enemy to kill. His eyes scanned me and then took in the carnage around us.

He stopped beside the first dead body he came to and then looked at us. "What the fuck happened?"

"We got ambushed," I said, stating the obvious.

Burn took the opportunity to stop searching. "Thought we were fucked for sure when this demon-looking thing dropped down out of nowhere and killed most of them. Then we blasted it and it took off."

"Uh huh," Ryker said, as if he'd expected nothing less. "A demon saved you."

"Burn thinks my monster is a demon," I said, waiting for the shock, because there should be some. That was big news. That wasn't an *uh huh* moment, that was a *holy magic* moment.

Ryker was too busy taking in the details around us to notice my lack of enthusiasm over his lack of shock. We were lacking all around.

Ryker pointed to bodies. "Did you find anything on them?"

"I didn't find anything. Whoever sent them clearly has no connection to the demon." For all the demon's faults, it wants to keep me alive," I added, waiting to see if that would garner more than an *uh huh*.

It didn't. He finally stopped looking around, but his attention wasn't fully here.

As the adrenaline continued to seep from my body, my brain began piecing together ideas that I preferred not to have. I shook out my hands, as if that would unload the thought hammering inside my head. The chain of events that might've led to this moment. First it had only been a smell. Then I'd been able to feel it, hear it. Things were progressing in a bad direction, and I was afraid I knew why.

"It's never materialized before." I chewed on my lower lip as Ryker's attention settled back on me.

As our eyes held, I realized where his mind had been, because I'd met him in the same dark place. Had my demon been behind the theft of stones from his place? Was that why it had been able to talk to me? Did my demon get to the stones I'd left behind, and that was why it had materialized today? Instead of collecting them to build our strength, were we collecting them to build its strength?

Burn stepped closer to the two of us. "I don't know what you guys are thinking, but if the looks on your faces mean anything, I'm not sure I want to know."

I ran a hand through my hair, looking off the other way. The last thing I wanted to do was share my deepest fear: the demon had more of our stones.

"Where's Sneak?" I asked.

Ryker hooked a thumb back toward the direction he'd appeared from. "I left him behind about halfway here. Sneak moves slower, and once I was drained, I figured there was trouble."

"Drained? As in empty?" Did he just say I'd pulled all of his magic out of him?

He tilted his chin down to give me a stare. "Yes. I feel like I've been turned inside out and wrung dry."

"Oh." I got it. I knew what it felt like when he'd taken mine. I'd been left with nothing.

Don't smile. Don't laugh. It was horrible. It was bad

on an epic scale. Dammit, that made me want to smile even more. It wasn't like he didn't deserve to know how it felt. Hopefully he'd be a little more careful in the future.

Ryker didn't say anything, but I knew he sensed my satisfaction. Did that make me a heel? Possibly, but I couldn't quite stop the feeling anyway.

"Do you want to take a little time to...recoup?" I bit my lip so that I didn't smile.

He cleared his throat. "No. I'll be fine," he said.

Ha! No way he'd be fine, but if he wanted to play it off like all was good, let him.

"Let's get going," Ryker said.

"What about the bodies?" Burn asked. "Maybe we should torch them?"

"No time. We need to get into Crisp before curfew, when we can blend. It'll be harder to move around afterward," Ryker said.

I shook my head. "If their buddies don't come back, the wolves can have them."

TWENTY

I COULD SEE THE DEAD PILE FROM WHERE WE HID in the trees outside Crisp. The dirt mountain was one place forever scarred into my memory. There wasn't a patch of grass in sight on the hill they used to layer and bury the dead.

The shovels and digging machinery were scattered about, waiting until morning, when work would commence. I couldn't see the top of the hill, but vultures flew above, dipping down repeatedly, lightening the load for tomorrow's workers.

I pulled my gaze from the hill to the watch guard as they walked the wall of Crisp. A wall that looked like it extended forever.

"That's where we go in," Ryker said, pointing to the northern corner.

"Sneak can get in, but how are we going to get past the watch?" That was another thing I remembered clearly from my childhood. *Don't get too close to the wall,* my mother would warn me. Bad things happened to those who looked like they wanted to leave. It had been drilled into my head.

"We already bribed the two that watch this area," Ryker said.

The watch was one thing. They didn't realize that the place was crawling with spies inside. If you saw something and didn't report it, you'd lose an eye. You saw someone steal and they thought you knew, you'd lose a hand. There were some things that never left you, and the punishment ceremonies on Sunday were one of them. Attendance was mandatory, so everyone in the city knew exactly what happened if you didn't toe the line.

"How's your magic?" I asked Ryker.

He looked at me and said with no hesitation, "Not good."

I didn't say anything else. He knew mine was scraping the bottom, or I wouldn't have had to use his. Waiting until tomorrow for another ambush would be even worse. At least Sneak could still do his thing.

I looked back at the wall. It was now or never. "If we're going in while it's light, this is how we do it. When we get in, you come with me," I said to Ryker. "A couple might look less menacing. We'll go ahead." I turned to Burn and Sneak. "You two should follow a good distance behind. They'll only see Burn, and you'll draw less attention than a couple of strange men. When we get close, we'll give you a signal. There's wards and traps everywhere, so we need to get in and out. Consider everyone that looks your way as an extension of the watch."

They nodded. I'd been secretly hoping they'd disagree and we'd end up in a fight. Maybe a drag-out brawl where someone refused to do as I said and decided to call it off and turn around.

Ryker took a step forward and then waited for me. Damn, that man was a constant thorn in my side.

We stepped out from the trees together, and I looked up. Both men on watch seemed to notice us at the same time, probably because we were walking into a large field with nothing but grass and they weren't blind. My lungs seized up like they were made of steel, not tissue. They both paused. Then one continued walking as if we weren't there. The other quickly followed suit, walking in the other direction.

Ryker wrapped his hand around mine, tugging me forward. I hadn't realized my legs had stopped moving. He led us over to a large shrub and then behind it. There was a crack in the wall and the dirt was packed down in front of it, as if it were a common doorway.

"How'd you know about this opening?" I asked.

"I know smugglers that get in and out this way. There's always an opening somewhere."

He bent low and then squeezed through it, his clothes snagging as he did. He waited on the other side, a building right behind him, offering cover.

"Come on," he said, holding out his hand.

I took it, hoping my gut wouldn't be whispering, *I told you so*, again.

A chill hit my core as I stepped back inside Crisp. I never thought I'd come back here. Definitely never wanted to, that was for sure. It looked the same as I remembered, but different. Like a dream that was painted in bold strokes, and the finer details didn't hold up when you opened your eyes. The streets I'd romanticized looked dirtier. The houses lining them were smaller. The few people walking them appeared gaunt and dingy. The only thing that was as grand as I remembered was the castle that loomed high above the rest of the buildings.

Ryker glanced behind us as we moved down the street.

"Are Burn and Sneak there?"

He nodded. "Yes. Anything look familiar?"

"Sort of. Let's head this way. If my memory is correct, that's where all the important places are."

He tightened his fingers around my hand. He hadn't let go of it since we'd made our way in. I had a feeling even if he was drained, he might know how to milk blood from a stone. Or I'd suddenly become an optimist.

I paused as we passed a small street with only a few houses on it. It had a weird bend to the left.

"What's down there?" Ryker asked.

"I think I lived down there." A hazy picture of a woman holding my hand and walking down the road on a weekend morning creeped over me. That life had been as fragile as the images in my mind.

"Do you want to go look?"

"No. Let's keep moving." The only thing I'd find down that road now were strangers and painful memories.

We continued to walk, and I sensed Burn and Sneak behind us. The roads opened up, and there was a chipped cement pool in the center. When I was a child, there had been water spouting up in the center, and on hot summer days, we'd splash around in it until someone complained. The watch would come chase us out, but we'd laugh as we ran. If the watch chased us tonight, I didn't think there'd be any laughter involved.

The buildings around it were clustered and formed a square, the pool in the center. Some were stores; some had foodstuffs. A couple didn't display anything in the windows. This was the place. The building that had the records were here. My mother would have to come and collect copies once a week to bring to the King and Queen of Crisp.

"They're in one of these."

I saw Burn's figure across the way. Sneak was probably with him, but I wasn't sure where.

Ryker moved his finger in a circular motion as we backed into the shadows of one of the buildings. I couldn't see Sneak, but I knew he was peeking inside all the buildings right about now.

"He's got it," Ryker said, and then pointed to where Sneak had appeared and was signaling us over.

We made our way to the other building, following the same path Sneak had taken around to the backside. He was waiting by a door.

Burn pointed to a corner farther down with a better vantage point. "I'm going in with Sneak."

"Hurry," Ryker said.

Sneak lifted his foot and, with a single kick, the door swung open. The clock started ticking with the sound of the bang.

It was an easy find. The place was a single room with walls lined with books lettered with the alphabet. I made quick work of grabbing the one with "RO," and then we were out of there.

There were footsteps approaching as soon as we stepped out of the building. Someone shouted, "I heard it over here."

Sneak disappeared, and Ryker grabbed my hand, pulling me forward before I had a chance to think which way to run. Burn fell in beside us. I heard someone scream, "Stop," behind us.

Windows were being thrown open as we passed. People screamed to the guards chasing behind us, letting them know which direction we ran.

A guard shot out in front of us from a road up ahead. Burn didn't slow as he knocked him off his feet, sending him reeling and clearing the way. I didn't know where Sneak was until I heard people falling and curses behind us.

We made it to the crack in the wall. Burn went first, and then I was half dragged and half shoved through, with Ryker following behind me. Sneak must've followed after, but I couldn't be sure.

We stepped around the bushes and stopped short because twenty guards had circled in front of us.

I was near empty, and so was Ryker. Burn didn't have the chops for this kind of fight on his own, and Sneak's magic would only save him.

They edged closer, swords out, and my gut started chanting, *I told you so.* I would've disemboweled myself at that moment if I could've.

"Who are you?" the guard in charge asked, staring at our group.

So the ambush hadn't come from Crisp either. Useful, but the least of my concerns at the moment.

I squeezed Ryker's hand before I said, "Take it all."

"You've got nothing."

The lead guard moved forward, sword extended. "Who are you?" he yelled.

"*Almost* nothing," I said. "Make it count."

Burn grabbed Ryker without another word said. Sneak was either smart enough to get out of range and or do the same.

They wanted to know who we were? I'd oblige them with one name. I inched closer to the guard's outstretched sword. "You want names? How about the Cursed King? Now move out of our way before we walk over your corpses."

The guard looked at me, then at Ryker. He was shaking as he said, "Bullshit."

I braced myself for what was going to happen next. It felt as if someone was taking a rusty-edged knife and scraping out my insides.

The lead guard went down, and I nearly followed him. That was all it took for the rest of the guards.

They parted like dried leaves in a strong wind. We walked through them, hand in hand.

"Burn, grab the book," I said as soon as we were out of earshot.

He took the ledger that I'd been about to drop. Ryker edged closer, pulling me to his side.

"They're watching. Do not pick me up and make us look weak," I said, annoyed I had to squander the last of my energy fighting with him.

"Then don't fucking fall." He shifted his hand up until it was under my arm, taking some of my weight.

I was hefted over a shoulder as soon as we hit the trees, and all I felt was relief.

Sometime later, I was deposited onto the ground. Sneak was kind enough to build the fire right in front of me as Burn started riffling through the book.

"Burn, don't singe that page," Ryker said from somewhere close by. I didn't care enough to see how close Burn was to burning it. That would involve opening my eyes.

"I won't, but I can't see without it."

"Well?" Sneak asked, eager to hear what Burn was reading.

"Rokke, right?" Burn asked.

His surprised tone made me want to laugh.

"Yes," I called.

I heard pages flip. Then flip again.

"Well?" Sneak asked. Feet shuffled around.

Pages flipped back and forth again, and laughter bubbled up in my chest because I knew what they were finding.

"Burn, what do you see?" Sneak said.

"Nothing. Like, really nothing." Burn sounded shocked. "Farmers, maids, some masons."

I couldn't stop laughing. I didn't know what was funnier: that they'd imagined some mysterious past or that I'd almost believed them.

TWENTY-ONE

Switch leaned down close to where I was lying in the dirt by the fire. I hadn't moved in the last four hours. "How much longer do you think it'll take before you've got some juice?"

Switch had been asking me how much longer every ten minutes or so.

"I think I've had enough rest." I stretched my hand toward him, looking for a little help getting up. My insides were only beginning to lose that raw feeling. I knew if I juiced him now, I'd pay for the overexertion later. I still stood. It was better than listening to that question another fifty times.

Ryker didn't argue. Burn and Sneak jumped to their feet and were forming a circle a few seconds later.

We landed in front of Ryker's place, and I swayed on my feet. My eyes were burning and my stomach was doing somersaults. I planted my hands on my knees and managed to stay upright.

A hand landed on my back, the tingle of Ryker's magic accompanying it.

"You did good," he said softly, his fingers moving in a caress of sorts.

I might've done good, but this was definitely not. This was the shit that made me think we were something other than what we were. This was what lured me into emotional heartache.

"Thanks," I said, straightening as soon as I could and moving a step away, dislodging his hand with the effort.

There was a flash of sadness in his eyes that chafed my soul, as if I'd wounded him. I didn't know if I should scream and demand to know what weirdo mind games he was playing, ignore him completely, or apologize for no logical reason.

"Switch, where the fuck were you?" Knife asked, walking over and saving me from having to decide what to do with Ryker.

Switch and I looked at each other. I gave him a nod. I'd make this right for him and Ruck somehow, but not this very second. I was still running on empty and didn't have a lick of an idea how to fix things.

"I thought you'd be back hours ago," Knife continued.

Switch's right eye twitched. "Sorry."

"We ran into some trouble," Ryker said, steering Knife's annoyance toward him.

Knife took a look at our group. I might've looked the worst, but Sneak had bags under his eyes, Burn's clothes were ripped, and Ryker looked like he might really kill someone today, as opposed to his normal *threaten to kill* look.

The fight seeped out of Knife's stare. "Okay, well, I've got some people who need to get over to Dorley, so go get them."

"I don't think I can do it right now, not even in singles," Switch said, his nose twitching as his eyes shifted to me. He didn't have to tell me what he was thinking. I knew. Knife was trying to use his people to get Switch back to Dorley and keep him there.

Knife turned to me. I'd been afraid of this. Now what? Did I plead exhaustion, which was true, or flat-out refuse, start a war, and have it out with him?

"She's already pushed too hard today," Ryker cut in, his hand landing on my shoulder.

Knife's gaze landed where Ryker's fingers had.

"He's right. I feel pretty drained." I was way too tired for a war. I wanted to skip right to the end and sleep like the dead for a day or so. I took another step closer to Knife, losing Ryker's hand for a second time in minutes.

Ryker crossed his arms and glanced at me before he told Knife, "I'll lend you a chugger for the people who have to get back."

Knife was still looking at the spot where Ryker had placed his hand. I took another step away from Ryker, finally dislodging Knife's preoccupation with the spot.

"I don't think one chugger will be enough, but I could make do if you have some extra fire stones," Knife said.

Unlike the magic stones we were hunting, fire

stones came from the Eternal Volcano and were used to run chuggers. They were more valuable than gold. Knife would be better off asking for Ryker's left arm.

"I might be able to spare a couple," Ryker said.

Knife's eyes swelled, and I could see him counting numbers in his head. "If you could spare three, I could make that work."

"I'll have them delivered," Ryker responded.

Switch was gone before Ryder finished talking. Burn and Sneak followed suit.

As soon as Knife walked off, Ryker's eyes shifted to me. "I don't know what deal you and Switch struck, but you can't keep him forever. He's going to have to settle his own mess."

"I'm not trying to keep him," I said.

"You're not?" Ryker crossed his arms, and his head went into the *don't bullshit me* downward tilt.

"Letting him stay here is not keeping him. No one should keep him. He's a free man. He should come and go as he pleases."

"Like a bird, maybe?" he asked, eyebrow raised.

I shrugged. "I guess a bird would be a good analogy."

Ruck snuck up on me, linking an arm with mine. "Got a second?"

Ryker looked at us for a few seconds too long before he said, "I've got to go get some fire stones."

As soon as Ryker was gone, Ruck said, "Knife's been looking for Switch for hours. I think he's catching on. We've got to do something. We can't let Switch go back."

"You've fucked more guys than I've met, and this has to be the *one*?" I asked. "You couldn't find a slightly more convenient *one*? You had to pick the guy that has the best fucking magic ever?"

"He really does, doesn't he? Don't try to talk me out of it just because it's going to be tough."

"I'll figure it out somehow. Now go find your boyfriend. I need some sleep."

His scowl was still in place, but it softened as he turned to find his boy. Mine deepened as I headed toward my place. Would the stones still be there?

The second I walked up to my one-room building, I knew the ward was gone. I paused before shoving open my door. If I didn't check, they'd still hypothetically be under my mattress.

I had to check. Had to know for sure, even if it were for the worst. I shoved a hand under the side where I slept. *Please be there.*

Nothing. I pulled the mattress off the bed, in case I'd pushed them farther back than I thought. I looked under the frame. Maybe they'd fallen through the wooden slats. I sat, my back against a wooden frame, my mattress on the floor. They were gone.

Ryker walked in the room, and I knew why he'd come.

"They're gone," he said, looking at my mattress in the center of the room.

Arms wrapped around myself, I shook my head. "It got through my ward. I don't think it can take them from me when I'm carrying them, but nothing else stops it."

He shut the door and then walked farther in, taking a seat on the wood base of the bed, not far from where I was leaning.

"When it came for you the other time, you said it felt like it was trying to get inside you," he said.

"Yes."

"If it comes for you again, you need to fight it with whatever you have or can get. I mean *anything*. Use everything you've got, and mine as well. If this thing manages to get into you somehow, access your magic, it might be able to access mine."

If it accessed both of ours, what kind of beast would it become? It would be unstoppable.

"Does that mean what I think?" I could tell from the set of his eyes, the tense lines of his mouth, that it did.

It could cloak itself in my magic and kill with his. This creature could wipe out thousands of people in a blink of an eye if the setting were right, the people close enough to it, like they were at the Valley.

"I don't think we should replace your stones."

He leaned forward, leaning his arms on his knees, his leg brushing my shoulder.

"We need to get one more for you to keep on you at all times."

"I know."

I waited until he left before I crept over to my favorite worming spot and knelt. I knew the second I plucked up a worm it wasn't going to work. I tried anyway. And tried again and again.

TWENTY-TWO

I LEANED AGAINST THE BUILDING, HIDING FROM the moonlight as I stared at Ryker's place. My thoughts and feelings were wrapped in a ward so tight that Ryker wouldn't sense me even if he was about to trip over me. I'd been standing here, counting the minutes as I waited for the blonde to leave. She'd been walking in as I'd arrived twenty minutes ago.

Knowing my demon monster had broken through my ward had blown through the last feeling of security I'd had. My heart had spread the contagion to the rest of my body, because somehow my feet had brought me here.

Twenty-five minutes and my internal clock was chiming that it was way past time to leave. She wasn't coming back out, and I knew what that meant.

We weren't together. He could be with whomever he wanted and do whatever he wanted. It was his life, his call, even if she did walk like a troll.

What was I doing with my life? Snooping. Spying

from the shadows of a bush. Letting a green monster rip me apart. And I had the nerve to call the blonde a troll?

I could keep on watching, spying, and lamenting over everything he did or I could get on with *my* life. Do what I needed to do. *Do* being the important part here. I needed to kick myself into a different gear, because I wasn't leaving here anytime soon, and this current game of *does he like me or not* wasn't fun.

I tipped back the flask filled with Burn's booze and walked away. I should've stuck to the alcohol in the first place. I might've been passed out in bed by now instead of roaming the streets of the Valley, being miserable.

I needed someone to drown my sorrows with, or bleach them clean with tons of alcohol. Ruck wasn't on the tower tonight, but I knew where I would find him.

It didn't take long to get there. When I stepped in the door, quite a few familiar faces greeted me. "Hey, look who's finally decided to play," Tommy, one of the tower's night shift, said.

The night tower guards often played cards in the storage building on their off nights. It was tough to find other things to do when you were used to gearing up for the day when everyone else was settling into bed.

"Figured I'd see what kind of action you had going on," I said.

I made my way between two different tables of coins and cards to grab an empty seat by Ruck.

"You playing?" he asked.

"Playing and drinking," I said, placing my flask on the table. "Deal me in."

It was two games later, and I was a few coins

lighter, when Knife walked in, always a regular when he was in these parts. I realized that I might be able to solve at least one problem tonight.

I flipped my hair back and leaned an arm over the back of my chair.

"You here to play?" I asked Knife. My words were innocent enough, but the way I licked my bottom lip wasn't.

Knife's eyes narrowed, and there was a hiccup in time before he said, "Hadn't decided yet."

I twisted slightly, arching my back as I did.

His eyes dropped to where my breasts were pressing against my shirt.

"I think you just did," I said, flirty smile and all.

Ruck gave me a side-eye. I gave him a kick under the table, hoping he'd keep his thoughts internal for once.

There was the slightest tip of his head, as if to respond, *All righty, then.*

Knife inched closer and straightened, taking in all I was offering, from my moist lips to the fullness of my hips. I wasn't a natural flirt, but I'd learned a few things as I watched woman after woman—and a few men— throw themselves at Ryker. It wasn't exactly heavy lifting.

"What are you up to?" Knife asked, his brows dropping a fraction lower.

I kicked out the chair opposite me. "What's wrong? Too scared to find out?" The one thing I knew best about Knife was his brimming ego.

The second he grabbed a chair and swung it

around to sit opposite me, I knew I had him. He couldn't sit and then bail, not without looking like a jerk in front of these people, some of which were his. He'd accepted my terms as soon as he took the chair.

Knife sat, and the table's other occupants either slid back or got up. They didn't know what was about to go down, but one thing was clear: we wouldn't be playing for coin.

I took the deck of cards and began to shuffle. "You call the game, I call the stakes."

He smiled. "Blue-Eyed Boo."

I didn't return the smile, but I wanted to. I knew from around Dorley that Blue-Eyed Boo was his game. What he didn't know was that it was also mine. It was what I'd been hoping for.

"Stakes? Unless you need time to rethink them now?" he asked, as if he had everything under control.

Man, sometimes he made it almost enjoyable to get one over on him.

"We play until one of us goes bust. I win, Switch is mine. You win..." I gave him a smirk and leaned forward, flashing him a little cleavage as I did.

Ruck tensed behind me. He knew I could play well, but Blue-eyed Boo wasn't skill alone. There was luck. Either way, win or lose, I was ready. The way I saw it, I either won Switch his freedom or I slept with Knife and maybe it would help me move on from Ryker. Ruck thought it would, and I was tired of being in limbo.

"You think I'd give up Switch for one night with you?"

I shuffled the deck of a hundred as I said, "Yes, I do. I'm worth it."

"I bet you are." He inched forward, leaning his elbows on the table. "Deal."

I slid him his first card and the game was on.

I SENSED RYKER BEFORE I SAW HIM. HE STOPPED right inside the doorway. The room had been quiet before, as we'd battled out a hard hand with seven kings spread out on the table in between us. Now it seemed as if everyone had decided to hold their breath as well as their words.

I'd thought I was the only one who'd imagined something more between Ryker and me. The way the room was all eyes and ears, seemed it was a mass hypnosis. We'd all been duped. Too bad the blonde he'd spent the last few hours with hadn't come along for the walk over here to prove it to the rest of them.

Either way, it didn't matter. It was time to cut the cord on whatever it was we had. Once, we'd been sort of friends, partners of a sort. Now we were two people stuck together. He did his thing, as evidenced by earlier tonight. For the first time, I was doing mine.

"Heard there was some action going on over here tonight," Ryker said.

"Friendly game of cards," Knife said.

I mumbled a yes. So why couldn't I look at Ryker? I had nothing to feel guilty about.

"Very friendly, from the sounds of it. Figured I'd

swing by and see what all the talk was about." Ryker walked to our table, looking at the cards displayed and the damning lack of coins.

Look at him. You have nothing to be ashamed of.

Look. At. Him.

I tilted my head back, and the rage boiling in his eyes helped me find my voice.

"Stopped by your place earlier, but you were very busy. I figured I'd find another way to pass the time."

His jaw shifted. "This is how you prefer to relax?"

"Yes. This is exactly what I prefer."

Ryker's smile was so cold that I thought my soul was going to get frostbite. Instead, I burned in response. How dare he judge me. He walked in here and acted as if there was more between us when every night he threw away any possibility of it.

I broke my gaze from Ryker's, the accusation tasting too bitter for my liking.

Ryker stayed focused on me, magic bursting around him riling our connection. "I'm glad I stopped by. It's good to know how someone likes to spend their time."

"I guess we all have our leanings."

I could feel Knife's look cut into me, almost as sharp as his magic probably was. Okay, so he'd realized maybe I'd had some other motivations for my bet. He had no right to act offended. When you were willing to bet with live people, you couldn't turn around and play Mr. Sensitive.

The second Ryker walked out, it was as if someone else walked in and dumped a bucket of cold water on me. The fire died. I was a pile of ashy, smelly soot. Not even my irritation over being so pathetic could ignite my soggy ass now.

I glanced down at my cards. The only motivation to win was so that I could get the fuck out of there and go sit in a dark room alone. It was the exact opposite of what I should do, which was win and then fuck Knife for the hell of it. I couldn't wait around for Ryker anymore. That was clear.

It took me ten minutes more to finish Knife off. I laid my cards out, a splendid array of kings, queens, and fools, and Ruck exhaled beside me. At least some good had come from this night.

Knife slumped back, but the disappointment didn't seem to make it to his eyes. "You got me. Switch is yours."

He stood without a fight.

TWENTY-THREE

"I can't believe you want this in writing, with an official seal, no less. I don't even know if I have a seal in here." Knife dug through the trunk in his room. "Isn't it bad enough you're taking Switch from me?"

"He's a person. He deserves to be free, and with an official letter of release. What if you're too drunk to remember you lost?" Plus, Switch wasn't going to believe it was a done deal until I handed over something he could hold and point to. If Switch was uptight, it would spill over to Ruck. I'd have the duo haunting my steps until I was back here, doing this very thing.

Knife's jaw dropped. "Too drunk?"

I ignored the question, waving a hand in front of my face. "Why is it so hot in here?"

"I like it toasty." He pointed to an iron thing standing in the corner, with a tube extending toward the ceiling.

It looked a lot like the one I'd found in my room when I returned.

"You burn stuff in that thing?" I asked, pulling off my jacket. I'd been using mine for storage. Who knew?

Knife didn't have a chance to respond before the door slammed open. Ryker strode toward me like a man who'd taken a sucker punch and was about to hit back harder. Now what had I done? He didn't have any stones left to steal, but that didn't mean a biscuit didn't go missing, or an errant sock. Everyone knew you couldn't keep a pair together for more than a month, but damned if he wouldn't be demanding his sock back from me.

Knife had stopped digging in his trunk. He stood there, shaking his head. "Even if I had won, I knew this was going to fucking happen. I don't know why I bothered."

I ignored his ramblings. He'd definitely hit the cups too hard, no matter how sober he thought he was. Besides, I needed to keep my attention on Ryker. He looked like he wanted to kill us both, and I was in no mood for accusations.

"Let me guess, you're missing a sock?" I put my hands to my waist. He better not start a fight tonight or I'd be punching someone.

Ryker stopped in front of me, his chest visibly rising and falling. He bent over, and his shoulder hit my hips. My hands lost their perch on my waist, and instead of a no-nonsense pose, I was waving my arms like a chicken trying to fly.

"What are you doing?" The tone wasn't good either. I sounded like I was squawking to match the flapping.

He didn't answer as he spun us both around so that he was facing Knife. "Touch her again and I'll kill you."

He'd completely lost his mind.

There was some more spinning, and I used my two wings as leverage against Ryker's back to look at Knife. Was he freaking out? Was he going to try and help me?

Neither. Knife was sitting down and getting comfortable on his chair.

"You two deserve each other." Knife toasted me with a bottle of wine before he took a sip. Last I saw of Knife was a sour puss on his face as he muttered, "Just how I wanted my night to end. Wonderful."

The cold air hit me as Ryker strode out of Knife's place. People must have heard the door to Knife's slamming open a few minutes ago. Curtains were drawn back as people peeked out their windows. Me putting up a fight wasn't going to change much about the scene we were creating with my current mode of transportation. No one preferred this mode of traveling.

I kicked, bit, and mutilated every part I could reach. I could only access a small portion of his back, but boy was that spot going to look bad tomorrow. He wouldn't be able to take his shirt off for a week.

"You're insane," I said.

He didn't answer as he marched us toward his place.

"I am not going to your place," I said. "And for the record, I'm getting a little tired of being hauled around here like a slab of meat."

He continued on as if I hadn't spoken. He didn't

put me down until we'd walked into his place and then into his bedroom.

He dropped me onto his bed, and I immediately stood up and tried to dodge around him. One arm looped around my waist, dragging me back.

"One warning. You're not fucking him, not while you're in the Valley. You try to leave here tonight and I'll tie you to the bed."

That was it. He'd completely lost his mind. He'd lived too long with too much magic, and it had broken him.

"You think you can sleep with anything that walks and I'm supposed to be chaste? Are you bonkers?"

I shoved at his chest with both hands. He stared down at me, rage still burning in his eyes. He turned and walked back into the living room.

I chased after him and watched as he settled on the couch, resting his head on his arm and closing his eyes. Not an inch of him appeared relaxed. He looked like a tightly wound coil about to spring.

I didn't glance at the door. I didn't want to leave anymore. I wanted to fight. Plus, I wasn't an idiot. Whatever was holding him in place was about to snap, and would if I made a step toward the door.

I stood at the foot of the couch. "I don't care what you say. I can sleep with Knife if I want."

He didn't say anything, but his chest rose and fell more rapidly.

"Is this because of the weird way our magic inter-acts? It bothers me too, but I don't try to dictate your comings and goings." If he thought he was going to get any rest tonight, he'd never miscalculated so badly. I'd stand right here and hammer home how crazy he was all night. We'd see who broke first. I had every bit as much tenacity as he did. If I couldn't beat him one way, I'd beat him another.

Another deep breath before he said, "If you sleep with someone else, I'll kill them. It won't bother me, but I'm sure you'll feel horrible about it. As far as 'comings and goings,' there's been no one since the merge."

I huffed, making sure it was loud enough for him to hear. That didn't deserve a comment, but there was no way I'd let him think I was buying his bull.

I leaned both hands on the couch. "You don't go more than a couple of days without fucking something. I saw a blonde entering your place tonight."

One eye cracked open, as if he couldn't believe he was about to have this conversation. "That would be Rhonda. I didn't fuck her. You can ask her if you'd like."

"Ha! Well, what about the girl I saw half-naked on your couch the day before I left for Dorley? Was she not here to screw either?"

His eyes snapped open and then crinkled in the corners. "You saw Marly the day before you left."

"Yes. So you're a liar." I stabbed my finger in his direction.

The lines of his neck eased. The anger that had been simmering in his magic suddenly calmed. A calculating look replaced it.

There was a tease of a smile about the corners of his

lips. "She let herself in. I told her to leave as soon as I saw her here."

"Sure you did." My snide tone did nothing for his uplifted mood. He'd definitely cracked.

He stood and walked to the door.

Knew I'd break him. This was when he got tired of being caught lying and told me to get out. Good. I was quite ready to leave. I'd only stayed because he'd forced the issue on me.

He turned around, and I stopped. "Where are you going?"

"Huh?" I asked, freezing in my tracks.

He didn't explain anything as he swung the door open and hollered, "Mikey!"

A kid of ten or eleven came running over, bright, bushy-tailed, and thrilled to be called upon. Mikey was probably excused from school the next day because he'd covered the night shift.

"What's you be needin', boss?" He smiled widely, showing off a newly budding front tooth.

"Go by and collect Rhonda and Marly for me. Wait." Ryker turned back to me. "Is there anyone else while he's at it?"

"You're going to drag them out of bed?" I asked. "To come here? Now?"

"Yes. Anybody else?" he asked, straight-faced.

"Uh..." I ran a hand over my forehead.

"No?" he asked, hand on the door with Mikey waiting for his orders right behind him.

He turned back to Mikey. "That should—"

"No. I believe you. Don't go get them." Even if it

did turn out to be a lie, which might not be the case, the idea of dragging all his women here to testify to the fact made every inch of me want to shrivel up.

"You're sure?" He kept the door open, not sending Mikey away.

"Yes."

"Fine. Mikey, you can go." Ryker shut the door, but not before I saw the disappointment on Mikey's face. Dragging them out of their beds would've been the highlight of Mikey's week.

"You might not have slept with them, but that doesn't change anything." Except it did change some things. Muscles that were ready for battle softened, and my lungs inflated a little easier.

He shut the door and leaned against it, watching me.

"Why didn't you?" I asked.

His gaze lingered on my lips. "I didn't want them."

I crossed my arms. "I'm not going to swear off sex until you say it's okay. It's not my fault you haven't wanted anyone lately." I turned and walked to the other side of the room before I went too soft. So what if he wasn't sleeping with anyone? It changed nothing.

"That's not what I said. There's someone I want." He was still leaning against the door, his eyes drinking me in brazenly. The heat was back in his eyes, but this time it wasn't anger. His stare didn't waver from me as his magic cocooned me. "You want to fuck tonight? Take your clothes off."

It was the last thing I'd expected. Just like that, all my bravado fled like a herd of horses from a fire.

Thankfully, I still had some of Burn's booze flowing in my veins to rein them in a bit.

He thought he could bluff me or something? That this would drive me back into his room without a peep of complaint? That I'd turn meek? He'd see.

I'd stripped for him before, only to be turned away. Sometimes it felt like he'd been pushing me away longer than I'd even known him. He wanted me naked? No problem. I'd play his game.

We'd see who cried mercy first. He hadn't touched me the first time I'd stripped for him, and I didn't think he'd do it now. I arched my back, faking a confidence I didn't feel, and pulled off my shirt then tossed it to the side. My breasts weren't large, but I'd seen enough to know they were still pretty, with a pleasing fullness and tilt.

My nipples tightened, as if they were begging for his attention. His eyes burned as they took in every inch of bare skin on display.

I let out a breath that rattled. His stare alone drove a yearning inside me. It was clear that this was nothing like the first time I'd stripped for him.

He pushed off the door and walked toward me, stopping a couple feet away.

He reached out, cupping my breast. His roughened thumb brushed over my nipple. I couldn't take my eyes from his hand as I ran my tongue over dry lips.

His eyes rose to mine as he continued to mold my breast to his liking. "You still have clothes on."

He hadn't sent me running yet, so he thought to up the ante? A test of my determination to see if I'd cry uncle. It was a silly notion, since a part of me had been waiting for this for months. There was no losing for me in this scenario.

I kicked off my boots and unbuttoned my pants before he took over, grabbing my waistband and shoving them off my hips.

He wrapped an arm around my back, arching me with its pressure. His other hand dipped lower, fingers gliding along my opening. His fingers slid in easily.

A high-pitched moan broke from my lips. My feet left the ground as he walked us over to the couch. I landed on my back, with him following me down. I heard the seams of my pants rip as he pulled them roughly from my body. I tugged at his shirt, wanting to feel his flesh against mine. He obliged me by pulling it off and then shedding the rest of his clothes as well. His teeth nipped at my flesh as his mouth worked his way across burning skin.

My head was thrown back; his teeth teased the tendon of my neck as his hand cupped my ass and I rode the ridge of his cock. I felt the silky hardness against me as he shifted lower and the head of his cock teased the entrance of my pussy.

"Damn, you're small," he said, his voice strained.

He didn't understand. He'd thought I'd fucked Knife already. It shouldn't make a difference that I hadn't, but I feared it would.

I gripped his hard ass, pulling him forward. I arched up, urging him on.

He thrust into me, seated to the hilt.

I gasped. He froze.

His head lifted, his eyes level on mine. "Why didn't you tell me?"

"Because it doesn't matter." In that second, as I saw the shock cross his face, I was glad he hadn't known.

He might've disagreed, but he didn't say anything. His lips brushed mine in a caress, a softness I didn't think Ryker was capable of, as if to ease some of the harshness of his entry.

He dipped his hand between us, his fingers rubbing at the apex, right above where we were joined, and a delicious tickle warmed my insides.

I could feel his girth stretching me, but he didn't move as I breathed through a pain that was already fading as it mingled with pleasure. My body started to relax, muscles growing languid.

His hips shifted, slowly at first. The tickle grew into a stronger yearning. With every withdrawal and thrust, it was more urgent. I wrapped my legs around his waist, inviting him deeper, wishing for even more of him.

The pressure built until I was clawing at his shoulders and moaning with an abandon I didn't think I possessed, until my world felt like it was exploding open.

Ryker sank half on top of me and then shifted us so he was underneath. My cheek met his chest as the aftereffects pulsated through me.

Ryker was silent as he lay on his back, staring up at the ceiling. I tiptoed around his magic, but he was locked down like I hadn't felt in forever. I searched inward, where we were merged, and found that connection closed as well.

I leaned on an elbow. I wouldn't exactly call him grumpy, but he didn't look happy, either. Distant. That was the best word for it. I looked away, not wanting to see something else that would mar the moment forever.

I wouldn't regret it. No matter what may come.

It would've been so easy to lay my cheek back on his chest and curl into him, but then this would feel like something it wasn't. I knew people well enough to know one thing for sure. They didn't change. Ryker wasn't a one-woman man, and he never would be. I'd gotten the most he was capable of giving, and that would be enough.

Knife had summed it up well: Ryker would never be the right guy, no matter who the woman was.

I sat up, not happy but not sad either. I was a pragmatist and could take the moment for what it was, be happy it happened, and move on.

I forced myself to be strong, to get up—to not care too much. I reached down to grab my shirt.

He rolled onto his side. "Where are you going?"

Suddenly his attention was solely back on me, as if my movement had jerked him out of his thoughts.

"To my place." I searched for my pants, keeping my back to him, for once feeling less vulnerable showing someone my markings as opposed to my heart.

His shadow rose as he stood. His arm wrapped around my waist, dragging me with him toward the bedroom. "Can't let you leave yet. You'd have to walk right past Knife's, and you can't be trusted," he teased.

He dropped onto the bed, pulling me down with him until my cheek was back against his chest.

What is this? What are we doing? That was what I should've been asking him. Except then I might have to hear the answer. *Fucking.* That was what we were doing. There were no words of love. No hint of a commitment.

I should get up and leave. I'd gotten what I wanted. My heart might be able to handle the sex, but I wasn't sure it could handle a night of him against me.

Knowing that, I still couldn't bring myself to get up again.

A long time ago, Ruck had given me the best piece of advice he'd probably uttered in his life. We'd found a small dead cat lying on a flat stone beside a building, a drip of blood at its mouth.

"The cat probably leapt from too high a place. This is what happens when you don't know your limits," he'd said as he looked at the sad little creature. "You need to know what your limits are in life, with every-thing, physical, emotional. Test the limits, see how far you can stretch them, because that's how you grow. But don't push so hard you break them, because some things you can't come back from." He'd run a few fingers over the cat's fur, as if trying to soothe a hurt that could never be mended.

Right now, I was the cat leaping too high, and Ryker was the stone that would break me.

TWENTY-FOUR

The bed was empty when I woke, a plate with buttered biscuits beside the bed. My clothes were folded on the dresser, alongside a new set. I ignored the new stuff, pulling my old shirt over my head. My pants hadn't made it through the night, with a gaping hole on the side seam.

Damn, I'd had those pants since I'd lived in the Ruins. I'd planned on being buried in them every time I thought I was going to die, which had been more often than most people probably pondered their death. I shimmied on the new pair then grabbed the old pair to take with me. Nothing a needle and thread couldn't fix up. I'd be buried in them yet. I grabbed a biscuit, too.

I walked out of Ryker's, making a detour that would take me the long way around the food building. Ryker was probably there, and it was best to have some space. It wasn't like he'd been there when I woke. Obviously he wanted space too.

I got to a split in the road that would either lead me

to my place or in the direction of the grove. I turned toward the grove, looking to stretch my muscles and give my brain a rest.

I sat down on a grassy patch with trees all around. When I'd been at Dorley, this was the place I'd missed most, more than my room or the food building, or even hanging out with Ruck while looking at the view from the tower. This place, with its large grassy opening and the Grove of Souls abutting it. I pulled the biscuit out of my pocket, leaned back, and breathed in the fragrance of the autumn blossoms of the Winter Red trees.

My stomach full, my eyes drifting closed, the smell hit me. It wasn't as rotten as it had been in the past, but it was still unforgettably wrong. It was cloying, like it would seep into my pores, ooze into my skin, and would never leave me. As if I'd be smelling the rancid scent for years to come.

The smell wasn't the only thing that was different this time. The feeling of its magic was too, as it swarmed around me, my hair blowing upward.

The birds stopped chirping and the place grew unnaturally silent, as if all the animals in the grove had departed in the face of the coming storm.

A chill passed over me as I prepared for an attack, trying to build up a ward as fast as possible.

"Chiara..."

It felt like a giant fist wrapped around my body, blowing through my hastily made ward as if I had none at all. I rolled onto my side, trying to breathe through the onslaught of pain and pressure, as if I were being crushed from every side. I writhed in pain as it wrapped itself around me, trying to weasel into me.

"Why do you fight me? Let me in and the pain will stop."

I squeezed my eyes shut, afraid to speak, make any connection that might help it break me. Air whistled through my clenched teeth as I wondered how long I could fight this creature off.

"Let me in. Let me in," it said over and over again.

Something brushed my shoulder. A feel of claws trailing along my skin, ripping into me. Pain seared through me, following along its touch.

The claws moved from my shoulder to my ribs, to my hips and down the length of me. I kept my eyes squeezed tight, afraid to see it. Terrified I'd crack if I did. I could barely expand my lungs to drag in a breath through the agony. I panted, trying to curl into myself, find a place away from the pain, the poking of its magic as it tried to break through my defenses.

"Open for me," it said, as a mix of compulsion layered on pain.

I opened one eye a fraction and saw the feet of my demon in front of me. Six black claws dug into the ground, two legs of grey skin, both thick, cracked and oozing a black, tar-like substance that gagged my senses.

Beyond it, I saw Burtie the burier in the distance. He looked at me and nodded, his green tufts of hair waving in the air before he took off.

The message was clear: help was coming if I could hold on.

I didn't know if I could.

"In," it said. "Let. Me. In." It was pummeling me everywhere.

The pain was building, and I felt like it was going to rip me open.

Then it was over. The pain was gone. The smell disappeared. I heard footsteps getting closer as I lay prone on the ground still gasping.

"Bugs." Ryker's fingers grazed my cheek, my hair, his touch a bare whisper, as if he were afraid to break me.

I opened my eyes and looked at his face above mine.

"It was here." I could taste the blood on my lips as I spoke.

Ryker reached for me but then stalled.

"Bring her inside. I fear it's still near," Burtie said from nearby.

I reached out to Ryker, preferring the pain to staying here, where my demon might be able to still see me.

Ryker hands were gentle, but there was no place left on me that hadn't been battered. I bit my tongue when I wanted to cry out. My lungs didn't want to expand, and every part of me reeled from what felt like the worst beating I'd ever taken, which said a lot, since I'd had dozens.

We moved quickly, following Burtie to a door built into the cliffside. Ryker stooped to get in the place and then laid me on the small couch.

"I'll be back. I want to try and find its trail," Ryker

said.

Ryker left, and Burtie took his place. "You'll be safe here while he tries to find the demon." He patted my hand and then rushed about his living space, placing a kettle onto a hook before swinging it over the fire. "Nothing can breach this place. It's been enchanted every year for a decade by the fairies—one of the perks of having them as neighbors. Not even that vile creature who attacked you could get in here."

Burtie walked back to me and waved his finger at my shoulder. "Let me see?"

I pulled my shirt off where it was already becoming glued to the wound that ran the length of me. It was red and angry but didn't run deep. "Looks worse than it is."

Burtie leaned close, squinting. "Well, thank magic for that. I've got something to take the sting out of it either way. I'm no healer, but I've got some family recipes that might help."

Burtie returned to his kettle and filled a cup. He brought it back over, dropping a sachet of something into it before handing it to me. "Here, this will help ease the pain but not make you dull."

I inched up and wrapped my hands around the warm cup, breathing in the minty scent of it and letting it cleanse the foulness that clung to my senses.

I jerked at a pelting sound at the door, spilling some of the brew on myself.

Burtie went to pat my shoulder but stopped short. "It's all right. It's just the fairies."

He walked to the door. Sparks were flying frantically right beyond him. "I know, but it's gone now. No, it's all right. It's not your fault."

There was a flurry, the lights moving so quickly they seemed to light the entire door in a haze. "I'll tell her, but I'm sure she knows."

I went back to sipping the brew. A black ball of fur with a single yellow eye in the center of its head stared at me from underneath a chair near the fireplace. Actually, it might've been staring at my cup.

"You want this?" I asked, holding it out.

The sparks at the door were still flying as the ball of fur jumped onto the arm of the couch. It settled down and immediately lapped at the cup. It made a few slurping noises.

"Oh, no, Hadder, did you drink all her well water?" Burtie asked as he walked back into the room.

The ball of fur grumbled.

His hands went to his hips. "Is that how you talk to me? I should've left you back in the old country."

The furball made noises that could've been arguing as it leapt off the couch and disappeared into the other room.

"Don't mind Hadder. He came with me when I moved here," Burtie said as he poured a new cup and handed it to me. "The fairies are upset. They think you'll be mad at them now, and then Ryker will evict them from the grove because they sensed the darkness and fled."

I shook my head. "I would've fled too. Only sane move there was."

The pain was ebbing, but the soreness was rushing

in to take its place. I grabbed the arm of the couch to help me up. Burtie took my other hand as I struggled to my feet. There was nothing I wanted more than to find my own bed right now, go to sleep, and hope I felt a little better when I woke.

"Thanks for the drink, Burtie, and for calling for help." If he hadn't, I wasn't sure I'd be standing now. I might be lying bloody in that spot, never getting up again. Or worse, I might've let the creature in.

"Of course."

I walked with care toward the door, my left leg going a little slower than my right. My right hip felt creakier than the rest of my body, not to mention the stabbing pain if I breathed too deeply.

"You sure you don't want to wait here until Ryker gets back?" he asked, trying to hover as I made my way to the door.

I stopped to talk to him, mostly because it meant I wouldn't have to move for a couple of seconds.

"It's okay. It's gone." I turned back to the door and then paused for a split second before I opened it. What if I was wrong? Would it be waiting for me?

I couldn't think like that or I might never leave Burtie's again. I pulled the door open and walked out.

My entire life, I'd known one thing: if I saw the threat coming, I'd figure it out. The ones headed straight at me, about to shred, burn, or rip me to pieces? I could handle those. I'd darted this way and that and pulled off more than a few miracles. Over and over again, I'd managed to dodge them all and make it out—maybe by the skin of my teeth, but I was alive.

There'd been a ton of them, too. Slow and creeping starvation from a forever looming lack of food, because in a world that was constantly at war with each other, farming wasn't a priority. The constant target on my back because I was a Wyrd Blood. Being marked for death by the Debt Collector.

After all those years of getting by, I'd almost been taken out by something I couldn't even put a name to. But I guess that was how life went. It was the shit that came at you sideways, in your blind spots, that knocked you to your knees. The stuff you weren't prepared for that left you reeling and groping, begging for mercy and crying uncle. Sometimes it was in the moments you were exhaling your relief that you caught a blow to the chest.

TWENTY-FIVE

"Tommy, get out of my way, and tell your buddy to move too." Ruck's voice woke me from somewhere beyond sleep.

"Ryker said no one else was to come in," Tommy replied.

My door rattled, as if someone had just leaned against it. Why were they all out there?

And why was the sun streaming into my room? I didn't get afternoon sun, only morning. Had I slept away the whole day and night? I barely remembered getting back to my bed yesterday after I walked home from Burtie's.

"He didn't mean *me*. He meant the rest of the caravan you let in," Ruck said.

"Tommy, let him in," I called from my bed.

"Now step aside before I break your nose." Ruck pushed the door open a second later. He walked to the window by my bed and pulled the fabric across it.

I heard someone yelling from the other side of my

window and realized there had been another guard posted beside it. Had the guy been peeking in my window and watching me sleep?

"Thank magic you're finally awake," Ruck said, sitting on the edge of the bed. He tugged the blanket down to my waist. "I heard what happened, but you don't look too bad."

I glanced down and realized I had on a different shirt. "Has anyone been in here? And why are all these people outside?"

"Ryker posted them after what happened. As to visitors, who hasn't been here? Ryker, Dez, Knife, the healer." He paused and then started to back up. "Burn and Sneak, too. The lady that makes those good biscuits. She left a plate, but people kept eating them when they came by." He pointed to an empty plate with crumbs.

I didn't care that they'd eaten all my biscuits. I lifted my shirt, looking at my shoulder and seeing the marks were completely gone. Dammit, Ryker hadn't even asked me. That healer probably robbed him blind, and I hadn't been that bad off. Nothing a solid week wouldn't have fixed up.

Wait, how had I slept through all of that? Burtie. So much for his drink not dulling the senses.

"You want me to go fetch you breakfast?" Ruck asked.

I stretched out stiff muscles. "No. I'm good, and it's better if everyone sees me up. I'm sure the story is spreading with the spectacle outside my place."

Several minutes later, I was exiting my place with Ruck and three guards following behind me.

I stopped and turned around. "I'm going to breakfast. You don't need to come."

They stopped and looked at each other. "But we're supposed to report if you're attacked," one of them said.

"The food building will have plenty of people to do that. It's all right." I began walking with Ruck again. The group waited a good five minutes before they followed us. As long as they left a buffer, I could live with it. It wasn't such a bad idea.

We walked into the food building, and Ruck shot over to the line. I paused, looking to that same corner that always drew my eye.

Marra had probably heard I'd been attacked. I didn't want her pity, but I couldn't stop from checking to see if it had softened her anti-Bugs stance a hair. Was there any part of her that still gave a shit if I lived or died? Or had we reached the point of no return? Either way, it would be a relief to have clarity.

She was looking right at me, the coldness in her eyes giving me a chill. She turned toward her friends. Fake Ruck glanced at me before he said something to her. Her head fell back as a smile lit her face.

I didn't notice Ryker until his magic was hitting me like a brick to the head. His hand went to my back as he stood beside me, but his gaze was somewhere else.

Marra's smile slipped under the new attention. She caught it before it completely fell from her face, but I could see the effort it took to keep it plastered there.

"Do you want me to get rid of her?" he asked.

I broke my obvious stare, shrugging it off. "What, Marra? I don't care about her. She can stay."

I was the one who'd be leaving as soon as I could, especially if he was going to be acting even nicer than normal. I got it. We'd slept together. He thought he should be nice, but all it did was confuse the situation. The building I was leaping from kept getting higher and higher. I knew my limits and was flying past them.

I walked toward the line, where Ruck was already five people ahead of me. Ryker stepped in behind me, the food bowls getting replaced as he did. What a stroke of luck.

"You didn't need to get the healer," I said in between the eggs and the sausage.

"I need you at your full strength," he said, putting another link of sausage on my plate.

I'd already had two. Why was he giving me more? Was he telling me I was too skinny? Was that a jab? He'd sampled me and found me wanting?

"I don't need any more." I plucked up the offending link and dumped it on his plate. He could eat the extra sausage. Maybe if he put on a little more weight, all his muscles wouldn't bump out. After all, not everyone liked that.

He dumped it back and then raised me two biscuits. Now I had three biscuits on display when everyone knew that two biscuits on your plate declared you a hog. It wasn't done. There was a reason I snuck biscuits in my pocket.

"Are you trying to make me look bad? Is that what this is about?"

His wrinkled forehead told me otherwise. "You didn't eat yesterday. You need to make up for it."

I was on the verge of telling him that wasn't his problem when I noticed we'd slowly been getting more and more attention. The entire room seemed to be paying heed to our every move, word, intake of breath.

It was safer to take all three biscuits and get to the table than to continue. I sat beside Ruck, who was sitting beside Burn. There were two empty chairs across from me. Hopefully Ryker would take the one closest to Sneak and not across from me, so all the busy-bodies would stop watching.

The chair skidded backward as Ryker took the seat across from me. He leaned back, legs stretched out and ankles crossed, but there were ripples in his magic churning up the air. I was too close to the edge myself to ignore him. He was eating, but there was something else. This wasn't a Marra or food issue.

Did he know something about the demon? Had he found something when he'd gone after it yesterday? I'd assumed he wouldn't find any trace, and that if he had, we wouldn't have minced words over Marra. It would've been the first thing he said.

"Whatever it is, just tell me."

"I've located a stone," Ryker said, not appearing to have the same warm gush of relief that was spreading through me at those words. This could be my salvation.

I leaned in until the toes of my boots brushed the tips of his under the table. "Where? Who's got it? How did you find another one so soon?"

"There's been a rumor about it for a long time."

I didn't like the way Burn and Sneak put their heads down as Ryker talked.

"You all knew about this one?" I asked, looking about the table.

I got mumbled agreements from both Sneak and Burn.

"Well, I didn't," Ruck added, as if he should count in this discussion.

"Neither did I." I patted Ruck's shoulder.

Ruck and I smiled at each other, but everyone else seemed like they'd been told to prepare for a burial.

"Wherever it is, it can't be that much worse than some of the others," I said.

Burn shrugged a disagreement. Sneak kept eating. Maybe they thought so, but they hadn't been nearly destroyed a day ago.

The only one who met my gaze was Ryker. "Yes, it could be, but I don't think there's a choice—unless you tell me differently?"

He was asking me if I could withstand another attack without a stone. He'd seen what the last had done. I'd been gnawed up like a chew toy and then spit out. I bit the inside on my cheek as pride and desperation warred within, keeping me from answering either way. Logic told me it was my only chance of surviving another visit from my demon, but damned if I was ready to say that aloud.

He nodded, his eyes locking with mine, telling me he'd figured as much. It bugged me that he thought I couldn't handle another attack, even if it were true.

"We can go tonight if Switch is up for it," Ryker said, turning to Ruck.

How'd he know about Ruck and Switch? If Ruck didn't look as surprised as I was, I might've gotten angry.

"He'll be there. He owes her, and he'd do it even if he didn't," Ruck said, after a long swallow.

"This stone never leaves your grasp," Ryker said to me.

If anyone didn't need that pointed out, it was me. "You're enchanting the enchanted."

Ruck leaned back in his chair, staring at me with his head tilted. "Enchanting the enchanted? What the fuck does that mean?"

I rolled my eyes. "It means I already know not to let the stone go—obviously."

"Not so obvious," Ryker said before he went back to eating.

You make one goof and no one could let it go. I'd wanted to be able to sleep in peace. Was it really that huge of a mistake?

Dez swung out a chair, taking a seat between Ryker and Sneak. "You're finally awake!"

I smiled because it was Dez, but the reminder of sleeping a day away chafed. The reason I'd slept hurt like a brick to the back of the head.

No one else was smiling, though. "Why's everyone look so bad?" Dez asked. "It's not like she's dead. She's right here."

"We're going for the pit stone," Ryker said, his magic rippling again.

"You're kidding, right?" She looked around the table. "Wow. Okay, then. I'm coming. I could be helpful."

Dez was coming? I still didn't know what she could do. I didn't think anyone knew.

"What can you do?" Ruck asked.

I wanted to give him a nice pat on the back, but it might've been too obvious.

She kept her eyes on her dish. "I can't say, but you never know when it'll come in handy. And if it doesn't, I can fight as good as anyone here."

Everyone was quiet, and I didn't know if that was because they knew what she could do or they were bursting with curiosity as much as Ruck and me.

Dez began talking to Ruck about a guard giving her a hard time getting in my room, which spurred a few more comments.

I drifted off, wondering what they'd all heard about this stone. I was too afraid to ask. I either died trying to get the stone, or the demon won. If it managed to get inside me somehow, we were all dead anyway.

If that thing managed to break me, use my magic and then Ryker's... Death swam around me in every direction; every decision could lead to catastrophic losses. The air in the room thinned as my pulse did a frantic dance. My skin grew clammy and everyone around me felt like they were casting verdicts, knowing I'd fail somehow.

"I'll see you guys later tonight," I said, my fork clattering. I jerked out of my seat like I'd just learned to stand.

I dumped my plate in the wash bin, and by the time I turned around, Ryker was waiting at the door. I stopped walking, but only gave him my profile. Still, I felt his nearness and shivered slightly when he stepped close enough that his arm brushed my side, his heat reaching toward me. It was too much—it all was. The other night with him, the demon, the never-ending ride of chaos that was my life, which I couldn't disembark from—at least not in the way I wanted to.

"Where are you going?" he asked.

"I have a couple of things to get done."

He dipped his head down until his lips nearly brushed my ear. "Is that the only reason?"

"Yeah, what else would it be?"

I walked away.

The last thing I wanted to do now was to have a big heart-to-heart on why it wasn't right to play pretend when you were only fucking.

TWENTY-SIX

W<small>E WERE IN THE MIDDLE OF NOWHERE WITH</small> nothing for landmarks but trees way off in the distance and a massive hole in the ground. No wonder someone had dumped a stone here and figured it would be safe. No one would ever come here.

I looked over the edge. "You said it was a pit," I said to Ryker. "I can't see the bottom of this thing. *Pits* have bottoms."

Dez couldn't stop looking from Ryker to me. "There's something going on with you two. You're different somehow. Are you in a fight or something?"

Or something.

"I don't know what you're talking about." I looked back over the edge of the pit. It was safer.

Ryker walked over and gave Dez a head tilt. She walked away, but her eyes never left us.

He stood beside me. "Are you scared? I can go first."

"I'm not scared, and we both know you can't." I'd

have to go down first. There'd be a ward. Wards were my jam. As tough as Ryker was, nobody could break into shit the way I did. What made that offer even worse was he was serious. It wasn't a joke. He wasn't teasing. He was treating me like I was too fragile to handle it, and he was doing it in front of people.

I looked over the edge again, trying to see this promised bottom. It had to be there.

It would be all right. I'd break the ward and Ryker would kill everything. We were a perfect team, at least with this. All was good.

"We can go down at the same time."

He might as well have been coddling me. He didn't speak like this. Did he not realize people were listening, even if those people were Burn, Sneak, Switch, and Dez? "Why? I told you I've got it."

"It's all right to be—"

"Shut. Up," I said under my breath.

He didn't even look annoyed. He looked worried. It was horrible.

"I've got this," I said loudly, hoping it would undo Ryker's damage.

Switch began twitching, jerking his head toward the side.

"I need a second." I walked to Switch and then had to follow him another five feet away, as he wouldn't stand still. "What's wrong?"

"I can get you out of here if you need. You don't have to do this if you're scared like Ryker thinks. I told Ruck I'd keep you safe." He was rubbing his arms and acting as if he were about to impart the world's greatest secret on me and was risking death by doing it.

"No. I want to do this." Ryker was contaminating them. He'd have everyone thinking I was soft. I wouldn't be able to show my face at breakfast if he kept this up.

Switch nodded, but his eyes were squinty.

Ryker was going to have everyone thinking I was a ninny because I wasn't thrilled to leap into a black hole. Who would be? It had nothing to do with bravery and everything to do with common sense. I had some. That was all my nerves proved.

I left the squinty-eyed Switch and made my way to Burn and Sneak. "Come on, guys. Give me the rope. I'm going in."

Burn held out a looped end. "Step on the end and we'll lower you down.

I didn't climb in gracefully, but I did it fast. See? No chickens here. After I was dangling about ten feet down, I looked up, waiting to see Ryker following me, gripping the rope tighter than needed as I did.

My rope stopped moving. Ryker appeared over the edge and continued to lower until he was eye level with me. He wrapped his hand on top of mine, where it was gripping the rope. He pulled me closer to him but didn't say a word. I didn't tell him to let go. Damned if I didn't feel a little better with him being near.

We began dropping again, and the need for the rope signals became more obvious as the time ticked by.

I was looking down when he cupped the back of my head and drew me in. His lips covered mine, his tongue caressing. He broke the kiss, his face still only inches from mine.

"You've got this," he said, before dipping back in, sucking on my lower lip.

Before I could digest Ryker's actions, I felt it. I tugged twice on the second rope beside us to signal the guys above to stop lowering us.

I waited another minute, making sure I was right. The feeling was so slight that it could've easily been missed.

"Do you feel it?" I whispered.

"No."

The ward itself was a beauty. Barely perceptible at all. What hit me first was some magic beyond the ward we were closing in on. It sent a shot of warmth through me, but a kind that made my hair stand on end.

"There's going to be something really strong beyond this."

"How strong?"

I took a deep breath, pulled my hand from Ryker's, and then bent at the knee to get closer. Leaning over and leading with my hands, I found the ward. A shiver shot through me as the dark magic boiled beneath. I'd never thought of magic as light or dark before recently. Whatever was brewing beneath this surface felt like it could turn my heart black if I gave it enough time.

I let my senses reach out, skimming the ward. I could feel a slimy magic churning below the surface. "Strong, but we can do this."

"You sure?"

I stared at him. "Yes. Just be ready to kill it."

I ran my hands over the surface, feeling the pattern of the magic, learning its grooves and idiosyncrasies. No two wards were ever alike. They were as different as the people who created them. Their weaknesses were as well, and there was always one.

The second I felt the crack, it was too late to warn Ryker. It was as if the pressure from the inside had been building, waiting for me to nudge it enough.

The ward burst open in an explosion of energy. The place lit with a green glow. Magic shot around me, rippling in currents. I went flying back, slamming into the cave wall, my head bouncing against it as I dropped another twenty feet to the bottom.

My eyes blurred as I shook my head, trying to clear it as the creature rose to its full height. I understood why that pressure had been so immense. Covered in scales that looked razor thin and shining silver, green glowing from its eyes, a Grodian towered twenty feet over me. I'd heard about these mythical creatures from childhood: spawned from experiments with dragon eggs, they killed by fire and then ate your charred remains. They'd been used during the Magical War of 810. They were responsible for more than one ruined city until a pact between all the countries made them illegal.

Ryker was nowhere in sight. I didn't know if he'd been thrown into one of the small offshoot caves or maybe been blown straight out of the pit itself. For now, I was alone.

It took in a mighty breath, its chest rising, and I knew I had less than a second to protect myself. I channeled everything I had into putting a ward between me and it. I didn't even wrap my sides, focusing on one direction: where it was standing.

I was right. The fucker breathed fire. I crouched, trying to make myself as small as possible as waves of flame hit my ward and singed my sides.

There were a few seconds of respite as it took another deep breath before it hit me with round two. I didn't know how well I was going to fare this time or how long I could continue. Getting out without a rope was impossible.

That was when I saw Ryker, his rope gone, as he attempted to scale down the rock wall toward me. He'd been blown upward and had to be a good hundred feet up, with the Grodian in between us.

"Kill it!" I screamed, hoping that the way our magic was merged would somehow save me from dying too.

"I can't. It's too close to you," he yelled back.

The monster took a deep breath, its head jerking toward the sound of Ryker's voice.

"Do it anyway." It was a risk, but I was willing to take it.

He kept descending as if he didn't hear me.

The monster was gasping, looking as if it were a little rusty at getting his fire back. As soon as it did, it was going to blast one of us. The way it was looking toward Ryker, he'd be dying first.

I'd have to watch him being charred alive.

"Do it," I screamed.

He ignored me, climbing down as fast as possible considering the slickness of the walls, waving a hand here and there as if trying to keep the Grodian's attention on him.

If he wouldn't listen, there was only one thing to do. I felt for that connection we had deep inside, the one I normally tried to ignore, and shoved everything I had at him. The bulk of my magic and then every drop I could squeeze out after that was shoved toward him. Giving it felt every bit as bad as having it taken.

His head swung toward me, and I could see the confusion in his eyes.

The Grodian was filling its lungs, and I knew it was about to char him right to the wall.

I moved from my spot of safety and started screaming, "Hey, fucker! Don't forget about me!"

The Grodian's attention shifted from Ryker as I prepared for the worst. One of several things was about to happen. (A) The monster would burn me alive. Very probable. (B) Ryker would kill the monster and take me out with it, which was what I knew he feared. Also very probable. Or (C) Ryker would kill the monster and I'd still be standing because his magic couldn't hurt me. At least if I did die now, I'd die literate and a non-virgin.

The Grodian's mouth opened, and I saw the flames gathering in his throat, about to shoot at me. Then I felt a sweep of something else graze by, a mere tickle to my senses.

The monster fell to the ground, shaking the earth beneath it. I remained standing.

Ryker landed beside me. Even in the dark, I could sense his glare. I moved around the clearing, and the big, dead Grodian, while avoiding the glare as much as I could.

"Where is it? It has to be down here. I can feel it." I talked to myself, afraid to speak to Ryker yet, as the adrenaline kept me moving.

Ryker pushed a boulder out of the way. "I got it."

"Good. Let's get out of here."

He dropped a nice-sized stone into my palm. It was perfect pocket size. I would've thanked him, but I was still worried about opening up communication with the stare he had going on.

He jumped up, grabbing what was left of one of the ropes. Mine had burned off higher in one of the blasts of fire.

More rope was quickly lowered down. He put his foot into a quickly made loop. "Put your foot on mine."

I did and then grabbed the rope that was between us. He wrapped an arm around me and tugged a signal.

The second we were off the ground, he started. "What the fuck were you thinking?"

What I was thinking now was that I'd almost made it out of the pit without having this conversation.

"Bugs." The way he said my name was enough to start a battle.

Fine, he wanted to fight? We'd fight. "I was thinking of how to save at least one of us. You call me stubborn, but what was that about? And while we're at it, what was the shit up there about? 'Am I too scared'? What's gotten into you?"

"Don't change the subject. That was idiotic."

"Your caution was going to bring about both our

deaths. Where's the man that had us brazenly robbing from Bedlam and screw the consequences?"

"That was thought out. What you did wasn't."

"Bullshit. You're just mad because it was my call."

We were nearing the top, and Burn reached down and yanked me up.

I could see from the expressions as I landed topside that they'd heard part of the fighting.

I gave a wave with the stone in my hand and then smiled. "All good. Got the stone."

TWENTY-SEVEN

"Switch, go back and tell them to send a chugger." Those were the last words Ryker would say for three hours.

We were a miserable-looking group as we sat around the fire waiting. Occasionally someone tried to break the silence with some gossip or small talk. It never launched into a full-fledged conversation. By the time the chugger arrived, everyone was running to jump into the uncomfortable spots in the cargo area. I derailed Dez and shoved her into the center of the cab so I'd have a buffer for the ride back. The glares from her were easier to handle.

I expected Ryker to rip into me on the way back, but he didn't say anything. By the time we were pulling back up to the Valley, I wasn't sure Ryker would be speaking to me again after this. At least it would make the goodbyes easier this time, if the hole it was putting in my chest didn't kill me first. I'd done it to save him, and this was what I got? Well, fuck him.

Ruck was there as soon as we pulled up. I jumped out of the cab before the chugger came to a complete stop.

"Hey. Heard it was a rough night," Ruck said.

Switch must've filled him in, but I could see questions in his eyes.

"Come on, let's go to my place," I didn't wait to see if Ruck followed. Putting space between Ryker and I was more important.

Ruck glanced back before following me.

He asked me the only question I wasn't ready to answer: "You fucked him, didn't you? Switch said he noticed a weird vibe between you two."

My face was blasted with heat. "We broke out a Grodian and all you care about is if I slept with Ryker?"

He opened his mouth and sucked in a breath. His entire frame froze for a couple of seconds and then he said, "You did do it!"

I pushed into my room, dropped my bag, and sank onto the bed. "You know, you need to realign your priorities. This should not be the most important conversation right now."

"I'll realign at a later point when I decide to give a fuck about the order of my interests." He sat next to me, shoving a bit so he could get more real estate. "You're alive, so it couldn't have been too bad. Now let's get to the good stuff. How was it? Is he big? I bet he's huge."

I ran a hand through my hair, my skin growing even warmer as I remembered Ryker's hands on me.

"Shit, that good? You've got the smile that says he rocked your world. Damn. I knew it. If I wasn't so happy with Switch, and you weren't crushing on him like a quarry, I might've tried to convert him. I bet it wouldn't be that hard, either. A man who likes to fuck as much as he does tends to be easier to swing around to the right side of things. How many times you do it?"

"Just once, and it's not going to happen again. It's not a thing. It was a moment."

There was a long pause before he said, "You know, I haven't seen women coming and going out of his place like they used to."

I held up a hand. Hope could be a dangerous thing. If I followed Ruck up this mountain and stuck my head in those clouds, my heart wouldn't be able to handle the bumps when I rolled back down.

"It's very clear what we are, and it's not hearts and flowers. I don't want to build this up into something it's not. I slept with him and I probably shouldn't have, because I'm already struggling to keep my feelings in a neat little compartment. I can't afford to buy into any delusions of what this could be. We both know Ryker. We both know this won't end like some fairy tale." He wasn't the right guy and never would be. He'd never be faithful. It wasn't who he was.

"I get it." The corners of Ruck's lips dropped, and his tone lost all its excitement.

This was one of those times that it hurt when he didn't argue with me. The fact that he was rolling over so easily shined a spotlight on how right I was. We both knew it, and his face was a mirror of my fears.

"Maybe you shouldn't do it again," he said, doubling down.

"I'm not planning on it."

I WOKE TO MY DOOR OPENING. RYKER WALKED IN and shut it behind him. He crossed the room until he was standing over me. Tension mingled with his volatile brand of magic.

"Don't ever force my hand like that again," he said softly, but seriously.

I flipped from my stomach to my back, meeting his hard gaze with one of my own. I wouldn't lie to him to make peace. I'd rather war with him daily than mourn peacefully at his grave.

"I'd do the exact same thing tomorrow, and there's nothing you can do that will change that."

He fisted his hands at his sides, as if he wasn't sure what to do with me next. Join the club. No one ever had.

Then his hands were fisted in my hair, his body covering mine. If he'd meant to intimidate me, it had quickly taken a different turn. His thigh between mine, his erection pressing into me.

My lips parted, my breathing hitched as I arched into him.

"You're going to be my undoing," he said, his lips grazing mine before claiming my mouth.

He'd almost died today, but here he was, warm flesh and beating heart pressing against me, and that was the only thing that mattered. I'd worry about distance tomorrow.

TWENTY-EIGHT

I flipped through the book Sneak had stolen from Crisp, generation after generation of my family history laid out. Having lost my family so young, part of me had always felt like I'd come from nowhere. Here was proof, though.

Dez walked through the door I'd left wide open. It was to let the sun in—not that I was paranoid about getting attacked with no one around to notice. I had a stone, after all. I patted my pocket.

"What are you doing?" she asked, falling onto the bed beside me.

"Looking at where I came from." Page after page of names, not a one with magic. It was so strange how Wyrd Blood happened, just springing up out of the blue to ordinary folk.

"Can I see?" She leaned over my shoulder, already looking.

I handed her the large book. She took it and rolled

over onto her stomach, running her fingers over the names.

"Wow, they kept really good records." She tapped her finger on the top of the chart. "They've got your lineage by more than five hundred years before the Magical War of 810." She traced her finger down the line of names, all listed with date, place of birth, and occupation beneath. "Your family really got around."

"What do you mean?" I leaned over to look.

"I don't know, it's just weird. Most people stay in the same country their entire lives, or maybe move to a nearby one. Not your people. Your mother was born in Crisp, but your father came from Burrunda, which is pretty far. Your grandparents on your father's side came from two totally different countries that were far apart too. It goes on and on." She dropped the book back in my lap and pointed to the different places listed. "It's like your family all had itchy feet or something."

I was still scanning the pages as she got up.

"I gotta go shower. I'll see you at lunch."

"Sure," I said, looking over my lineage with a sharper eye.

"Hey, you eating all these?" Dez asked, pointing to the basket on my table.

"No. Take them. Sylvia has been dropping off way too many." I didn't tell her I suspected it was at Ryker's request. She hadn't asked me about that situation, and I didn't want to tell.

"Sylvia makes the best. Thanks," Dez said, grabbing a couple before giving me a wave goodbye.

I FLIPPED THROUGH THE BOOK FOR ANOTHER HOUR as I munched on some biscuits. It only covered people whose paternal line started with "RO," but it was a good sampling. Not one other family had itchy feet, as Dez called it. There had to be hundreds of other families listed. If they moved to a neighboring country every other generation, that seemed to be a lot. Not my people. We were globetrotting all over this world.

I put down the book, patted my pocket to make sure the stone hadn't fallen out, and headed to lunch. I'd ask Dez to think about it some more. There had to be other families like mine.

I walked into the food building, and Marra's gaze snapped to mine. Was she finally concerned? She didn't seem overly worried. She stared, and for the first time ever, I looked away first. I didn't care what she was thinking anymore.

I found a seat at the usual table, where Burn and Sneak were already eating.

"You look like shit," Burn said.

"You do," Sneak added.

I hadn't slept well, and it had been worth it, but that wasn't a discussion I was looking to have.

"Where's Dez? She said she'd be here." I scoured the food line, but she wasn't there either.

"Haven't seen her," Sneak said, then took a bite of his sandwich. "You're not eating?" He pointed to the lack of food in front of me.

"Too many biscuits."

They both nodded, more interested in getting back to their conversation than whether Dez was here and how many biscuits I'd eaten.

I waited another five minutes, listening to them talk about the shape of some woman's ass, before I got up.

"I'll see you guys in a bit," I said, leaving the food building and heading to Dez's.

It was only a few doors down from Knife's, and the itchy feet of my family were weighing heavily. Once she'd pointed it out, it stuck in my brain like a gnat in a web. Was there something funny about my family?

Knife was walking out of his place as I was walking toward Dez's. Although he'd seen me when I was passed out, it was the first time I'd seen him since the night Ryker had carried me out of his room.

"Hey," I said, raising my chin.

"Hey," he replied.

A couple more awkward moments passed.

"You see Dez?" I asked, rocking on my heels.

"Yeah, she went into her place not long ago." He nodded his head a couple times.

"Okay, I'll see you later," I said.

"Yeah, see ya," he said, walking off.

Well, that was awkward. I stood on the stoop of Dez's place as I watched Knife disappear around the corner.

I knocked on her door and waited. When she didn't answer, I took a fist to it. Dez always answered.

Nothing. I put my ear to the wood, listening. There weren't any sounds inside.

"Dez!" I yelled through the door, and then moved to the window. Knife didn't know what he was talking about. The room was empty.

I was about to walk away when I caught sight of her foot hanging out from behind the bed. Oh no. Acid boiled in my stomach, about to burn a hole right through me.

I pounded on the door again. Then I took a step back and landed a kick right beside the doorknob. The door swung open and crashed into the wall. I was grateful I'd kicked down plenty of doors in my thieving days.

I ran inside and stopped short. Dez was lying on her back, eyes open, chest still. She was dead. I didn't need to check her pulse to be sure. I'd seen enough of the deceased in my life to know. Logic wasn't needed either. My gut screamed it. I ran over, pressing my hand to her skin that had already lost some of the heat of life.

I turned, and fell to my knees. My palm hit the ground and I did something I thought I was too strong for. I threw up a few feet away from her body.

Ryker was by my side before I was done heaving, angling the door shut so no one could see inside. He walked farther in, stopping in front of Dez's body.

I sat back on my heels and wiped an arm across my mouth.

"I was walking past and heard the banging," he said before I asked.

I got to my feet, giving my face a last wipe just to be

sure. "I saw her an hour ago. She'd been fine. Maybe the healer..."

He looked at me, and the answer was the sadness in his eyes. It was too late. I'd known it when I touched her. I just hoped I was wrong.

"How did this happen?" I asked. No one had died in so long that I'd begun to think those deaths were behind us for good.

"I don't know."

My legs felt weak and my skin chilled as I stared at her body. She'd been bouncing around happy an hour ago, and now she was dead. We didn't know why, and there was nothing to do to fix it.

Ryker brushed my back. Instead of pulling away, I leaned into him.

"Do me a favor; go tell the Burtie we're going to need a ceremony tonight. I want to get her buried quickly," Ryker said.

Tonight. He was afraid of contagion. If this was the Boom, it hadn't acted like any outbreak I'd seen before. Coming and then disappearing for months on end. No, this was something different.

I turned to leave, and he reached out again before I did. He patted the pocket I used to carry the stone.

I nodded and walked out. I'd only gone a few paces before I broke into a jog, then a run. I bumped into people here and there but didn't slow down once.

I walked down the path to the grove and then wandered. I'd made it as far as the line of trees when I stopped, sitting on a mossy mound.

I'd survived slavers, nearly died more times than I could recall. I'd raided chuggers to keep my crew from near starvation, and yet I couldn't remember ever feeling this defeated, not since when Sinsy died. I'd just seen Dez. She'd been fine. How could she be dead? It made no sense. If she'd been back at Dorley, would she still be alive? If I'd stayed at Dorley, if I'd never come to that party, she never would've been here.

I looked at the ground beside me, and for the first time, I was afraid to worm because it might answer. If it said yes, I was somehow to blame for this, what would I do? Could I handle that kind of truth? Was I a poison that spread to all around me?

I dug a hand into the soil until I found a worm. I cupped my hands together and asked my question. "Am I the reason she's dead?"

I placed it down. Before the thing could move, a flying spark swooped down and grabbed it.

What the fuck? If fairies ate worms, that was fine, but they could dig for their own.

I dug for another worm. Before my hands were cupped around it, another fairy grabbed it.

"Why are you stealing my worms? Dig up your own. I'm trying to do something."

I knew they were close by. All I'd have to do is dig up a worm to prove it. I put my hand into the soil. "I'll do it!"

A fluttering light flew right up to my face and squeaked again. I had to squint to make it out, but it definitely had a little head, and I thought the mouth was moving. I heard a squeak.

"What?"

It flew closer to my ear, and another joined it. "No."

"Why can't I worm?"

It didn't say anything this time. Awfully convenient.

I saw Burtie walking through the trees toward me. Some more fairies flying about him, spreading a dusting of gold as they did.

He tilted his head back. "I know, we've got a problem. I see her," he said as he made his way to me. He put a hand on the ground and then eased himself down beside me, joints creaking. "What happened? They say your energy is off."

"We're going to need a tree. Dez is dead."

His mouth turned down. "She was a lovely soul. I don't have her in my records, but we'll pick her out a lovely tree."

"Yeah." I leaned my arms on my knees, leaning forward.

Burtie patted my back. "People make their own footprints where they see fit. Denying them that is akin to denying them their free will. Wherever those steps led them, it was their path, their freedom to own."

My vision began to blur, and I knew I had to get out of there before I ended up watering all the trees in the grove with the sorrow that was tearing at my insides. I got back to my feet and locked weak knees in place.

"I'll have the tree ready," he said.

"Thanks, Burtie."

THE CLOSER I GOT TO THE HEART OF THE VALLEY, the slower I walked. Ryker would've told Knife already. If there was one person in this world that Knife loved, it had been Dez.

As much as I didn't want to be the bearer of bad news, I had to find Ruck.

I could tell word had already spread by the sporadic clusters of people talking softly and glancing at me as I made my way back.

I was halfway to Ruck's place when I spotted him. He met me halfway, and his downcast eyes and frown told me he'd already heard.

He shoved his hands in his pockets.

"I can't hug you. I'll break if I do. I'm barely holding on," he said, his eyes liquid and shining like the stars.

"I know." I swallowed so loud it echoed in my ears. I dragged in a breath, trying to hold back the shudder in my chest.

I took a step away from him and then tilted my head in the same direction. "Come on. I want to show you something."

"What?"

"Can't describe it. You have to see it," I said.

His steps were slow, but he followed. I walked him back down to the grove, where Burtie had already prepared the burial for Dez.

I'd watched her being carried down here a couple of hours ago. I'd watched Burtie carry a Blessed Tree, twice his size, to her grave. In the spring, it would be covered with golden blooms that would glow when the sun hit them, as if it were being blessed by the sun. Burtie had chosen well.

He'd placed it above her and uttered words I didn't understand. As he spoke, the tree's roots wrapped around and cradled her. Then the fairies had come.

They were still there now as Ruck and I approached. They circled the tree, dusting the entire area with their magic as a sweet melody filled the air.

"What are they doing?" Ruck asked.

"Helping her and her magic move on to the next life because they loved her." I motioned to a mound not far away, where we could watch them without getting in the way.

We sat shoulder to shoulder, and I continued to repeat what Burtie had explained. "Burtie said they're using their magic to help release her from this world so she can move on easier. It's a great honor. They only do it for those they believe had pure hearts."

"Move on where?"

"To a place where your spirit roams free. Burtie told me that the fairies can go there, that they aren't bound to this world. That they'll help her find her way. He said she's not really gone."

The sun began to set. The sparkling of the fairies seemed to rise higher above the tree and then glide across the sky, bringing their tinkling chorus overhead.

When they were right above us, just before they disappeared, I heard the echo of Dez's laughter.

Ruck wrapped his hand around mine, and I knew he'd heard it too. A single tear tracked a path down his cheek, but the corners of his mouth rose a little. I squeezed his hand. Our friend would be okay.

TWENTY-NINE

I woke up in Ruck's room the next morning, remembering the night before. We'd watched everyone say their goodbyes to Dez. It had taken hours for everyone to come.

The crowd had been dwindling when Knife finally appeared. I'd started to fear he wasn't going to come at all. He'd been a shadow of himself. He hadn't spoken to anyone, and it seemed as if he didn't see anyone either.

He'd knelt beside her tree and hadn't gotten up. I'd walked forward, laying a hand on his shoulder. He hadn't budged.

Ryker had walked over to me. When I glanced at him, he'd given me the slightest shake of his head, as if to say there was nothing I could do.

It wouldn't help. He needed time.

A fist pounded on Ruck's door, jolting me back to the present. I got up, stepping around where Ruck had crashed on the floor with Switch, both of them sleeping off all the booze we'd consumed here last night.

I opened the door, and Bobby, one of the messengers, handed me a note with a smile.

MY PLACE, NOW.

IT DIDN'T HAVE A SIGNATURE, BUT IT DIDN'T need one.

I PUSHED OPEN RYKER'S DOOR A FEW MINUTES later. He was standing beside a fresh pot of coffee. By the smell, it had been brewed recently.

"You needed me?" It hadn't escaped me that he'd summoned me here by messenger instead of finding me himself. I knew he'd probably come looking for me afterward. As I walked from the grove, I'd seen the look in his eyes.

Crashing at Ruck's hadn't been a complete accident. I would've ended up in Ryker's bed again, and that was something I needed to avoid.

Ryker poured himself more coffee as he said, "I want you to try and worm."

"I can't worm. I *try* every morning." I walked around to the side of the table where he kept his mugs and helped myself to the coffee. I knew when Ryker was about to dig in. Seemed he had stamina in every aspect of his life. I pulled out a chair, slumped into it, and kicked my feet up onto another.

He perched his hip on the table in front of me. "Humor me. We've got a demon on the loose, Dez is dead, and I have no answers."

I looked over the rim of the cup, meeting his eyes, the ones that were locked on my lips. This morning was going to go in one of two directions: outside, where there were witnesses, or toward his bedroom, where there weren't.

I wasn't in the mood to worm and fail, but it was too risky to do anything else. I couldn't sleep with him again. Once was a fluke. Twice was an accident. Three would be a habit, and a bad one at that.

"Fine. Let's go." I put my cup down before his lips followed his eyes. I jumped out of the chair, flung open the door, and made it to the witnesses before I could breathe. There was a nice place under a tree not far away that had plenty of traffic passing it. Perfect.

He was close behind me. "Practice field," he said, and then took a step in the opposite direction.

"What about that nice, shady spot?" I pointed, in case he missed it.

"You don't like worming with an audience."

Somehow, in between sleeping with everyone in creation, he'd taken a few minutes to notice that little quirk of mine.

"I was trying to make this quick for you." I spun on my heel, heading toward the field, swearing I'd keep a five-foot buffer between us. If he didn't get close, we couldn't have sex.

I hurried my steps. Being alone with him was

becoming dangerous. I knelt on the ground as soon as I got there, drawing a circle with my finger and marking it with the requisite yes and no.

The second I plucked the worm from the ground, it wiggled like a lunatic.

"It's not going to work."

He didn't need to speak. His glare said, *Do it anyway,* loud and clear.

I cupped the worm and brought it to my mouth for one reason only: when it failed, I could nonverbally reply, *I told you so.*

He squatted down so he could look me square in the eye. "Wait, why aren't you giving me a hard time?"

I sat back on my heels. "Easiest way to prove I'm right."

He laughed. Between the laughing, smiling, and generally nicer behavior, he was laying a real head trip on me. I stopped giving him my attention. It was better to ignore him in his good moods.

I whispered a real easy question. "Did I sleep at Ruck's last night?"

I laid it in the circle, and it went straight down. Ryker's amusement disappeared with the worm.

I went to stand, and he was already shaking his head. "Try again. This time do it where you put your hands in the ground."

"I've tried it. Do I need to prove I'm right again?" I wiped the dirt from my knees as he watched.

He didn't press me to continue, as I'd expected. When I looked to see what was up with him, his eyes were on my lips, before they slowly moved to my eyes. My breath hitched and my center warmed. I also itched to run, all at the same time. I turned and headed toward the path, looking for a subject that would kill the mood that seemed to be never-ending.

"Did you see Knife this morning?" I asked. That should cut the warm and fuzzies into chopped meat.

"He's going back to Dorley soon," he said, his tone cooler than his eyes had been a second ago.

Knife was leaving? Without me? Dez was gone; Ruck was shacked up with Switch most of the time. I was running out of buffers. All Burn wanted to do was shove me at Ryker. Sneak didn't talk.

"I should go with him for a little bit. He's mourning. He might need me."

Ryker stopped walking and grabbed my arm so that I'd do the same. "And what about the demon?"

"I've got a stone. I'll be okay as long as I keep it on me." I hoped, anyway. Either way, I'd take the chance. I'd get out of here for a few days at least and let whatever was brewing between me and Ryker calm down. It was a phase that would pass. A new skirt would catch his eye and he'd move on.

"Why are you so set on getting back to Dorley? Why are you constantly running away?"

"Helping a friend isn't running away."

"Bull. You're using Knife as an excuse to leave."

"Why are you so set on making me stay when I don't want to be here? Let me go home."

"Stop. Calling. Dorley. Home."

"Why? It is. Let me live my life."

"Don't you think I would leave you alone if I could? I can't."

"I don't want to be the only one who can get these stones. I don't want a monster trying to kill me. I don't want to be special. *Special* sucks."

"You think if you got rid of all the magic in your blood you wouldn't be special? Is that why you think I can't leave you alone?"

"Yes. No one would want me then, and I could go live a very happy and boring life."

He cupped my face, forcing me to look at him. "You could purge every drop of magic from your blood and I can guarantee I'd still want you."

Who the hell talked like that? I wanted to groan in misery, because I knew at that moment I was utterly sunk. Any resolve to not sleep with him melted like snowflakes in the boiling heat of his stare.

He reached out and wrapped his hand around mine, towing me to him like a rudderless boat that didn't have an oar of its own.

He dropped my hand, but I didn't move away.

He moved his fingers to the waist of my shirt, dipping underneath it and grazing the skin of my back and waist while his mouth hovered so close to mine that we breathed the same air.

"You have no idea how much I want you."

His words anchored me to him when I knew I should've been walking away. My brain still screamed to leave, but my heart and body held the majority vote, and they weren't going anywhere. He smoothed his hands up my ribcage, dragging my shirt with it, and I lifted my arms to help him along.

His hands froze. "Something really strong crossed the outer ward."

I didn't know if I was worried or relieved.

THIRTY

Sneak was running up the path as we were heading down.

"Who's here?" Ryker asked as soon as we got close enough.

"The Queen of Cacoy is on the eastern border along with some others." Sneak rested his hands on his hips, and his cheeks were flushed. It might've been because of who was here or because he ran most of the way to find us. Either were possible.

He couldn't have really said Queen of Cacoy, could he? "*The* Queen of Cacoy?" I asked, as if there might be another.

Sneak nodded. "Says she wants to talk to you two."

"The one who wanted to kill me with her fake bean now wants to chat?" I didn't need a strong survival instinct to know this was bad.

"Yes. The Queen of Cacoy wants to speak to you. Am I going to have to keep repeating everything?" Sneak asked.

I let his snippiness go. It was clear his heart was pumping overtime, and I didn't think the sweat that clung to his shirt was entirely due to the jog over here.

"How many are with her?" Ryker asked.

"She's got about fifty Wyrd Blood in tow. Some heavy hitters are with her." Sneak sucked in a breath that hollowed out his throat.

Fifty? Not good, but we had more than that here. We could take them, maybe. If hers were all high level, maybe not. Easy, calm breaths. We could do this. And even if we couldn't, I didn't want to die looking like Sneak did right now. That would be way too embarrassing.

"Who?" Ryker asked.

"New King of Bedlam, one of the royals from Burrunda. Remember the weirdo from Villoy?" Sneak asked.

"Strange hair?"

"Yep. That one."

"Not the worst," Ryker said, shrugging and heading toward the border.

I wasn't sure what would constitute "bad" if fifty Wyrd Blood marching on you didn't.

We hit the bottom of the path, and he stopped. With a hand to my back, he tried to steer me in a different direction. "Go to the grove and wait there."

I turned myself back around. "I'm not going to the grove. I need to see what she wants."

"What she wants is to kill you," he said, as if I should've remembered that very obvious point.

I shook my head. "She wouldn't have shown up at

the front door if that was her plan. She doesn't hit straight on, and she wouldn't do it herself."

"She's got a good point," Sneak added.

Ryker took one of those long, calming breaths he'd been doing more and more often, while looking off at the distance. After a second of regrouping, he said, "Fine. But can you do one thing I ask and stay within arm's reach?"

"Not a problem," I replied. Especially since I'd been planning to anyway. Sometimes he acted like I had a death wish.

I knew what arm's length entailed as well. We might need some more burial holes later. I'd dig them myself, but that queen was definitely not getting buried near Dez. I'd dig a hole over in the forest, outside the valley. Maybe in a bog. That was the best she'd get.

The closer we got to the border, the more Wyrd Blood I noticed heading in the same direction, and the more dulls heading in the opposite. It was a smart move. This wasn't their fight.

Burn came running over to us. "I've got every abled Blood heading over."

"Good," Ryker said. "You and Sneak make sure they stay out of range."

"Got it," Burn said, and the two of them took off, trying to organize.

Ryker and I walked side by side, a path clearing for us up ahead. With all the Wyrd Blood standing together, it was hard not to feel the power pouring out around us. Most of them were low level. If I'd walked among them a year ago, I might've killed them. Now I recognized most of their faces, and when they looked upon me and Ryker, striding out to confront the queen, pride shone in their eyes. We must've had a hundred on our side, all nodding as we passed, looking ready to back us up any way needed.

Sneak and Burn were walking a line in front of them on either side, warning them to keep their distance.

Ryker's hand found mine, and I held on to it. I felt the magic from the other group before they came into view. There was no denying they were stronger, but I wouldn't trade sides for the world, even if it meant death.

There were four people that stood front and center, but one who stood out the most.

"Is that the Queen of Cacoy?" The first thing that hit me was how smooth her skin was, how lush her brown hair. A white fur trailed down to her feet, hiding any chance of seeing a marking. From her looks alone, she might've been under thirty. Her reputation told me she was probably much older, but the stronger the magic in her blood, the less she'd age.

"Yes," Ryker said, confirming it.

"Who's the guy beside her?" He was a few inches shorter than her. Black, crisscrossing marks covered both hands and climbed up his arms.

"Never seen him before, but from the markings, I'd say the new King of Bedlam. At least one thing now makes sense. It wasn't a revolt. It was a takeover."

I didn't need him to tell me who the other two were. One of the men didn't have normal hair but tufts all over his head that stood straight out for a few inches each. Markings wove all around the rest of his scalp. That meant the other person was from Burrunda.

Ryker kept moving forward, and I followed his lead. We didn't stop until we were closer to the enemy than our people. Good thing I didn't mention anything about digging those holes out loud. There were a lot of potential dead bodies here. This was quite a commitment.

The Queen of Cacoy broke from the group, walking toward us. Her companions took a step to follow. She raised her hand without looking back, and they all stopped like well-trained dogs.

She continued until she was standing a few feet in front of us. Her eyes skimmed me, pausing on my torso, as if she already knew who I was. The way they dropped to my pants and the boots I wore, that was an altogether different message.

"What brought you slinking all the way over here today?" Ryker asked.

If I did love Ryker, it was because of moments just like this.

She pursed her lips for a second. "We need to talk."

"Then talk," Ryker said.

"Are you going to let me in, or are we going to stand out here and create a spectacle?" If she'd given my dingy clothes a disgusted look, it was nothing compared to the way she stared at Ryker.

"We're going to stand out here," he said jovially, smiling.

I feared if the queen kept insisting, he might actually laugh. He truly seemed to be enjoying thwarting her.

She crossed her arms. "I could force the issue."

"Mutual destruction? Go ahead. You should let your dogs know too," he said, waving his hand toward her entourage.

She swallowed so loudly it was audible, and the little vein at her temple started to throb in the worst way, ruining her perfect complexion. "I'm doing you a favor coming here before your plans ruin us all. I suggest you invite me in and hear me out."

"A favor? You mean like the bean that would've killed her?"

"No matter what you believe, I'm not stupid enough to walk into your country intending to kill her."

Damned if I didn't want to hear her out. It was clear I might've been the only one. Ryker seethed hatred from his pores. The lines of Wyrd Blood behind us were nearly showing their canines.

I looked beyond her to the Wyrd Blood she'd chosen to bring. I reached out, feeling their energy, drinking up their magic. None of them met my eyes; their magic pulled away from me. They weren't here to fight. Would they under the right circumstances? Probably, but that wasn't the plan. They were as much an adornment as the fur she wore.

That was it. I had to know what she'd come for. Considering everything, we couldn't let hatred blind us.

"We should let her in and hear her out."

Ryker snapped his gaze to me, and his lips parted as

if he were holding back from calling me crazy in front of the queen.

"Only her. The others stay behind," I said, trying to sound saner than he was giving me credit for.

"Fine. They'll stay," she said, without a care. Proved she didn't need them. They *were* here for show only. I would've been happier about being right if it hadn't made her scarier.

Ryker wasn't budging. I squeezed his hand and tilted my head, hoping to get him moving.

His eyes kept insisting I was crazy.

I tilted my head again, ignoring the silent comment.

It was clear he was going to relent as soon as the smile completely disappeared from his face.

"We'll let you in, but only because she's taking pity on you." Ryker stepped toward me, making a clear path for the queen.

She sucked in a breath through clenched teeth. Her eyes narrowed, and the little vein in her temple was near to bursting. She straightened her shoulders and walked past us as if we were invisible.

With a nod from Ryker, Burn stepped in front of her, leading her toward Ryker's, as we followed. Every Wyrd Blood in the valley looked on as she passed, gawking like they were watching the devil walk into heaven. The way she strode through the throng of condemning eyes made it clear the devil didn't think she was a sinner.

"Thank you," I said to Ryker as we followed her toward his place.

"Mark my words, you're going to regret this," he replied.

A few minutes later, Burn pushed Ryker's door open and stepped aside.

The queen walked into Ryker's place while Ryker paused by Burn. "Anyone makes any moves…"

"I'm on it."

She was already seated at the table when I walked in. I could feel her power but also her control. Her magic was locked down the way Ryker's had once felt to me, before things had gotten all tangled up between us.

I moved to the other side and sat across from her. I didn't care what title she gave herself. We were equals. Ryker pulled out a chair and sat beside me. United, if only for now.

He shook his head, as if he'd rather have killed her than what we'd come to, sitting civilly across from each other. It was clear I was going to need to take the reins with this meeting.

"What do you want?" I asked.

She didn't hesitate to get right to the point. "You need to stop gathering stones."

I let out a huff. "So you can have all the power?"

"You don't tell us what to do regarding the stones," Ryker said. "People have been trying to get them for decades. You expect me to sit back and let someone else collect them and then beg for their mercy as they rule this world? Never going to happen. As it was, that nut Harvo from Bedlam had already managed to seize one. Mushroom Man had gotten another. This was happening whether you wanted it to or not. I got an opportunity and I took it before things went to shit."

"Do you understand what happens when you gather these stones?" she asked, eyes narrowed on us.

"We'll have more magic than you," I said. There might've been a little gloating involved, but the woman had tried to kill me.

She stood, her palms on the table. "You little idiot. You're going to ruin us all. I was running half the world while you were playing in caves."

She hadn't pulled that out of the air. This woman knew something about me, about my past, and wanted me to know it. Her eyes burned hot as she looked back and forth between us.

Ryker remained relaxed but his tone was glacial. "Take it down a notch with the theatrics or this talk is over. You'll be out wandering the field again."

She swallowed back her pride but was choking while she did. When she sat down, the table had scorch marks in the wood where her palms had been. I had a bad feeling she could light this place up in a second if she wanted. No one should have to worry about being burned alive twice in one week. It was redundant.

"What do you know about my history? It's clear you're dying to share." I'd lived through it, so if she thought the retelling was going to rattle me, she was delusional. She better have something I wasn't aware of.

"Which part would you like to know? The part where your mother poisoned you? Or the part where she sold herself to the Debt Collector? Or how your flake of a father sold that info to the slavers to buy his freedom and that of his floozy?"

I knew enough of the details for her story to ring true. But she'd filled in a crucial part of the picture. That was how my mother had gotten me out. She'd poisoned me so that I'd be tossed out with the dead. Then sold herself to save me. Once my markings had started to show, it would've been that or hand me over to the ruling house of Crisp. Remembering what I did, I would've done the same.

It would've been a good plan if my father hadn't botched it. I'd already known he'd walked away from me, and I'd walled off any hurt.

Ryker reached under the table, giving my thigh a gentle squeeze, supporting me without letting the queen know her words might've stung.

They hadn't. This woman couldn't touch me, not where it counted.

"Anything else?" I skidded my chair back a couple of inches and then kicked my boots up on to the table. Let her highness look at my muddy soles.

"Unless you have more than a history lesson, we're done here," Ryker said, standing.

"The stones you've been gathering aren't just stones," the queen said. "Have you ever heard of the Black Abyss?"

Why did that name sound familiar?

Ryker didn't move, didn't change his breathing or say a word. But deep within, where I could feel the place our magic connected, I felt the beginnings of a tidal wave.

The queen looked at him. "I see you recognize that name?"

"Might've heard it mentioned before," Ryker said, and it was clear he'd more than heard of it. He knew exactly what she was talking about.

"What is it?" I asked Ryker. After all, I was the person who'd been collecting the stones. Details would be nice.

"It's legend that there was a place deep in the mountains that was the origin of the magic wave that spread across the world," he replied. "That there were miners who accidentally broke into this place called the Black Abyss. Once that chamber was opened, it released a surge of the magic into the world. That's where the stones originated, from a larger one that was in that chamber."

The queen leaned forward. "It's not a legend at all, and you know it. I lived at the foot of that mountain. I was a young girl, a normal human then, before the magic flooded into me. I saw the things that came out of the Black Abyss before the miners sealed the chamber up again. Over the course of just weeks, my town was destroyed by dragons and monsters you'd never seen the like of."

"Wait a second—if the chamber was sealed up again, how did we get any of the stones in the first place?" I asked.

The queen looked like she was thinking back to another time altogether. "To see the original stone was to know its power. Before the chamber was sealed, pieces were chiseled from the larger stone in secret. No one knew what happened until the people who'd stolen some of the stones heard whispers in the night, calling to them, as if they were being haunted. Asterol, they named this invisible creature, knowing and fearing it was some sort of manifestation of the stones dark magic. No one would risk reopening the chamber, and the stolen stones couldn't be destroyed. They were broken down as small as possible and separated for a reason, sent to all different parts of this world on purpose, never supposed to come back together. Most were warded by the first Wyrd Blood.

"But even then, we could feel the magic trying to unite itself. The magic wants to come back together, and now you're helping it."

Ryker scoffed. "But it was okay for the Mushroom Man to have it because he was another one of your pets?"

She slammed a hand on the table. "I had that under control. Before you, I'd never had to think of those dark times. Every time you collected another stone, you put another piece of the dark evil back together, fed its strength. It might already be too late if it can get the stones on its own. Damned if I'll be destroyed because of you two."

She thought it only wanted the stones. It didn't. It wanted something within me as well, and something inside Ryker. I hadn't shown up on her doorstep looking to share, and felt no urge to do it now.

At least I knew why she wanted me dead. I wasn't sure I could blame her, either. I might've killed me too.

"Is that why you tried to kill me? Bought my life from the Debt Collector?"

"Of course. Do you think I would've cared about your life otherwise? Bothered with that freak of magic? I've hated him for centuries. I'd kill him again if I could."

"You killed the Debt Collector?"

"The Debt Collector sold me a bad soul I couldn't collect on. Once you merged with him, the contract was worthless. His death was a magnificent display when he died, let me tell you. Sorry you couldn't be there." She smiled.

Dammit! I clamped my teeth together and swallowed every curse I wanted to spew, and there were many. I remained seated but wanted to slam my hands on the table. The only thing stopping me was I'd just make noise. Who could compete with scorch marks?

She might've been getting under my skin a tad now. She was quite irritating. I peeked over at Ryker. His glance said, *I told you so.*

"I had an opportunity and I seized it. Clearly you're disappointed, but life doesn't always work out the way you want. I should know. I'm here, after all, and you're alive." She sat across the table gloating, stroking the fur of her jacket like it was a beloved pet.

"I knew this was a bad idea." Ryker turned and sat on the table, giving the queen his back. "Are you done listening to her? I'm finding this quite tedious myself."

I wasn't sure if tedious was the right word. I'd rather have pins shoved under my fingernails than talk to her again. I'd learned some things today, but I wasn't going to plead a case to let her continue.

The queen stood, brushed off her fur where she'd been sitting, as if the place had contaminated her, and crossed her arms, staring at us.

"I was finished anyway." She pointed at me. "You made this problem, and you'll have to fix it. I'll never be able to get close enough to kill it. Neither will he."

"Thank you for stating the obvious," I said. I'd already suspected that as well. The demon had disappeared as soon as Ryker had gotten close.

She turned and headed for the door but stopped right before she left.

"By the way, tell that little mute friend of yours to stop using my poison. She's lucky the idea of being here another minute is repulsive, or I'd find her myself." She waved her fingers in a girlish goodbye as she left. I could tell by the gloating look in her eyes that she knew she'd finally taken a shot that hit home.

Ryker didn't say anything. He didn't have to. Anger was filling the room. My contribution to the magical mix was panic. There was no way Marra would've poisoned people. She might've gotten messed up in the head since her sister died, but she hadn't become a killer.

"That woman's trying to cause problems. We have bigger issues right now than her lies, like what we let loose with these stones. How much did you know?" I asked, standing and pacing halfway across the room before leveling him with a stare that would've burned someone else to the ground.

He followed me halfway over. "Are you asking if I knew about the Black Abyss? Yes. If you hadn't hidden most of your life, you would've probably heard about it too at some point. Did I know it would unleash a monster? Of course I didn't, just as you probably didn't realize the girl you were defending was a murderer."

"How can Marra be behind the deaths? When I wormed that last time, the lines said it was caused by someone you'd heard of. Not someone here or that you knew."

"Are you sure that's how you asked the question?" He spoke like someone whose jaw was locked.

"Yes." I wasn't defending the Marra who hated me but the woman who'd been in my crew. The one who'd starved with me, fought with me. I was speaking as the family member of a person about to get hung.

"The worm might have thought of the poison as the cause, or the person that created the poison."

"But what about the queen? She said it was hers, and you *know* her. That directly conflicts with what it said." If I didn't drive enough of a shadow onto the queen's accusations, someone was going to die.

"The queen doesn't make her own poisons. And yes, I know *of* the Wyrd Blood that does it for her." He turned and walked out.

"Where are you going?"

He didn't answer. He wouldn't kill Marra without being one hundred percent sure.

He probably wouldn't.

I let out a groan before I ran out the door.

THIRTY-ONE

I'D WATCHED MARRA EAT DINNER AND THEN PLAY cards for hours. I'd sat in a tree, got rained on, and now hovered in the shadows across from her room while she was probably toasty in bed. What I was doing made no sense. I should let Ryker kill her if he wanted. If I was drowning, she wouldn't throw a rope to save me, and yet I was here.

The worst part about all of this was that I hadn't even seen Ryker. If he *was* going to kill her, he would've done it by now. He wouldn't have waited until she crawled into bed. He would've walked right up to her and killed her in the middle of the food building.

That didn't mean Marra was off the hook. He was probably waiting to see if there was some proof besides what the Queen Bitch of Cacoy had said. Now we'd have to see if some turned up. She was an emotional mess, but I still couldn't believe she was a killer.

I *hoped* she wasn't a killer. Was it possible to be that

wrong about someone? Could the past blind you that much? Yeah, it was possible. If all those deaths were her doing, she deserved whatever she got. I wouldn't be there throwing her a rope, either.

Someone sneezed in the empty space beside me.

"Magic bless you," I said.

Sneak sneezed twice more before he appeared.

"How long have you been here?" I asked.

"I've been on her since lunch. You were a little late."

Ryker had disappeared somewhere. I should've guessed it would be to get Sneak on the job.

"Why didn't you tell me you were here?"

He shrugged. "I don't know. I guess I wanted to see how long you'd sit in the rain for some asshole who shits all over you. It was dumb but somehow admirable." He chuckled.

Glad he was amusing someone, because I sure wasn't laughing. I pushed off the wall. "Looks like she's going to live through the night. You'll let me know if something goes down?"

"Oh, don't worry, I'm sure you'll know," he said, his eyebrows halfway up his forehead as he turned toward me. "You're lucky Ryker's in charge. I would've gotten rid of her as soon as her cracks revealed her rotten insides."

Ryker had protected her? Why would he do that? Sneak was confused. That might happen to him more than I realized. Perhaps it was why he didn't talk that much.

I kept quiet, waiting to see if he'd say more.

"After the shit she pulled, getting people worked up against you, he was dying to kick her ass out," Sneak said. Then he stared forward, not offering anything else.

"He said that to you?" I asked, hoping to get the information flowing again

"Of course he didn't, but I know him." He turned back to Marra's place. "Fuck. She's on the move again. I probably gotta go wait for her to take a dump or something."

Sneak grunted and disappeared again. The only sign of him was the crunch of gravel under his feet.

Ryker had left Marra alone for me? It didn't make sense, unless he'd thought he could use her to control me somehow? Or maybe Sneak had no idea what he was talking about. Ryker hadn't said that. Sneak had assumed it. Not exactly reliable info.

I turned to head away from Marra's. Sneak would cover the rest of the night, and Marra would be alive in the morning. A redheaded young girl caught up to me as I was walking out of the alley. The shadows were a busy place these days.

She handed me a piece of paper with a smile. "Ryker wants you at his place. He's called a meeting."

"Are you supposed to read the messages?" I pocketed the note. No need to read it, since she already had.

"I don't recall anyone saying not to." Her slender hands went up in the air.

I ruffled her hair. "Good girl. That might keep you alive one day."

I was in my corner of the couch. Ruck was on the other side, which I'd now come to think of as his corner. Switch was sitting between us. I didn't think it had much to do with being close to Ruck. It was more about having a safe zone around him so Knife couldn't get too close.

I'd been trying to not stare at Knife since I'd gotten to Ryker's, but it had taken all my self-control. This was the first time I'd seen Knife since the burial. He hadn't even ventured out yesterday, when the queen had shown.

His sorrow was a magnet to my own. Part of me wanted to get him alone so we could fall into the oblivion of depression together. The other part of me wanted to stay put to protect Switch. Free or not, Knife was glowering at Switch from across the room, misdirected anger looking for a home.

Burn was leaning on the table, one leg swinging, a little closer to Knife than normal. Burn seemed to be keeping one eye on Knife's movements, as if he were afraid of the swelling anger around Knife finding the wrong home as well.

Sneak was still off trailing Marra around.

Ryker strode in from the bedroom. "Good. Everyone is here."

"Why *are* we here?" Knife asked. He might be in the room, but he had one foot out the door. The foot left behind looked like it was ready to kick someone.

Ryker walked over and stood by my corner of the

couch. "We know what's coming for Bugs. The queen called it Asterol. It's connected to the Black Abyss."

"The Black Abyss?" Switch said.

"I thought that shit was made up," Knife said, his attention fully inside the room for the moment.

"According to the Queen of Cacoy, it's not," Ryker said.

"Well, if anyone would know, that old crone would," Burn said.

Ryker filled them in on the other pertinent details shared by the queen. I didn't stop holding my breath until he'd finished and not brought up Marra. As of right now, she was still innocent, and Knife didn't need to hear any speculation about her guilt until proven.

Knife's head dropped back as he let out a long groan. "I knew I should've left yesterday."

Ruck turned to Ryker. "How's Bugs supposed to kill this thing? She can't even see it without catching a beating."

Ruck was right. I couldn't. But I'd had hours to think this over and had the beginnings of a plan.

"We have to set a trap," I said. "The only way to lure it out is to get it more stones. It always comes for the stones."

"Isn't that dangerous, considering what we know?" Switch asked.

I glanced at Ryker to find I already had his full attention. His jaw was locked down and the vein in his neck was a little bigger than it should've been. But he said nothing. He agreed. It was our only shot.

"We know we can lure it with that. We get one

more stone to lure Asterol. I keep one on me, to buy time. This way, maybe I'll be able to keep it around long enough for Ryker to come in and kill him."

Ryker didn't say anything as he sat on the arm of the couch beside me.

Knife took a couple of steps, cracking his neck. "It's a risk. If it gets more, it might become too strong to kill."

Burn stood, his gaze bouncing between Ryker and me. "They can do it. It's a good plan. Bugs will lure it. Ryker will kill it. They've got this."

"Now we need one more stone," I said.

"We've got some feelers out up north still. We might hear something soon hopefully," Burn said.

"I can help with the search," Switch added.

Ruck was offering to go with him, but I only heard every other word. Knife's head dipped an inch, his lips pressed together as he shoved his hands in his pockets.

I got off the couch and took a step toward him. "Knife? Do you know about one?"

He sighed so loudly that the whole room's attention shifted to him.

"Knife? Do you know of another one?" Ryker asked.

Knife shook his head. "Durroker, that old Wyrd Blood that lives out on his own over in the Glades, supposedly has one stashed. He told me when he was deep into his cups one night. Word is, he's off his rocker these days, so don't approach him alone." He walked to the door and stopped. "I won't be going with you. I'm done. I've lost enough blood for a lifetime."

Knife didn't say goodbye or look at anyone as he

left. The room went quiet. My sorrow urged me to follow Knife out the door, but I didn't have that luxury.

"Anybody else want out?" Ryker asked.

"We're in," Ruck said as Switch nodded next to him.

"You know I've always got your back," Burn said.

"Day after tomorrow, we go to Durroker," Ryker said.

"If you guys don't need anything else, we're going to get out of here," Ruck said, looking at Switch.

I smiled and tilted my head toward the door.

Switch grabbed Ruck's hand, and they were gone without getting up.

Burn stirred on the other side of the room. "I'll go check on Knife. See you guys later."

I was sitting on the couch, scratching my head. As all the things the queen said repeated in my head, there was something that kept mentally tripping me.

Ryker's eyes narrowed on me. "What is it?"

"I've got to check something. I'll be right back."

THIRTY-TWO

I LUGGED THE HEAVY BOOK MARKED "RO" BACK with me to Ryker's a few minutes later. He was reclined on the couch, waiting.

I sat beside him. "I've got to show you something." I flipped open the pages until I was at the first entry of my family tree. "Look at this. They were miners." I flipped another page. "More miners." I pointed over and over again. "I've got a miner at the beginning of every branch of my tree. Some of them might've been there when they first broke into the Black Abyss."

"Let me see." He reached for the book, skimming over the many branches of my tree.

I reached over, pointing. "See the way they all moved around, from country to country, over such a short span? Dez said that wasn't normal. Do you think it's possible that some of my ancestors were there, they absorbed magic, but it didn't show until the lines commingled in just the right way?"

"As if the magic were trying to find a way to come

together again in the right combination until it created a Wyrd Blood that could get to the stones," Ryker said.

I leaned back, too sick at the thoughts running through my mind to keep looking. I wrapped my arms around myself. Generation after generation of manipulation until it birthed me?

Ryker shut the book and tossed it on the table, turning his full attention to me. "It doesn't change who you are. The majority of the magic in this world originated there."

"Yes. But my magic might've been strategically created by this thing. What if I can't worm because it?"

"It's blocking you, at best. It can't control you, or it would've broken you."

I pulled a knee up to my chest. "Maybe it's time to try and undo the link we have before we go any further with this plan?"

"No." He stood, giving me his back.

"You know the consequences if I fail. I'm in a fifty-foot hole and you're standing beside me. But one of us has a rope to climb out. It's time to climb out."

"That's not on the table."

"If I go down, so will you."

He turned slowly, moonlight streaming in the window and catching his profile, casting the rest of his face in shadows. I could feel the heat of his eyes and the churning of his magic, so much deeper since the merge.

In this second, with the idea of him dying with me, there was no denying that I loved him. It ran through me to the very depths of who I was, as if it were part of my identity now.

He might never feel the same, but he'd never have this connection with another woman. This part of him would always be mine. This, at least, would be sacred.

"Stop talking as if you're going to fail. Like you think you might die. You're not," he said, as if his force of will would make it so.

He'd saved me before, but this time was different, and we both knew it. This fight was mine, and I had to figure out how to not take him down with me if I failed. "I'm exploring all the possibilities, is all."

"Undoing the merge isn't one of them."

I didn't have the burning rage needed to fight. I didn't feel like I had much of anything left inside me right now but desperation. I leaned forward, my palm the only thing keeping my head up.

"You look drained. Are you sleeping?"

I shoved the hair out of my face. "Are you? Is anyone?"

"Stay here tonight," he said.

His eyes were soft on my face, my lips, but with a burning hunger that called to me. He was my refuge. And every time I curled up into him, I wanted to leave less and less.

There was a knock at the door.

"Ryker?" It was Tommy from the watch.

"What is it?" Ryker asked, without opening the door.

"The tower scheduler is brawling with Leroy from construction," Tommy yelled. "I can't find Sneak, and Burn is more likely to punch Leroy than stop the fight."

Ryker cursed under his breath.

He walked to me, bent down, gripping the back of my head, and closed his mouth over mine. His tongue dipped between my lips before he broke off the kiss. He hovered right above me. "I'll be back soon. Be here."

He walked to the door and yanked it open.

Five minutes after he walked out, I left.

Burn's door was closing as I walked out of Ryker's. I ran over to it, managing to get a palm on it before it clicked shut.

"Ah, shit," Burn said, shaking his head as I followed him into his place. "I gotta bad feeling I know what you want."

"Is there any way you can separate me and Ryker without him knowing? I need you to undo the merge."

"Even if I could, I wouldn't. He'd kill me if I did," he said as he walked around the place, grabbing up scattered laundry.

Did that mean there was a way? If there was, I'd torture him until he did it. "So—"

"I didn't say I could. It can't be done without his knowledge. Anything I tried, I'd need him there for."

"If you don't and this goes bad, he might end up dead. Are you sure that's your answer?"

"You could tell me I'd end up dead right beside him and it would still be my answer. When I did it, I needed you two, plus a shitload of other Wyrd Blood, *and* the fairies kicking in. Do you really think I could slink off and undo it with the snap of my fingers?" He stopped moving around, a pile of laundry in his hands.

I could tell by the pain in his eyes that if he thought it were possible, no matter what he'd just said, he'd try in order to save his friend. It was what I'd feared, and Burn knew enough to fear what might be coming.

"If I were you, I'd go have a good time while you can," he said with a smile. "Now, if you don't mind, I've got some company coming."

"You do?" I asked, trying to sound happy for him, but it was all bittersweet.

"Yes, I do. You know the teacher I might've been eyeing up?"

"Oh, I know the teacher." I'd thought she wasn't interested, but from the way he was hustling around cleaning, something must've changed.

"Yeah, well, it might be happening after all."

"Good for you," I said.

He opened up an already full trunk on the side of the room and began pressing his armful of clothes into it. "Great, now get out. I don't want her to see you leaving and get the wrong idea in case she's the only one who doesn't know you and Ryker are doing it."

He smiled as if he were funny.

"Go fuck yourself," I said, but not unkindly.

"Not tonight," he replied, laughing as I left.

———

ANOTHER NIGHT STRUGGLING FOR SLEEP, EXCEPT this time I could nearly taste the Zs. It was right there, within reach, if I could only shut down my thoughts for a little bit. I tried to lie still, but my brain kept racing past at a hundred.

All I could think of were monsters and power merges, life and loss.

Dez...

Fuck. I flipped over onto my stomach. What if it had been Marra? I should've made her leave as soon as she turned on me. I should've told Ryker to get rid of her when he'd offered. No, I'd screwed up long before that. I shouldn't have come back here. Then Knife and Dez wouldn't have stayed. I'd been weak, and Dez had paid for it.

There were so many turns that could've been different and maybe she'd be alive. If I hadn't merged with Ryker, I'd be dead, but Dez's body might not be lying in the Grove of Souls in a spot that should've been mine. And now I was going to get another stone and lure the monster out? How many more people would die before the end?

My door opened. A few minutes later, a warm body covered mine. I didn't panic. I would recognize Ryker's scent, his feel, his energy anywhere. I didn't need to see him to know him. Sometimes it felt as if I'd memorized everything about him.

He nipped at my neck and then my earlobe, his scruff rubbing against my skin. "Why weren't you in my room waiting like I told you?"

Pull back. Tell him you're tired. Do something before it's too late.

I arched my ass into his groin. That was definitely the wrong "something." His arm slipped between my body and the bed, and he cupped my breast, arching me into him further.

"You weren't there."

"You knew I was coming back. You should've waited." He wrapped his arm around my hips, hoisting them upward while he kneaded and then pinched my hard nipple. "You're going to have to pay for that."

I swallowed hard.

You can still stop this. It's going to end badly.

He yanked my nightshirt up to my waist, and I could feel his naked thighs as they parted mine. The head of his cock pressed against me, teasing, barely dipping in. I arched back, trying to press him further into me, but he held me back.

"Next time I tell you to wait in my bed, are you going to do as you're told?"

There was no way I could stop this. I wanted him too much.

"Yes." I would've agreed to anything right then, even handing over all my magic.

His cock dipped a little farther in before teasing my entrance again.

"Are you sure about that?"

"Promise."

His cock rammed fully into me, filling me. I felt as if I were dissolving into him, fading from the pieces of myself and becoming whole with him. With each stroke and caress, we merged into something new, and it was terrifying. I clung to him as our bodies shifted together.

His lips knew every part of me, moving lower, only for him to fill me again with his tongue. I glided over him, our bodies slick with sweat, to take him in my mouth, wanting to know him as well. And then he was pulling me upward and filling me again, wrapping around me until we were both shaking with release, and I still wanted more. That was when I knew there would never be enough with this man. I'd want him ceaselessly until the day I died, and it didn't matter if it was tomorrow or centuries from now. He was a drug to my soul.

He settled into my small bed, pulling me into the nook of his arm and shoulder. He dragged up the blanket around us both.

Any second, he'd get up. He'd go back to his nice, large bed.

The seconds kept adding up.

"You're sleeping here?" I asked. It was a stupid question, because he was closing his eyes, his head on my pillow and his arm wrapped around my waist.

"It's comfortable, and you're warm." He pulled me closer to him.

More comfortable? I never used the heater thing in the corner. My bed was narrow. I was forever out of water in the pitcher.

What was this? What were we doing? How long could this last before he grew bored of me?

I should tell him to leave, that I couldn't sleep like this. I glanced up. His eyes were closed, his lips soft.

"What is it?" he asked, sensing my stare or the rigidness of my spine.

"Nothing." I pressed my cheek back to his chest, breathing in the scent of him. He smelled different after we had sex, and I liked it. I needed to log it into my memory, file it away for when this was over.

He opened his eyes slightly. "You know, there's this thing I've seen other people do called talking. We could try it."

He rubbed down my spine, trying to coax the steel from it.

"Okay but not now. I'm too tired."

I closed my eyes. I didn't want to talk. I wanted to enjoy the feel of him against me as long as it lasted.

His hand paused. "We've got some things that need discussing."

"Another time," I said.

He rubbed the length of me until his hand found a home on my hip.

THIRTY-THREE

Banging on my door startled me awake.

I was in the same position I'd fallen asleep, my cheek pressed to Ryker's chest, our limbs intertwined.

"Let's ignore it," Ryker said, shifting closer.

The door banged again, and Sneak called out, "Ryker? I gotta talk to you."

Ryker sighed loudly, and I knew he was going to get up. He climbed out from underneath me and then yanked on his pants.

"Hang on," he called. He pulled the blanket a little higher up my body. "I'll be right back."

I rolled onto my back, realizing that anyone who didn't know I was sleeping with Ryker would know now. He was standing outside my door, shirtless, at the crack of dawn. I wasn't stupid enough to think it would deter any women from throwing themselves at him.

My system jolted as the sleep cleared. Why was Sneak here, anyway? I scrambled out of bed, throwing on clothing as my hands shook.

I swung open the door. Both their heads snapped to me as they stopped speaking. My stomach dropped.

Sneak's eyes broke from me first as he said to Ryker, "I'll go and..." He jerked his head in the opposite direction.

Ryker nodded. I stepped back, letting him in. He shut the door.

"Whatever proof he has better be beyond solid. Not that she was spotted somewhere, near someone else, who might've had a shady look about them."

He grabbed his shirt and threw it on, taking a painful minute of silence before he stopped moving. He turned to me, looking like he'd taken a punch to the gut. "Bugs, there was a partially eaten biscuit in Dez's room the day she died. To be thorough, we brought it to the healer on a fluke. Turned out it was poisoned."

I stepped back, letting his words sink in.

"We immediately questioned Sylvia. Turns out Marra has taken up baking recently, but only on select occasions. She was in one of her baking moods the morning Dez died."

I circled the room, his words sinking in like fangs in my jugular. No. It didn't fit.

I waved my hands, shaking my head, as a heady relief came. "You're wrong. She got that biscuit from my place. I ate them too. It wasn't poisoned."

Ryker turned with me. "Bugs, the healer confirmed it."

"Then the healer is wrong. I would've died too."

He walked to my door and opened it. "Come on."

"Where we going?"

He looked like he was carrying a two-ton weight on his shoulders as he stood by the door. "You need to see something."

WE WALKED UNTIL WE CAME TO A SMALL building, set off by itself. It was where the healer stayed when she was here.

Ryker knocked on the door.

It didn't matter what she showed me. Those biscuits weren't poisoned. I'd eaten too many. I remembered the day clearly. I'd seen Marra at the food building right after I ate them.

I remembered seeing her. The way she stared at me...

I put a palm flat against the building, leaning.

Ryker glanced at me. The blood had drained from my face, and I must've looked like a ghost.

His lips had parted, as if he were going to ask something, when the door swung open.

"Been waiting for you," the healer said, leaving the door open and walking back inside.

"Do you still have it?" Ryker asked as he followed her.

"Of course I do. I can follow instructions," she replied.

Ryker stopped a few steps in and looked back at where I was still standing on the threshold. I let go of my grip on her building and forced myself to enter.

"You need to see this," he said, as if he knew how hard this would be.

The wooden snake she used to heal was already out on the table, the creature all too familiar to me.

First, she picked up an apple and waved it in front of the snake. It immediately came to life and took a chunk out of it, then swallowed. The chunk expanded in its wooden throat before smoothing out again a few moments later.

"That's how normal food looks," she said.

The healer walked to the corner, grabbed a bag, and removed a small piece of a biscuit.

She held it in front of the wooden snake. It didn't move.

"One more time if you want more apple," she said.

The snake suddenly nipped off a tiny piece. Its mouth and head turned black before it regurgitated the biscuit onto the floor.

Its color quickly returned to normal and she held the apple back to its mouth, letting it gobble the rest of the thing down.

"That's what poison looks like," the healer said, stating the obvious.

I reached out to the wall, bending forward slightly. "How can it be? I ate the same thing and didn't get sick."

"If I had to guess? It could be the stone you've been carrying on you. It increased your warding ability so much that your body rejected the magic. Or maybe the merge helped block it. Aren't you immune to poison?"

the healer asked Ryker, all the while feeding the snake more apple.

"I am," he said.

"Maybe she's tapping into your specific abilities," the healer said, shrugging.

"Thanks," Ryker said.

I turned and walked away, pulling deep breaths as soon as I got outside. Ryker wrapped his arm around me, pulling me back against his chest.

I leaned against him. "Now what?"

"If it were up to me? I'd kill her."

A ragged breath shook my shoulders, and he rubbed my arm.

"But it isn't. This is your call," he said. "What do you want to do?"

"I've got to talk to Ruck. If she was behind the deaths, she nearly killed him as well."

Ruck leaned sideways until his shoulder hit the side of the tower, as if he didn't have the strength to stay on his feet by will alone. I knew the feeling.

"What do you want to do?" I asked.

He shrugged as his eyes glazed over, shaking his head repeatedly. "If I didn't know her the way I do, I'd kill her too."

I looked out at the horizon. "But we do. No matter what she is now, she wasn't always like this. I feel like we're not only killing the person she is but the other Marra I loved."

"I don't know if I can do it. Even after what she did to me. Somewhere in that fucked-up, broken head of hers, there's still the Marra we grew up with." He lifted his shoulder. "Look, you want to make the call, go ahead. I won't hold it against you."

I sighed, the warring parts of me overflowing outward. "I don't think I can either."

"Then what? She can't stay here. She's too dangerous. What about banishment?" he asked.

"She'll have to find a new crew if she hopes to survive. Can't make it without someone watching your back." I dragged my hand through my hair. "At least we wouldn't have her death on our hands."

"Letting her leave comes with risks. She might still cause problems. She knows a lot about this place, the people, the vulnerabilities."

"Can you give the order to kill her?" I asked.

"When I think of Dez? I could kill her with my own hands. When I see her, it might be a different story. How do you think she got her hands on the queen's poison?"

"That's an easy one. The queen smuggled it in for her to kill me."

"Another reason why letting her live isn't safe," Ruck added.

"Let's talk to her. See what happens," I said. I leaned over the tower, where Tommy was waiting to take Ruck's shift, and waved him up.

There was a guard posted outside Marra's

place when we got there. He stepped aside to let us by. I knocked on Marra's door to no answer. I would've knocked again, but Ruck pushed the door open.

Marra was sitting on her bed. Her legs were stretched out in front of her, ankles crossed, as if she were taking an afternoon break.

"Why? How could you?" Ruck asked, getting closer to her than I could stomach. I remained by the door, watching as she smiled. She was really gone. If we did kill her, it wouldn't be Marra dying but some sick and twisted version of who she'd been.

"How could you do that? To Dez? To me?" Ruck asked.

My insides twisted as he begged her for answers.

She made a stabbing motion toward me before her eyes shifted in my direction. Pure venom shone in them.

"You sided with me against her," I said.

Everyone had something that would undo them. Sinsy's death had been Marra's.

"What about the other deaths?"

She smiled and then used her hands as if she were building something invisible. It had been the signal she'd used back in the Ruins when she thought we needed to practice before a raid. She always wanted to do dry run after dry run. Always needed to be prepared.

I edged closer to the door, my need to get away from her warring with a desire to stay close to Ruck. His head dropped forward, his spine slumping with it.

I reached out and grabbed his arm, dragging him

out of there. I kept pulling him until we were on the side of the building and she was out of view.

He slumped against the wall, banging his head back. "She's gone. She's really gone."

I'd thought when I saw her, it would be harder to make the call. It would still be hard to kill her, but I knew what had to be done.

Ruck tilted his head toward me. "Can you do it?"

"I can't have someone else do it." I pointed to his hip. "Give me your knife."

He reached to the one he had hanging at his waist and handed it to me.

I wrapped my fingers around it and then turned back to Marra's, before I lost my nerve. Ruck followed me.

The guard stepped out of the way, and I swung the door open. She was still on the bed, but there was a stillness to her now that hadn't been there before.

I walked closer, and her eyes stared off to nowhere. Her chest didn't move.

"She's dead. She must've had some of the poison in here."

The first thing that hit me was a sigh of relief. It wasn't what I expected, but I wanted to slump into a chair and thank the gods of magic that she'd taken it out of my hands. I wouldn't have to murder someone I'd once called sister. Those memories wouldn't walk hand in hand with when she'd helped bandage up a cut on my arm or defended me when we lived in the Ruins and Willoby had called me a scrawny nobody.

Ruck's head dropped, eyes on the ground. His chest

expanded and then deflated in a whoosh, washing away the hard line of his shoulders as it did.

His eyes were as dry as mine when he finally looked up.

Neither of us would say it, but we were both thinking it. It had worked out for the best.

I SWUNG MY LEGS OVER THE EDGE OF THE TOWER platform, thinking about Marra's lifeless body. Ryker had come in and laid a hand on my shoulder, offering me his silent support. Switch had also shown up. In the end, Ruck and I had gone off alone, back here. No one but us would mourn her loss, and we needed to do it together.

Ruck didn't speak for an hour. When he finally broke the silence, he said, "Today sucked. It really, *really* sucked."

"Tell me something good. One really nice thing that warmed your heart. I need it," I said.

More than anything, I needed something good and beautiful to think on, a lifeline in the dark.

"Switch has the softest hair. When I sleep next to him and it fans out on the pillow, I rest my head on it. I feel like I'm surrounded by kittens." He smiled, as the thought of it flooded him. "Your turn."

My answer was instant and surprising to even me. "Ryker cuddles."

"You mean, like hugging and stuff after it's over?" Ruck asked, as if he couldn't merge the two.

"Yes." I laughed at the shock on his face.

"Wow. He didn't strike me as the type."

I wrapped my arms around myself, as if I could feel Ryker with me. "When he does, I feel like nothing could ever hurt me. Like he'd protect me from anything." I shrugged, wishing I'd picked something else. Hearing it aloud made it seem more ridiculous than it had in my head.

"I can see that."

"You can?"

"Yeah. The day you left for Dorley, he came to the tower and yelled up that I had to get my ass down from there right this second. I nearly jumped half the way, because when Ryker's in a mood, you sort of do that. He said, 'You're leaving with Bugs today.' I told him I didn't have a replacement for my shift. He said, 'I don't give a fuck. Your girl's upset. Get your ass moving.'

"This thing with you two might never work out, but I don't doubt for a second he'd protect you if he could."

I dropped my head, biting my lip. "Thanks, Ruck. I needed that today."

THIRTY-FOUR

RYKER LOOKED AT THE CLOCK ON HIS WALL. BURN
and Sneak were hogging the couch, and I was sitting on
the table.

Ryker walked to the open door. "Where the fuck is
Switch? We were supposed to leave for Durroker
twenty minutes ago."

"I'll go get him." Fetching Switch was better than
telling Ryker what I thought was holding him up.

"He's at Ruck's again?"

"I don't know. Figured I'd try a few places." I'd try
Ruck's first, though, because I'd heard the noises
when I walked by a few hours ago. Still, it was only a
guess.

I ducked out and jogged over.

They were definitely still going at it when I
knocked.

"Switch? You ready? Everyone is waiting." I used to
barge in, but not these days. Ruck and Switch went at it
like rabbits, and creative ones.

Someone said, "Oh shit," on the other side of the door.

"I'm coming!" Switch yelled.

I leaned a shoulder against the building as they rustled around inside. Switch stepped out with hair sticking every which way and a shirt that was leaning to the left.

"Bugs, swing by after you're done," Ruck said from inside, where he was flopped on the bed.

"See you in a bit."

Switch was running his fingers through his hair, trying to flatten it, as he rushed toward Ryker's. "I'm sorry. I lost track of time."

"Don't worry. You're not that late." I grabbed the sleeve of his shirt and tugged it down, evening him out.

Three stares were leveled on him as we walked up.

"They look cranky," he said as we got closer.

"They always look cranky," I said. "Okay, we're all here, so let's get going."

We formed a circle and then we were off.

I had one hand wrapped around Ryker's and one around Switch's.

Suddenly I was alone, crashing to the ground.

"Dammit and magic, Switch!" I yelled, knowing he wasn't there to hear. He'd dropped me off in the middle of nowhere, again. I'd been juicing him, too. Where'd he drop everyone else? What a clusterfuck.

I got up and dusted off my bruised butt and then patted the pocket I kept the stone in. It was empty. It must've dropped out during the fall.

I scanned the ground, looking for it. It had to be

here. Dammit. I was going to kill Switch when I got to him.

I froze as the smell hit me, that rotting, putrid smell that made me want to dry-heave and run. It was here.

I scrambled around on the ground. I needed to find that stone, and now. I saw a glint a hundred yards away and made a dash for it.

Then I stopped short as Asterol appeared in front of it. He picked it up and held it in front of him. The stone glinted in the sun, looking as if it were exploding. The sparks that shot off absorbed into its skin. It opened its arms, its chest expanding, and stretched as if it had eaten a good meal.

Then it turned its attention on me. "Chiara."

This wasn't a mistake or Switch's fault at all. The first time I'd dropped, I'd ended up near a magical stone. This time, I ended up here, with it. This thing had broken my connection with Switch, and he'd done it again, now.

"You're the one that made Switch drop me."

It bent its large body forward until its face was a foot away. Its upper body rested on its knuckles. "Give up, Chiara. You're not strong enough to fight me. You're not strong enough to win."

"What are you?"

Its form broke from the beast until my mother was standing before me. "I'm whatever you need. Whatever you want, if you'd only let me in. Give me what I need."

The voice sounded exactly like hers, the hair and

skin as if she were the same age as the last time I'd seen her.

I stumbled backward.

Ryker stood in front of me. But it wasn't him. The true Ryker wasn't here. "Is this better? Is this what you need? Will you let me in now? I could be everything he isn't. I want you like he never will. I'll never leave you. We'll be together for eternity." It continued forward, its hand outstretched to me.

I jerked back. "You're not him."

"Does it matter if I look like him, sound like him?" It reached out and brushed its fingers over the flesh of my cheek. "Feel like him? I want you, not like the rest of them. Your parents threw you away. He turns from you. Ruck has someone else. Marra betrayed you. But me, I'd be all yours. I'd be the one that never left you. After all, we're the same."

I recoiled, clinging to what Ryker had said about most magic coming from the Black Abyss, not just mine. But I was nothing like this creature.

"No we aren't."

"We need to be one. He'll never want you now. You have to know that. You're different. You're like me."

"No, I'm not." It would say anything to break me. I knew that. It wanted me, and once it had me, it would get Ryker.

"You hold my magic, so much of it, and with my help, we can get it all. You're special, Chiara. Don't make me hurt you."

A tickle of pain started, flaring across my skin. I stumbled to the ground as the pressure began, and the agony would follow. This time I didn't have a stone to help me, and no one would be getting me help.

This time I'd break, he'd take everything I had, or I'd die.

The pressure built and nothing I did relieved the pain, as if I were being stabbed from every direction. He was going to break me, find his way in. I could feel his magic snaking into me through sheer pressure. I opened my eyes, trying to find a weapon to end my life with. I couldn't beat him, but I could stop him from getting Ryker.

"Bugs!"

I heard Ryker's faint shout in the distance and knew this was really him. I could feel his magic reaching out to me. I searched the horizon for him. Ryker was trying to get to me, but it looked like he was fighting against a wind I couldn't see or feel.

Asterol's arm rose, and Ryker was flung even farther away. I saw him try to get up before he was lifted and tossed yet again.

A blast of magic surged within me. It was Ryker's. He'd given me all that he could, all he had left, and all he'd done was seal his fate. I was going to lose. Asterol would find his way in, break me, and then kill Ryker as he lay weakened.

The pressure increased, and with every push, I felt its magic claw closer to that special spot within me.

This was it. I was going to break.

I could feel Ryker's magic pulsing inside me, mixed with my own. If I had Ryker's magic, why couldn't I wield it the way he did? If I could break any ward, why couldn't I break through the force Asterol was pressing down on me? It said the same magic pulsed through us both. If it could block me from worming, why couldn't I do the same to it?

As if it sensed what was going on in my mind, another wave of magic blasted everything from me but pain. I gasped, trying to hold on. I hugged my knees to my chest, my eyes watering. I rolled onto my side, feeling as if I were in a vise that was crushing everything I was.

Two spots appeared high above. Then there was only one. Switch had just dropped Knife out of the sky.

His magic waned for a second, as if he sensed the coming attack.

"I'll do it if you promise not to hurt Ryker," I said to Asterol, trying to keep its attention on me. I only needed a second before Knife dropped down on upon it.

Its full attention swung to me again. Before it said anything, Knife landed on the monster in a blur of movement. Asterol screamed in agony as slices appeared everywhere across its body. Asterol howled in pain as more slices appeared, but none of them were deep enough. The damage was widespread, but there were no killing blows.

Willing myself to find the strength, I got to my hands and knees as Asterol ripped Knife from its back. It snapped Knife's body in two before dropping him to the ground like a discarded rag doll.

Black blood oozed from all over Asterol's body, and it wobbled on its feet.

Knife's eyes were glazed, blood coming from his mouth. I heard him whisper, "Kill the bastard."

As if he'd been hovering nearby, Switch was there and gone in a second, and so was Knife.

Asterol was unsteady, but quickly regaining its strength. If it disappeared this time, I might never have another chance. I had one shot at this. I needed to be close. To touch him, even. This had to work.

But it was injured. Would it let me close now? I turned, ignoring its presence as I stared at Ryker's lifeless form.

I fell to my knees, praying I could pull this off.

"He's dead," I said, letting the tears fall freely. It wasn't all an act. Ryker wasn't yet, but he might be soon. So might Knife. I couldn't let them go unavenged.

I folded in on myself, slouching forward, broken.

"I have nothing left." I looked up at Asterol as the tears continued to flow. "Can you show me him whole one last time?"

It hesitated, and I dropped my gaze to the ground, letting the sorrow of failure soak into me. If I couldn't do this, Ryker would be dead.

"I can be him if that is what you desire."

I looked up. Ryker stood, healthy, in front of me. It was a mirage, but maybe the last time I'd see Ryker whole.

I reached a hand out to it, and it walked forward.

Its fingers wrapped around mine. I felt the ragged hide of what I was really holding. I saw the black tar substance that dripped from the illusion.

Eyes closed, I dropped as much of the protective

ward around myself as I could. Nothing could be between us. One shot at this. That was it.

With my magic and every drop of Ryker's flowing through me, I reached inward. I couldn't use his magic like it was my own—I had to use it the way it was meant to be wielded. I went to that dark place I'd sensed, and this time I didn't only dip my toes into the abyss—I flung myself into its mercy and hoped I didn't take out the rest of humanity.

Ryker's dark magic filled me like nothing I'd ever encountered. My magic had always felt like it wanted to curl around me, protect me. This magic felt as if it wanted to strike out. Fear battled with need. I knew I could kill everything around me, including Ryker. If I didn't, we were dead anyway.

I let it surge out of me like the wild beast it was, unleashed in Asterol's direction. I blasted it, and it struggled, pulling back from me with immense power. I clung with a tenacity born of desperation and grief.

It switched to the offense, battering me with its magic. I held on, wrapping both hands around it, unleashing everything I had, everything Ryker had given me, and then pulling for more, hoping it wouldn't be the final blow that killed Ryker in the process.

Asterol dropped, shaking the ground beneath me as I became the Cursed Queen, walking death. A blast of heat hit me, sending me sprawling backward and feeling like it settled into my soul. As if part of Asterol's essence had become one with mine.

I fell to the ground, nothing left.

Asterol lay dead. It was a sight I would've stared at

for hours if it weren't for the puddle of blood beside it belonging to Knife. If it weren't for Ryker's body lying nearby.

I crawled most of the way over to Ryker, who lay all too still, and pressed my ear against him. A strong beat thumped below. I collapsed beside him, my cheek pressed to his chest.

My lids parted slowly, and a hand smoothed the hair back from my face. A fire's heat soothed me as I was lying on my side, covered in Ryker's jacket.

"How are you feeling?" he asked.

I sat up, wrapping his jacket more firmly around my shoulders. That strange sensation I'd had right after I killed Asterol was still there, as if a part of it had been injected into me.

"Okay. When I killed it, I was able to use your magic. Something strange happened. I feel..."

It was a hard thing to put a name to.

"Fuller?" he asked.

"Yeah. Full. Is it going to go away?" I searched his somber face, hoping he'd tell me this was something that went away.

"No, but you'll get used to it."

My gaze went to the spot where Asterol had been, a strange smoke billowing up from the area. "Where's its body?"

"It's been slowly shrinking for the last few hours. There's nearly nothing left now but a stain."

There'd be more than one. The puddle of Knife's blood would be right beside it.

"Knife was here."

Ryker didn't respond right way as he pushed some of the logs around. "I know. Switch told me he was going back for him after he left me. I saw the human blood beside the body and figured as much."

"Switch popped back in and took Knife away again. There's still a chance." If Switch had gotten him to the healer in time, I knew the magic that woman could wield. It was possible Knife was alive.

"How did you find me?" I asked.

"After Switch lost you, the rest of us got scattered. It took him a while to find me. Then longer to find where you were."

"You guys look like shit," Burn said as he appeared on the other side of the fire with Switch.

"Could you have taken a little longer?" Ryker asked, getting to his feet slower than he normally would.

"Not my fault." Burn gave Switch a nudge with his elbow. "Switch refused to leave until he found the healer for Knife."

Burn's gaze lingered on Switch, and the smile dropped.

"Is he okay?" I asked, fearing the worst but still clinging to hope.

Switch caught my stare and shook his head. "It was too late."

An ache opened up in my chest. Another death, another loss. But it was finally over.

"I'm sorry, Switch. I know you had your problems, but you were with Knife a long time."

"He wasn't a bad guy," Switch said.

How many times had I said the same?

"So that thing is dead, huh? It let you close?" Burn asked Ryker.

"Not me—Bugs," Ryker said.

"Well, I'll be. Didn't know you had it in you," Burn said with a smile.

"Honestly, neither did I." When you see the person you love and know they're going to die if you don't do something, it's amazing the things you can pull off.

"Let's go home," Ryker said. He reached out and pulled me to my feet.

THIRTY-FIVE

Two burials, less than twelve hours apart, and as different as night and day.

I sat on a hill in the grove of souls beside Ruck and Switch, watching Knife get laid to rest. Hundreds of people flooded in to pay their respects.

Marra's burial was earlier this morning. Only Ruck, Switch, Ryker, and myself had been there to see it. Not even her new friends had shown. The fairies had made it clear that she wasn't welcomed in the grove, so she'd been placed in a grave outside the perimeters of the Valley, a sunny spot on top of a hill. Ruck and Switch had carried over a boulder to mark her grave.

Those same fairies circled Knife's tree now, singing their song of passing and helping him transition.

"I'm glad he's here, but I would've thought he'd want to be laid to rest at Dorley," I said.

Switch leaned forward so he could see me on the other side of Ruck. "Knife wanted to be buried beside Dez. It was the last thing he asked for before he died."

Switch looked at me with a knowing eye, and I realized how stupid I'd been. Tears filled my eyes, then overflowed to my cheeks. How could I not have known?

"You knew," I said to Switch.

Switch nodded. He looked down and then leaned his head on Ruck's shoulder.

"Knew what?" Ruck grabbed my hand. "You all right?"

I shook my head. "I'm so stupid. Before I went back to Dorley, Dez had told me she'd been in love, but the man hadn't loved her back. She was wrong. Knife just hadn't realized it until she was gone."

Ruck's face fell. "Fuck. That's some heavy shit."

I dropped my head on Ruck's other shoulder. "She only told me because she was trying to help me. She knew firsthand how hard it was to live like that."

People were still moving around below us, and I saw Ryker glance up again to where we sat, watching the procession.

"So now what? We staying, or you still want to leave?" Ruck asked.

"I think I'll follow her advice. This time, though, I'll really move on," I said.

Ryker's stare was on me, as if he knew what I was planning. He couldn't, but it sure felt that way.

Ruck patted my outstretched leg. "Between the three of us, I'm sure we could cover enough ground to find somewhere good, if that's what you really want."

"When I saw Ryker lying in the field, I thought he was dead. It tore at something in me so deep that I didn't know if I wanted to live without him. I can't stay here and move on. I have to go."

"We're ready to go with you, wherever the road may lead us, whenever you're ready." Switch leaned over, patting my leg where Ruck had, as if he thought that was what their job was. Pat Bugs and make her feel better. It was helping as much as it could.

"Would tonight be too early? I think the sooner the better. The longer I'm here, the harder it'll be to leave again."

"You got it," Ruck said, then he and Switch knocked hands as they figured out who was supposed to pat me this time.

The fairies finished their song and were flying overhead when I heard a man's laughter in the air, and then I thought I heard a woman's join his.

"Was that Knife?" I said, looking upward, as if I tried hard enough, I'd be able to see him in the clouds.

"Dez is making him laugh one last time. That was her magic, but she only used it for him," Switch said.

I WAS SHOVING THINGS INTO MY BAG WHEN THE door opened. Ryker filled the room with his presence. I turned back to packing. It was eerily similar to the first time I'd left, except so much had passed in between.

He shut the door and walked farther in. "After everything, you're still trying to leave."

"It's for the best."

He walked closer, watching my hands as I put things into the bag. "Stop packing. We've already done this once. I won't do it again."

As if this wasn't hard enough without him standing here, being his stubborn self. I ignored him, grabbing another shirt and stuffing it in my bag.

The first time I'd left him had nearly broken me, but I'd gone about my day today as if everything were okay. This time I felt as if I were already cracked into a million pieces. I didn't know how I was walking or talking anymore, and I hadn't left yet.

He grabbed the bag I'd filled, dumped it out onto the bed, and then tossed it to the other side of the room.

His arms circled me. I planted two hands on his chest and pushed out of his embrace. There was no way I'd be able to have this talk as long as we were touching.

"I can't do this anymore." I took a few more steps away from him.

"Why?" His eyes narrowed as he watched my face intently.

"You knew I was going to leave. I never said I wanted to stay. Nothing's changed." I grabbed the bag from where he'd thrown it, brought it back to the bed, and stuffed things back in it.

"That's a lie, and you know it. Everything has changed." He pulled a folded piece of paper from his back pocket and held it up.

"Where did you get that?" My stomach dropped. It was the letter he was never supposed to get. With everything happening, I'd forgotten all about it.

I went to yank it out of his hand, but he held it out of reach as he began to read it. *"Ryker, by the time you get this, I'll have left for Dorley. I'm sorry I didn't tell you. I didn't have the nerve to tell you a lot of things face to face. I need you to know I didn't come by this decision lightly."*

I jumped for the letter, but he held it too high. I looked past him to the door, but he shifted in front of me. "We're having this out, whether you want to or not. You don't get to sneak away again."

I walked to the bed, sat down on it, and leaned back so I could look at the ceiling instead. "Fine. Go ahead. Let's get this over with."

He cleared his throat and continued reading. *"I wanted to tell you how much I care for you, but I know your feelings aren't the same. I thought I could stay here, be your friend, your partner, at least as far as the stones go, but I can't. It hurts too deeply to see you with other women when I know you'll never be mine. I'm truly sorry, but this is best for both of us."* He folded it back up carefully and returned it to his pocket.

"Where did you get that?" I could feel his eyes on me, and my skin burned like the surface of the sun.

"Knife gave it to me after he knew we were sleeping together. You should've given it to me."

"Don't put too much stock in it. I was drunk when I wrote it. That note changes nothing." Drunk on misery, to be precise. I rolled on my side, looking for a place to hide from his piercing eyes that saw too much.

He stood right beside me. "You're not walking away from me again, not when I know how you really feel."

I turned toward him. "How I feel doesn't matter. Don't you understand that? I've been settling my whole life. Happy to just be safe, to have something to eat, to not be chased with someone trying to kill me. Settling for a man who wants to sleep with me but can't love me? I'm not doing it anymore."

"Is that what you really think? That I only want to sleep with you?"

"Yes."

He squatted beside me. "Do you remember in the pit, when you forced me into killing that monster because it was the only thing that might've saved you?"

I sat up on the bed, looking for a way around him. "If you're going to start on that again—"

He dropped onto the bed, tugging me back down with him, dropping a leg over mine to keep me there. "Listen to me—"

"Don't feed me lies to keep me here. You didn't want me. You pushed me away over and over again."

"When was the last time I pushed you away?"

I shrugged. "I don't know."

"I'll tell you. It was before we got the stone in the pit. When that happened, and I thought you were going to die, it shredded me inside. I didn't know if I'd leave that pit if you weren't with me. But my magic didn't kill you.

"I'm the Cursed King. You've heard the stories. You know what happened. In a single night, everyone I cared for died."

"That was true?"

"Yes."

"And you're afraid you'll kill everyone again?"

"Not everyone. I was afraid I'd kill you. It's been a long time, and I have a lot more control than I did then, but that fear never fully leaves you."

I stared in his eyes, trying to find the lie in them.

"Why do you think I slept on that tiny fucking bed of yours?" he asked, smoothing the hair from my face.

"I thought you were cold. You didn't want to get up and walk home."

"And you believed that? Even I had a hard time swallowing the load of bull I was spewing."

"What does this mean?"

"Don't you hear what I'm saying? It means I love you. It means I'm not letting you walk away from me again. And before you tell me that it's your magic I want, that has nothing to do with it. The way you took care of your people, were loyal to them even when it drove me crazy because they didn't deserve it. The way you would read the picture books at night and spy on the classes. None of that has anything to do with your magic. Bugs, I'm a grown man, and I know who I am and how I feel."

"What about when you get tired of being with only me?"

"I'll never tire of you. Every time I see you, hear you, feel your skin, I want you more, not less."

"Are you sure?" I asked, biting my lip, my eyes getting watery.

"When you find the right one, you don't keep looking for the wrong one. I'll prove it to you, however long it takes. Either way, you're not getting away from me. If you leave, I'm going with you."

"If you break my heart—"

"I won't." He cupped my face, and I almost believed him.

THIRTY-SIX

Almost one year later...

"Why did you get to place all the furniture? What if I wanted to put the furniture somewhere different?" I asked as Ryker and I walked to the food building.

"It was the only logical place it could go with the door and the window. If we're going to stay in that room, I'm going to be as comfortable as possible."

It had taken Ryker a while to realize that we weren't moving into his place, or a different place. I had a perfectly good room I liked just fine. It was my room, now ours, and I wasn't giving it up.

"Why can't we put the couch on the eastern wall?" I asked.

"Because that's where the bathroom is going to be."

The bathroom addition had been a hard line in the

sand for him. I hadn't fought that one much. I didn't want to be totally unfair to the guy.

"If you'd like, you can block the door. You like to run so much, it might be a useful way to slow you down," he said.

"Or maybe it'll be a good way to keep the women out in case you have a relapse?" In truth, he hadn't touched another woman, and I knew it. Didn't stop me from poking him here and there about his past ways.

"The only strange women that show up at our door are for you. I'm not sure how you're getting the word out that we'll break out every man, woman, and child in need, but can we go and eat breakfast in peace before more show up?" he asked, holding the door open for me.

He knew exactly how I was doing it. Switch was spreading the word far and wide that there was a better way to live and there was help available. We'd started with Wyrd Blood. If we broke the power base of all the tyrants around, eventually things would run their course. I never wanted to hear about another mother selling her soul to save her child.

I smiled as I walked past him. I filled up a plate of food, and Ryker dropped an extra biscuit on my plate. I left it there.

Ruck, Switch, Sneak, and Burn were already seated when we got to the table.

"Don't forget our anniversary party tomorrow," Switch said.

"Wouldn't miss it." I squeezed Ryker's leg under the table, signaling him to stay quiet. Ruck and Switch had gotten married ten months ago, and they had a party every month. I thought it was sweet. Everyone else thought it was exhausting, even Ruck. He'd admitted it to me last week, but it made Switch happy, so he kept doing it.

"You two thinking about making it official?" Ruck asked.

"Can't talk about that for three more days," Ryker said.

"Shit, forgot," Ruck said.

It was one of the things I'd asked for when I'd agreed to stay. We wouldn't discuss commitment until I was sure he was really committed. I didn't want to live with my head in the clouds, only to crash one day when I saw him with someone else. I hadn't even caught him looking at another woman. He'd told me almost a year ago that he only wanted me. I hadn't believed him, so he'd proven it.

I couldn't believe I'd almost left him. Ryker's hand covered mine where it still lay on his leg.

A little while later, I ducked out of the food building before him. I went to my favorite worming spot. I reached down, dug my fingers into the soil, scooped up a worm, and whispered to it.

I placed it in the circle.

It went straight for yes.

"You better not be asking it what I think you are," Ryker said from behind me.

"Why? You scared the worm won't lie for you? You know it doesn't." I gave him a teasing stare, implying he was guilty of something.

"Because if you need a worm to tell you at this point, I'm going to doubt your sanity."

I stood, and he took my hand, tugging me after him.

"We're going to have to set up some rules. You can ask it whether you're going to eat lunch, or whether you're going to go for a walk with me after dinner, but not that other question."

He twined his fingers into mine as we made our way along the street.

"That's fine by me," I said. "I don't need to. You're very transparent."

"Am I?"

"Embarrassingly so."

"Do you think everyone reads me as well as you do?" he asked, smiling with me.

"Unfortunately, yes."

He stopped in the middle of the thoroughfare, forcing people to weave around us. He wrapped his arms around my back, pulling me tight to him.

"What are you up to now?" I asked, hoping it was what I thought.

"Just in case there's someone around here who needs a little more help." His lips covered mine as two people melded into one.

He was right. I didn't have to ask that question anymore. I already knew he loved me. Now I knew he'd ask me to marry him in three days, too.

Sign up here to be notified of new releases by Donna Augustine.

http://www.donnaaugustine.com
Twitter
Facebook
Facebook Reader Group
Follow me on Bookbub